I0649723

Blood and Hope

Battalion 1 Series: Book 5

Theo Mann

The Invisible Publishing Company

Battalion 1 Series

Contents

Chapter 1

C aptain Corban Rhodes launched himself off the ground and blasted his booster rockets to their highest speed.

Dirt clods and scraps of grass tore away from his face and body as the wind hit him, but he concentrated all his attention on the battle unfolding in the distance.

The Masks' city machine plodded along the ground on its rolling tread wheels. The giant spaceship never drove any faster.

The thousands of Masks marching south didn't march any faster, either. They advanced in a steady wave over the rolling grasslands that used to be a battlefield.

Hundreds of dead Legion soldiers covered the ground down there. Their bodies hung from and got crushed under the wreckage of dozens of Dusters and Predator fighter craft shot down by the newly released Masks.

Of the whole overwhelming Legion force, only the Ravager carriers remained. Explosions burst in the skies over the planet Sarus as the Masks' invasion ships throttled the Ravagers into retreating.

Rhodes blocked all of that out of his awareness. Only one thing mattered now.

The city of Estra lay right in the Masks' path with millions of defenseless civilians in the firing line.

Rhodes gained altitude flying his fastest. He had to get to the city before the Masks did.

More Ravagers descended from orbit to land platoons closer to the city. Those platoons wouldn't be able to stop a mechanized fighting force as big as the one the Masks just released.

The Legion's best platoons had already been on the ground fighting the Masks. That was the whole point of this campaign—to throw everything the Legion had at the enemy and hopefully stop them from slaughtering the whole population.

Everything the Legion had didn't stop the Masks. Whatever the Legion kept in reserve would be pitiful compared to what the Legion had already lost.

None of that mattered to Rhodes. Nothing mattered but defending the city.

All thought of attacking the city machine went out of his head. He wouldn't destroy it. He couldn't even get near it.

His last remaining hope rested on somehow protecting Estra, but he already knew he couldn't do that, either.

The rest of Battalion 1 caught up with him a few minutes later. How sad and pathetic the battalion looked compared to that massive tide of Masks down there.

Eight people. Rhodes had eight people including himself. No amount of weaponry, boosters, The Grid, or any of the battalion's other modifications could make up for the Mask's sheer numbers and colossal firepower.

Don't think. Rhodes commanded himself not to think. He wasn't here to think. He was here to protect those people with every ounce of his strength.

If he got shot down, so be it. Everything that made his life worth living was already over. He had nothing to lose.

He dove for the Masks, but he couldn't fly any faster than this. The platoons moved into formation across the Masks' path and opened fire.

The Masks didn't open fire on the platoons. The Masks didn't have to do anything. The platoons destroying a few Masks here and there at the front didn't make any difference.

The Masks didn't need to reserve their firepower, but they still didn't shoot. Their steady marching advance forced the soldiers to fall back almost to the gates of Estra.

Rhodes swooped over the city and banked back to the north. He raced over the soldiers' heads and opened fire on the Masks with lasers spitting from every weapons port.

He carved a swath of destruction through their ranks, but they only climbed over their dead comrades to keep on coming. They closed every gap left by fallen Masks.

The battalion wheeled in around him. Everyone joined their lasers together in a wide, sweeping curtain of destruction.

The battalion's combined lasers formed a wall. The Masks marched straight into it, fell over each other cut to pieces by the battalion's lasers, and more Masks kept climbing over the fallen to meet their own deaths from the same lasers.

The mound kept growing higher and higher, but the horde of Masks never stopped or even slowed down.

The Grid gave Rhodes a clear view of a continuous stream of Masks pouring out of the city machine. Nothing stopped them.

They packed behind the fallen and eventually realized they could walk around the pile to keep pushing south.

Lieutenants Ted Oakes and Dane Rhinehart wheeled left to open fire on the Masks coming from there.

Rhinehart bellowed at the oncoming enemy. "You bastards! I'll fucking kill you!"

Rhodes, Lieutenant Heath Lauer, and Corporal Jairo Dietz turned to the right. That left a gap in the center for Masks to keep climbing over the pile of bodies.

Alyssa Thackery, Corporal Eddie Coulter, and Corporal Rudy Fuentes couldn't hold off the Masks alone.

The whole battalion had to step back—and one step at a time, the Masks forced the battalion to retreat, too.

The process kept repeating no matter how many Masks the battalion destroyed. The battalion eventually ran into the platoons.

Even then, the Masks kept pushing....and pushing....

They widened their formation. It stretched the length of the city wall. The battalion couldn't stop the Masks from shooting their way into town.

Once they broke past the platoons, no force in creation would stop the flood. Masks streamed around and behind the battalion to invade the city streets.

The battalion and the platoons kept unloading on the Masks. Rhodes fired one Viper missile after another into the Masks horde, but it was already too late.

Civilians ran screaming from the invading machines. Once the panic started, it cascaded through the city in another tidal wave of bodies—human bodies this time.

The people of Estra must already have heard about the destruction of Veulia farther north.

The Masks swept into town in an advancing line exactly the way they conquered every other city so far. They demolished buildings, gunned down people who stumbled across their path, and leveled everything in sight.

Men, women, and children stampeded through the streets screaming and running from the Masks' assault.

Unlike last time, no Ravagers waited outside of town to evacuate these people to safety. The population was completely exposed and defenseless against an overwhelming enemy force.

Rhodes launched back into the air. He didn't take the time to explain to his subordinates what they had to do. Everyone knew.

The Grid looked more gut-wrenchingly terrible with every passing minute. The battalion raced between buildings, veered farther south over the fleeing mob, and headed north again to come at the Masks.

Rhodes opened fire. He joined his lasers together with the rest of the battalion. Each of them unloaded as many Vipers as they could as fast as they could.

"What's Plan B?" Dash murmured through the interface.

"This is Plan B," Fisher replied.

"This is Plan C through Z, too," Wild growled. "This is it. We got nothing."

"So....we just keep shooting until all these people die?" Van asked.

The noise of explosions and gunfire made it impossible for anyone in the battalion to talk, but Rhodes didn't see that he had much choice.

The herd of refugees ran into more people coming out of their buildings farther south. The newcomers slowed everyone down and then the fleeing mob poured out of Estra onto the vast open fields south of town.

Those people fled their homes with nothing more than the clothes on their backs. No one had food or vehicles to carry them.

Mothers and fathers carried their children in their arms. A few old people rode piggyback on their relatives just to get them out of town alive before the Masks caught up.

The Masks' own strategy slowed them down. Nothing else could.

They took longer to demolish all the buildings in their path. Then they searched the area to hunt down any stragglers who fell behind.

The citizenry bought themselves a widening gap between themselves and the Masks.

Then the reality set in once they got outside of town. Millions of people shoved, pushed, and staggered south to get away from the city.

Rhodes went into a mindless trance of shooting. He had absolutely nothing else to do. He only hoped to slow the Masks down a little more.

Thackery cut her fire. She lowered her arms to her sides even as she hovered in midair with the rest of the battalion.

Rhodes glanced over to scowl at her. Why wasn't she shooting anymore?

Then Lauer put his weapons down, too. Oakes and Dietz stopped next. Rhodes opened his mouth to order them all to keep shooting ….and then he stopped. What was the point?

The minute he stopped shooting, he understood even more clearly. The battalion wasn't making any difference at all. The Masks advanced at exactly the same speed whether the battalion shot at them or not.

"Now what do we do?" Fuentes asked.

Thackery gulped. Her voice trembled when she said the words Rhodes never let himself think until right now.

"We should turn ourselves over to the Masks," she croaked. "We should offer to let them recapture us in exchange for them leaving all these population centers alone. It's the only way."

"I would do it in a heartbeat if I thought it would work," Rhodes replied.

"Why don't you think it will work?" she asked.

"They'll never stop. Whatever is driving them to kill all these people, it isn't anything rational. They won't be able to stop. They'll just keep driving and driving and driving. I don't think they could stop even if they wanted to."

"Then.....it's just....over?" Coulter asked. "I can't accept that."

Rhodes spotted Ravagers descending through the clouds farther south. The ships landed in the fields.

Officers, soldiers, and medical teams joined the growing column of refugees to help anyone who needed it, but the Ravagers couldn't evacuate everyone. They didn't even try.

"Let's go see what the officers want us to do," Rhodes suggested. "We aren't accomplishing anything here."

He took off flying over the city. Lauer, Dietz, and Rhinehart took longer to tear their eyes off the disaster.

The three men stayed there in the air watching the Masks systematically carve their way into Estra.

The crowds of civilians came to a standstill waiting for those in front to leave the city first. Fights broke out in the rear as more people panicked.

The three men finally abandoned the front and caught up with Rhodes and the others. The battalion flew out to the fields and landed near one of the Ravagers.

Rhodes found a colonel in charge of coordinating the medical teams. His nametag read, *Wolanski*. He was busy bandaging a baby's head while the little one squalled in his mother's arms.

"Captain Corban Rhodes of Battalion 1, Sir," Rhodes reported. "Would you happen to know who I should report to about getting further orders?"

"Don't you have your own people to report to?" Colonel Wolanski asked over his shoulder without stopping what he was doing.

"I wasn't sure if you wanted my battalion to support the evacuation."

"We aren't evacuating. We don't have enough Ravagers. Trying to evacuate anyone would only cause a riot when everyone found out we planned to take some people and not others."

"So....." Rhodes glanced up and down the column.

The civilians stumbled past him heading farther south. They didn't stop.

The line of people disappeared behind the grassy swells. There was nothing over there to protect them from the Masks.

"We're directing everyone farther south to Triowa, the next city in line," Wolanski explained. "It's the only place we can get these people any shelter."

Rhodes opened his mouth to point out everything wrong with that plan.

Triowa already had a population of over ten million. The Masks were on their way right now as soon as they finished with Estra.

Once the Masks attacked Triowa, all those people would have to flee somewhere, too. Twenty million showing up from Estra would complicate things, to say the least—if they even made it that far.

Triowa was more than fifty miles south. All these fleeing refugees would be totally exposed to another Masks attack along the way.

As soon as the Masks left Estra, they would head for Triowa. They would find all the people they missed in Estra.

All those people would be sitting out in the open with no cover. No force in the universe would be able to stop the Masks from slaughtering all of them exactly the way the Masks planned.

Even now, people dropped out of the column and collapsed on the grass, either from exhaustion, hunger, dehydration, or from medical problems they had before they fled Estra.

The Ravagers didn't have enough medical personnel to take care of everyone. Most of those people just stayed where they fell. The column kept moving past them.

Wolanski finished tucking in the bandage, straightened up, and turned around to face Rhodes. "Why don't you check in with your own officers, Captain? They can give you orders better than I can."

Rhodes scowled at the column and everything that wasn't there to the south. "I don't like leaving the column unprotected."

"Don't you have a way to communicate with them without leaving the column?" Wolanski asked.

"I guess so, Sir," Rhodes muttered.

"If you absolutely have to, you can go on board the *Astridosia* over there and contact your superiors through the Legion channels." Wolanski pointed to one of the other Ravagers.

Rhodes mumbled, "Yes, Sir."

Wolanski walked away to help one of the other medical teams. That left Rhodes with no more answers than before.

"Do you want me to interface with the....?" Fisher began and then changed his tone. "Oh, wait a minute. We're receiving orders from the *Ero*. We're ordered to stay on the ground and defend the column."

Oakes rolled his eyes and gasped in exasperation. "How exactly are we supposed to do that?"

Right then, an old lady stumbled in the column. She and a younger couple had all been working hard to steer a group of ten young children forward to keep up with the column.

The line of refugees came to the crest of a swell and started down the other side. The old lady tripped on the long grass and somersaulted down the rise into the hollow below.

A bunch of the children she'd been helping screamed, broke out of the column, and raced over to her to try to help her up. The couple did the same thing.

Rhinehart stepped out of line, strode over them, and bent over to pick up the old lady.

The children shrieked in terror and scrambled over each other to get away from him. "The Masks!!" two of them screeched. "The Masks are here!!"

Rhinehart straightened up and scowled at them. Rhodes knew him too well not to recognize that scowl. Rhinehart didn't understand them at all. He had no idea what they were talking about.

The couple recoiled from him, grabbed the old lady, and wound up dragging her across the grass to pull her out of his reach.

Rhinehart kept frowning at them in confusion while they manhandled the old lady to her feet, rounded up their children, and pushed everyone back into the column.

All those people shot terrified glances over their shoulders at Rhinehart. He just stood there, stunned by their reaction.

The whole scene wrenched Rhodes in the guts. The battalion gave everything to protect these people.....and they thought the battalion was a bunch of Masks.

Rhodes walked over to Rhinehart and touched his elbow. "Come on, Lieutenant. Let's go."

Rhinehart stumbled away, too dazed to respond. He followed Rhodes back to the battalion without a word.

Colonel Wolanski appeared at Rhodes's shoulder. "Maybe you should fall back behind the column. You can protect the refugees better from there....and it won't cause as many problems."

Rhodes turned away feeling sick. So this was how it was going to be—again.

He headed north down the column. He could have made it back to the northern end in a few minutes by flying there, but he didn't.

The column offered every shade of human suffering imaginable. This could only end in another disaster—an even bigger disaster.

As soon as the Masks finished with Estra, they would come after the column....and then Triowa.....and then Chaivis....and then the Lilithea Cluster.

Rhodes racked his brain for some way to stop the impending catastrophe. There was no way to stop it.

"Those bastards!" Lauer growled under his breath. "They deserve to die!"

Rhodes looked up. Lauer glared at the people in the column. He compressed his lips and narrowed his eyes at them in barely suppressed rage.

"We tried to help them—and they treat us as their enemies!" he snarled. "Who do they think is going to defend them if not us?"

"We should stay here," Dietz suggested. "We should make them look at us. We should make them see us. We shouldn't crawl off and hide like we have something to be ashamed of."

Rhodes didn't stop walking north. He barely listened to their conversation.

"Sir?" Oakes asked. "Should we stay here?"

"You can if you want to, but I won't," Rhodes replied over his shoulder. "I don't mind moving behind the column where these people can't see us. At least that's one thing I can do to make them feel better."

Chapter 2

R hodes and his subordinates eventually got tired of walking and used their boosters to fly to the northern end of the column.

Rhodes rose into the atmosphere and widened The Grid to see what the Masks were doing.

They were still mopping the floor back in Estra, but they still had a few more miles of city to cover before they made it to the other side.

Only a half-moon of intact buildings remained of the once majestic city. The very rear of the column made it five miles from the city limits.

The rest of the population filed away for miles into the distance.

"They'll be out here for days before they get to Triowa," Lauer muttered. "They could be out here for weeks, even."

"Who the hell knows what the people of Triowa will be able to do for all these refugees once they get there," Rhinehart agreed. "The people of Triowa won't even be able to save themselves.

"That isn't our decision to make," Rhodes replied. "Just like all these other decisions everyone around here expects us to make."

"You mean they expect *you* to make them," Dietz countered. "No one is asking us to make any decisions."

"No one is asking anyone to make any decisions because there are no decisions to make," Rhodes replied. "There's only one decision to make and everybody already made it."

"Shoot the suckers," Rhinehart snarled. "Shoot every last mother-loving one of them."

"It's gonna be a while before they leave Estra," Thackery pointed out. "These people might make it as far as......"

She broke off when a crowd of Masks poured out of Estra. They left a sizable chunk of their force behind to finish off the city.

Hundreds more set off marching south—and they marched a lot faster than the column moved.

"Here they come!" Rhodes called. "Attack them now! We have to stop them here!"

He plunged into the attack again and opened fire on the Masks. These shootouts always played out the same way.

The Masks fired their fusion rifles at the battalion, but Rhodes and his people kept whizzing back and forth across the Masks' formation.

The battalion's lasers laid the Masks down faster than they could shoot. The Masks didn't send out an overwhelming force this time—not yet. That would come later.

Rhodes rose a little higher. This vantage point gave him a good angle to kill countless Masks.

Their bodies piled at the front and they clogged in behind the same way. Rhodes and his people flew over the destroyed Masks and cut down those trying to break through.

Staying airborne also gave the battalion a perfect angle to stop the Masks from walking around the bodies to continue their journey.

The battalion separated the same way as before. Rhodes, Rhinehart, Coulter, and Lauer cut to the right. The more Masks they killed, the more the four men created another wall of fallen bodies.

This one curved backward while Fuentes, Thackery, and Oakes did the same thing on the left side.

The two sides penned in the Masks more effectively than Rhodes ever dared to hope. They kept trying to climb over and walk around the curved pile.

They only succeeded in adding to their own barricade. They couldn't get through.

Rhodes' heart soared and Coulter laughed. "Hey! This is actually working!"

Rhodes didn't want to believe it. He expanded The Grid of Estra to see if more Masks would come out and assault the battalion, but the other Masks were all too busy for that.

Just when he thought the battalion might actually win this one, engines thundered out of the atmosphere.

Rhodes's throat went dry when fourteen invasion ships dropped out of nowhere right on top of the column.

"Fall back!" he roared. "Protect the column!"

The battalion wheeled away, but not fast enough. The invasion ships bombarded the column with vicious firepower. Explosions blasted bodies into the air all over the field.

Only the column's sheer size and length prevented a total slaughter. Civilians screamed and scattered, which actually wound up saving more lives than any fighting force ever could.

Dozens of Ravagers that had been supporting the column launched off the ground to engage the invasion ships, but the air battle wound up putting the civilians in even more danger.

"Spread out!" Rhodes bellowed. "Cover as much of the column as you can! Use your grid lines the way we did before! Cover the civilians!"

Rhodes dove for the nearest cluster of fleeing refugees. They shrieked even louder when they saw him plummeting straight for them.

That didn't matter anymore. They could be as scared of him as they wanted to be as long as they were still alive to be scared of something.

He aimed for a mob of three hundred refugees. They all broke away from the column and ran west in a swarm. None of them thought about anything other than getting away from the invasion ships.

Hardly anyone ran south and no one ran north.

These three hundred split off at a right angle to the column's original route. All those men, women, and children took off as fast as they could run across the fields.

The invasion ships didn't let them get very far before a dozen fusion blasts erupted from the closest invasion ship.

The shots detonated in the center of the mob just as Rhodes got near enough to defend them.

The group was nowhere near enough to the invasion ship for him to shoot back at it—as if he could do anything by himself to fight that ship.

He widened his grid lines as far as they would go. A second wicked blast of fusion fire smashed into the group, vaporized dozens of people, and another dozen screamed when they saw Rhodes falling right on top of them.

He clenched his teeth, stretched his grid lines to their farthest point, and landed all their ends on the grass. He wasn't a person anymore. He created a field to deflect those shots.

They plastered all over The Grid and threatened to blow him apart, but at least the people under his field were safe.

They cowered on the grass, held onto each other, and screamed themselves hoarse while concussion after concussion hammered his Grid.

He shut his eyes and dug deep. He couldn't help everyone, but he could help these people. A hundred people of all ages got caught under his field.

Mothers hugged their children and even clamped their hands over their children's ears to protect them from the noise. No one dared to look up for more than an instant before they ducked for cover again.

The constant, punishing boom of fusion blasts on Rhodes's field eventually wore through to his physical body. The Grid couldn't protect him from everything.

He winced and then groaned in pain as the bombardment stretched on and on for what felt like hours.

Keeping his eyes shut left him with no choice but to look at The Grid. The battle turned against the Legion in a matter of minutes, but the Ravagers put up a better defense than Rhodes hoped.

The invasion ships focused their gunfire on what was left of the column. The air battle migrated farther south to keep up with the remaining refugees. The column and all the other people in it got farther and farther away from Rhodes's position.

Rhodes stayed where he was for a minute trying to decide if and when it would be safe to let these people out.

Before he could make up his mind to change his grid lines back to their original configuration, the Masks ground troops that had been marching on the column from the north finally caught up with him.

They surrounded him in droves, fired their rifles into his Grid, and even climbed on top of him. They shot down into the field from above trying to get to the people inside.

They screeched louder than ever seeing the Masks so close, but he had enough to worry about apart from their distress.

"The Masks' gunfire is damaging your systems, Captain," Fisher informed him. "You can't hold them off much longer."

Rhodes didn't answer. He couldn't. He kept his mouth shut and did his best to block out the incessant punch of gunshots striking The Grid.

He didn't understand any of this, but The Grid must not protect him from physical damage. He should have realized that. It couldn't have worked out any other way, but he wouldn't have done anything differently either way.

He felt his lines starting to weaken, but he just had to hold on. The battle of invasion ships against the Ravagers drifted farther south.

Just when he didn't think he could stand the assault a second longer, the Masks climbed down off his field, fired a few more shots trying to hit the refugees, and then marched off south to catch up with the rest of the column.

Rhodes stayed where he was for a long time with his eyes shut. He didn't seem to be able to tear his eyes off The Grid.

More Masks left Estra, but they didn't stop to bother him. They kept right on walking past him.

The Masks ground troops assaulted the column from the north. That made the refugees flee faster to the south.

They kept putting more and more distance between Rhodes and the people underneath him. Now what was he supposed to do with them?

He stayed there for hours until Fisher informed him, "There are no more Masks in Estra, Captain. You can stand down now. Don't ask me what we're going to do about the damage to your implants."

Rhodes tried to alter his grid lines, but he couldn't move. "Um.... .something's wrong, Fisher."

"Your exterior housing has been damaged. Just a moment. I think I can help you."

Rhodes felt himself going rigid. The pain of both bombardments became overwhelming.

Just then, Fisher used his own grid lines to take hold of Rhodes's lines. It was the same process the Masks used to control the battalion but in reverse.

Fisher wrenched Rhodes's lines out of position. They came unstuck from where he'd fixed them to the ground.

The minute they released, they collapsed back into their default shape.

He toppled onto the grass amongst the refugees. They screamed again and a dozen of them had to scramble out of the way so he didn't crush them.

He groaned and rolled onto his side.

"I think the damage is superficial enough for your grid lines to repair the damage," Fisher told him. "Lie still for a minute. I think I can speed up the process."

Rhodes couldn't have moved if he tried. He writhed on the grass snarling in pain.

Fisher twined his own lines into Rhodes's and knitted up the damage to Rhodes's chest implant on his back between his shoulder blades.

Rhodes buckled where he was breathing hard and trying to pull himself together. He kept searching The Grid.

"The city machine......it's entering Estra......"

"It won't get here before morning at this rate. The ground troops are a bigger problem. We won't be able to rejoin the column and we can't interface with the rest of the battalion. We'll have to stay here. We're far enough away. Maybe the city machine will leave us alone."

"What is it?" a little boy asked from not far away.

Rhodes became aware of some of the refugees standing around staring at him.

"Who is he talking to?" a man asked.

"Maybe he's connected to the other Masks," an old woman suggested.

"He isn't a Mask," a younger woman countered. "Look at him. He's partially human. He has a human face and some of his body is human. He isn't a Mask."

"He's more machine than human," the same man pointed out.

Rhodes dragged himself upright, but he had to hold himself up with his arm. Fisher spread his grid lines all over Rhodes's body repairing all the damage.

Thank goodness it wasn't more serious or Rhodes would have been in trouble—almost as much trouble as these people.

"Whoa!" the boy whispered. "Did you see that? It repaired itself! It fixed all that damage."

"Stop calling him, 'it'," the younger woman told him. "He's a man. You can see that for yourself."

"He saved all our lives," a different man reminded everyone. "We should be thanking him instead of standing here talking about him like some inanimate object."

Rhodes dragged his head up and looked around at the group. Ten people surrounded him all gaping at him.

The rest of the refugees shrank away from him, clutched each other, and shivered at the sight of him.

The second man stepped forward and held out his hand to Rhodes. "Thank you for saving us. We're eternally grateful. I'm Vanus Herata. I was a mechanical engineer in Estra. Is there anything we can do to help you? Do you need medical attention—or any mechanical repair?" He glanced around. "I don't know where we would get it.....and the Ravager crews probably aren't qualified to take care of you...."

"I don't need medical attention," Rhodes husked. "Just give me a minute. The bombardment....It just hurts. I'll be okay....in a minute."

Vanus kept standing there with his hand out. "At least let me help you up. It's the least I can do."

Rhodes had to gather his strength before he managed to take his arm off the ground. He clasped Vanus's hand and pulled to get to his feet.

Rhodes forgot for a second that he wasn't a normal man. He almost knocked Vanus over. He staggered before Rhodes remembered and let go of his hand.

"Thank you just the same. I'm okay." Rhodes pushed himself up, took a deep breath, and looked around.

The Grid looked as bad from here as it ever had before. All the Masks that left Estra now assaulted the column from behind exactly the way Rhodes predicted.

"At least the rest of the battalion is there," Rhodes muttered to Fisher.

"Who are you talking to?" the boy asked again.

"I have an internal communications interface with the rest of my crew," Rhodes explained. "We can talk to each other when we're separated."

"Can you tell where the column is?" Vanus asked.

"They're a few miles south of here, but the Masks are assaulting the column from the north. The Masks are between us and the column. We won't be able to rejoin the column—not before the sun goes down."

Rhodes surveyed Estra one more time. "Keep an eye on the city machine," he told Fisher. "Let me know if you see it coming any faster—and tell me when it leaves Estra." Rhodes glanced westward. "We might have to go farther west to get out of its path."

"Even that might not take us out of danger completely," Fisher pointed out. "If the city machine is this intent on wiping every single human being, it will send out another force of Masks to intercept us."

"We'll just have to take our chances." He turned to the people around him. They watched him carry on a conversation with someone they couldn't see. "We'll spend the night here. Maybe something will happen and we'll be able to rejoin the column."

"What if we can't?" the old lady asked.

"Then I'll interface with the Ravagers to come and pick us up."

"Shouldn't they have done that by now?" Vanus asked. "Why isn't the Legion trying to evacuate us? We're sitting ducks down here."

Rhodes didn't tell him that the Legion no longer had the ships or other resources to evacuate anyone.

Fifty million people sat right in the Masks' path. A hundred refugees wouldn't make any difference if the Masks really, really wanted to kill everyone—which it sure looked like they did.

Rhodes didn't tell Vanus that. Instead, Rhodes just said, "I don't make the decisions. Try to settle down on the grass here. I know it isn't the most comfortable situation, but we'll just have to make the best of it."

"What if the Masks come back?" the boy asked.

"Then I'll do my best to protect you. Now the sun is going down. If any of you have any blankets or warm clothes, you might want to get them out and use them now."

Chapter 3

R hodes made a circuit of the refugees' camp. It wasn't even a camp. He told them to use any blankets or warm clothes, but he saw after a few laps around the group that none of them had anything.

Mothers and fathers took the clothes off their own backs to wrap around their children. That was the best anyone could do.

Rhodes gathered handfuls of grass from the hills and used his thermal cannon to ignite the grass bundles. He did this all over the camp. The refugees had to work in shifts to gather enough grass to keep the fires going.

Rhodes made his way back to the east side of the camp—the side closest to where the invasion ships first attacked the column.

"The city machine is halfway through Estra, Captain," Fisher reported. "There is a chance it could draw level with us before morning—or it could send out more Masks before then."

"We can't do anything about that now. Just keep an eye on it and let me know if it does anything dangerous." Rhodes turned his attention back to the column itself.

"The Masks seem to have backed off," Fisher pointed out. "I wonder why they don't attack in force and finish off the column for good."

"It still won't be safe for us to try to get back to the column tonight. We'll have to recheck the situation in the morning. Fuentes has taken damage to his right leg. The others are all unhurt."

"I'm receiving a message from Colonel Wolanski, Captain."

"Wolanski! Why is he contacting me?"

"He's on board the Ravager *Astridosia*. He's in communication with the *Ero*. The Legion wants to land your conversion stations with the column so the *Ero* doesn't have to stick around just to support the battalion."

Rhodes snorted. "We wouldn't want that, would we?"

"The Legion is converting your capsules to upright stations for ease of transport. Drs. Osborne and Trudeau are coming down to act as the battalion's medical and repair support staff."

"That's a small mercy. At least the Legion doesn't plan to leave us out here without any support at all."

"The *Ero* plans to land your stations and the two doctors near the front of the column...."

"That means I won't be able to use my station until I find a way to rejoin the column."

"Precisely," Fisher replied. "Setting aside that little challenge, the stations are mounted on a mobile carrier. They'll travel with the column as long as you're ordered to defend the refugees."

Rhodes sat down on one of the swells. "I guess I can look forward to that—as soon as I find a way to rejoin the column."

"You could fly there alone, go through a conversion cycle....."

"And leave these people undefended," Rhodes finished. "I wouldn't do that."

"Skipping conversion cycles for too long would degrade your systems. Eventually, you wouldn't be able to defend them at all. It would be better for you to go through a conversion cycle and then come back to them refreshed."

"I'm not there yet, pal. I'll consider it when I do get there." Rhodes glanced over at the refugees around the fires. They kept the fires going by themselves. They didn't need any more help from him.

"You held up amazingly well defending them against that bombardment," Fisher remarked. "I'm impressed."

"I'm all they have. They would all be dead now if I gave in one minute sooner."

"I admire you," Fisher murmured. "I don't know if I could do what you do. In fact, I know I couldn't. I don't have the emotional capacity to sacrifice myself for anyone the way you do."

"I don't know what to say, Fisher. I wish I could contradict and say you're wrong...."

"I'm not wrong. Who would know my emotional capacity better than I would?"

"You sacrificed yourself more than once to help me when we were the Masks' prisoners," Rhodes pointed out. "Does that count?"

Fisher remained silent, and before either of them could say anything else, the woman from earlier came over to Rhodes. The young boy came with her. He couldn't have been more than nine.

She sat down on the grass in front of Rhodes and burst into a huge smile when their eyes met. "A few people over there had some food. I thought you might be hungry. You've been out here alone for hours walking around guarding us." She unwrapped a piece of paper and held it out to him. "Take it. We want you to have it."

"Thank you, but I don't eat," Rhodes replied. "You should have it. Give it to the boy."

"He's already eaten." She looked at the boy. He gazed up at her with big, pleading, puppy-dog eyes. "Fine. Here." She handed it to him and turned back to Rhodes. "How come you don't eat?"

He shrugged it away. He found it difficult to look at her, especially considering the way she was looking at him. "I guess that's just the way it worked out. I don't have internal organs. We have equipment that gives nutrients and removes toxins from our organic tissue. That's all I know."

"How did you get like this?" the boy asked. "Did the scientists grow you in a lab or something? Did they put your body parts together in a factory?"

"Be quiet, Avi," the woman interrupted. "That's none of your business." She turned back to Rhodes. "Please excuse him. You don't have to answer that."

"It's okay. He's a kid and kids need to ask a million questions." Rhodes turned back to Avi. "My son Palmer would not stop asking questions from the minute he woke up in the morning until he went to bed at night. You couldn't shut that kid up to save his own life."

Avi froze with food bulging in the side of his cheek. "You have kids? Seriously?"

"I have three of them back on Preinea. I wasn't always like this."

Avi gulped with difficulty. "How did you get like this, then?"

"You don't have to answer that," the woman interrupted again.

Rhodes couldn't decide which of them he wanted to look at. He hadn't had a conversation like this with anyone since....he couldn't even remember when.

He never talked about his family or his former life with anyone in the battalion, not even Fisher.

Rhodes never talked about it with his men in the Legion, either. None of them talked about their families.

"Did you fall into a vat of radioactive waste?" Avi asked. "Did aliens implant their DNA into you to make this stuff grow on you? Is it alive and taking over your whole body?"

Rhodes laughed in spite of himself. "It was nothing as cool as that. I got shot on the battlefield fighting the Emal. A Duster crashed on top of me and would have killed me. The Legion sent me to a lab where they replaced my damaged limbs and organs with these implants. That's as interesting as it gets."

"It is cool!" Avi exclaimed. "You're the coolest thing I've ever seen."

"He isn't a thing," the woman told him again and made a face at Rhodes. "I'm really sorry."

Avi started to say, "Sorry....um....."

"Rhodes," Rhodes finished. "Captain Rhodes. Corban Rhodes. That's my name." He allowed himself to turn to the woman. "What's your name?"

She smiled and her cheeks colored. "Yira." She held out her hand. "Yira Kosna. This is my son, Avi, of course."

Rhodes glanced down at her hand. He made a few strategic mental calculations before he shook it. He made sure to use the right amount of pressure so he didn't crush it or break it.

She smiled even more broadly when she let go. She looked away and pretended to be checking on her son.

Rhodes studied her more closely. She wasn't exactly pretty. Her straight, light-brown hair was nothing to write home about.

She had a pale, careworn quality that made Rhodes think she'd probably had a hard life, but her vivacious nature radiated through her bright brown eyes.

She smiled easily, especially when she looked at her son. Rhodes found himself wishing she would look at him like that—and she did.

She kept blushing and smiling when she did look at him. She looked away too often.

Sitting here talking to these two brought up so many buried feelings and memories. This conversation made him feel far more human than anything else that had happened to him.

It made him feel more human even than most of the things that happened to him before he got taken into Battalion 1.

He couldn't remember feeling this way around anyone except his own family.

He didn't even feel this way around his own family—not most of the time. He did feel it sometimes, but not always. He never realized then that it could be any other way.

Now he knew what those connections and conversations were really worth.

He would have given absolutely anything—including his own life—to go back and feel that way again—even just for a few minutes.

He felt that way a thousand times after he lost them. That was the real tragedy. He didn't find out what they were worth until it was too late.

He felt that way when he found out about the Masks living in Stonebridge. This was what they were missing—this feeling of connecting to and actually caring about people—the feeling that they might actually care about him as much as he cared about them.

Yira noticed him watching her and looked away again. "Anyway, we'll leave you alone. I'm sure you have better things to do than talk to us."

"I don't!" he blurted out. "You don't have to go. Stick around....if you want to."

Avi jumped right in. "Those other people that go with you—did they get injured and almost killed fighting the Emal, too?"

"Most of them. Some of them got sent to the lab for other reasons, but most of them were soldiers like me. What about you?" Rhodes glanced at Yira. "What did you do in Estra?" He almost asked if she was married to someone in the column, but he didn't ask that.

"I worked in a hospital—in the emergency social services unit," she replied. "I spent all day dealing with people who'd just lost loved ones in the hospital and either couldn't cope or didn't have the resources to take care of themselves afterward." She tried to make a face, but it turned into more of a wince. "I guess this column is where I really belong."

"Wow," Rhodes remarked. "That sounds hard."

"Not as hard as this."

"I went to school in Estra," Avi interjected.

"I certainly hope so," Rhodes replied. "I would be worried if you didn't. So what's your favorite subject in school?"

"Sports." The boy stuck out his tongue. "I hate sitting at a desk."

"You would get along really well with Palmer. That kid couldn't sit still for anything."

"What other kids do you have?"

"I have another son—a younger one—and a daughter. They all like sports, too. That's all they ever do—when they aren't in school."

"Are they here?" Avi asked.

"Of course they aren't here," Yira interrupted. "He said they were on Preinea."

"Oh. Right. Sorry," Avi mumbled.

"That's okay," Rhodes replied.

"So…do they come to visit you?" the boy asked.

Rhodes hesitated and Yira jumped cut in again. "You don't have to answer all his questions. It really is none of his business."

Rhodes took a second to decide how to answer. His past wasn't technically a secret—at least, no one at Coleridge Station ever said it was.

"My family doesn't come to visit me,'" he finally murmured. "They think I'm dead. The Legion told them I was dead when they took me into the battalion. None of us can go home again. My family doesn't know where I am or what happened to me. I wouldn't want them to know. They're better off thinking I'm dead."

Yira winced. "I am so sorry! He shouldn't have asked."

Avi turned white. "You mean....you can never see your kids again ....or your wife....like—ever?!"

"Avi!" Yira whispered. "Leave him alone. You can see this is hard enough for him."

Rhodes didn't contradict her, but he didn't exactly mind them both acting so shocked. At least someone else realized how bad it was.

Avi's questions and both of their reactions somehow humanized Rhodes even more—more than he ever thought possible. He saw himself from their perspective. He really was human if they could understand him like this.

They were total strangers and yet they both got it instantly. He didn't have to explain. Of course losing his family would be hard for him. How could it be otherwise for anyone human?

That was the other crushing tragedy about the Masks. They didn't feel a thing when one of their number got destroyed or melted or cut apart by lasers.

They just replaced each other in the Stonebridge landscape. If the father got killed, some other Mask took his place. The new person looked, talked, and behaved exactly like the old one.

Yira struggled to control her features. "Is there anything we can do? I don't know why I even ask that. Of course there isn't, but if there is anything....I mean, you're the one out here doing everything for us. I don't know what to say. Your story...."

"Don't worry about it," Rhodes replied. "I didn't tell you so you would feel sorry for me. I don't need you to do anything for me."

She flinched again. "It's one of the worst stories I've ever heard....and all your comrades went through the same thing, didn't they?" Her cheek spasmed. "I didn't think the Legion could be so cruel as to put someone through that—or several people."

Rhodes didn't tell her about all the people who died going through the Battalion 1 project.

He wouldn't have believed the Legion would be capable of something like this, either. He wouldn't have believed it if he hadn't seen it with his own eyes and gone through it himself.

Avi saved the situation by changing the subject. "So where do you live when you aren't here? Do you have a base somewhere?"

"The original lab where we went through the project is on a secret Legion base in the Dalea system." Rhodes pretended to frown. "Maybe I shouldn't have told you that."

Avi laughed. "You just did."

"Anyway, we've been on a Ravager since we went into combat. Now we're here. I don't know how long we'll be here."

"What do you do at the base when you aren't in combat?"

Rhodes found himself smiling at the boy's endless questions. "Me? I like to draw in my free time."

"No way!" Avi exclaimed. "That is so cool!"

Rhodes felt the organic side of his face burning. He never knew he could still react that way. "It's pretty cool. One of my people liked to carve figures out of wood. We do whatever we feel like to pass the time. Sometimes we play card games or dice games or gamble."

"You don't play sports?" Avi rolled his eyes to heaven. "That sounds so boring."

Rhodes laughed. It felt strange to laugh. "Not those kinds of sports. Sometimes we play other kinds of games."

"Like what?"

"We have training sessions in The Grid...."

"What's that?"

"It's complicated. We go into a simulated landscape and run obstacle courses against pretend enemies to accomplish an objective. It's kind of like sports but with weapons and targets and stuff like that."

Avi brightened up. "That's cool! I want to join the Legion when I grow up."

"No, you don't," Yira interrupted and made another face at Rhodes.

"You can't stop me," Avi fired back.

"You wanna bet?" Yira told him.

"You might be able to stop me now, but you won't be able to stop me forever." Avi turned back to Rhodes. "I will join the Legion. You'll see."

"I'm sure you would be great," Rhodes replied.

"Okay, I think that's the end of that conversation." Yira stood up and pulled Avi away by the shoulders. "Good night, Captain. Thank you for everything you're doing for us. It was very nice to meet you and talk to you and everything. I guess we'll see you tomorrow. Come on, Avi. It's getting late. You need to go to sleep."

He started to resist. "I don't want to leave yet...."

His mother pulled him away. They passed one of the fires and disappeared into the dark.

Rhodes watched them go struggling with a confused tide of emotion. He leaned back against the hill behind him and stared up at the stars.

How many years had it been since he did this? How many years had it been since he lay on his back in the grass in an open field and stared up at the stars like a normal person?

Everything about tonight felt so different from the world he'd been living in with Battalion 1. This was what it felt like to be human.

Fisher broke in on his thoughts. "Your system is exhibiting a stress response from not going through a conversion cycle."

"I'm sure I'll make it through one night," Rhodes replied. "I went longer than this on Drion."

"That conversation caused you to exhibit a stress response."

"This isn't a stress response," Rhodes replied.

"What is it, then? Your brainwave patterns are outside the normal range."

Rhodes burst out laughing. He couldn't stop himself.

"What's wrong, Captain?" Fisher asked. "Are you malfunctioning?"

"I'm not malfunctioning, pal. I'm happy."

Fisher frowned. "Happy? Why?"

Rhodes looked away. "You wouldn't understand."

"I know I don't understand. That's why I'm asking."

Rhodes couldn't stop laughing. This feeling bubbled out of him. Would it ever stop? Maybe he would keep being happy from now on. That would be wonderful.

"Look, pal," he replied. "Those people....They're like the family I lost. I can't explain it any other way. Being around them is like being around my real family.....or maybe this feeling is what I was supposed to feel in Stonebridge, but I couldn't because it wasn't real then. I don't know. I just feel.....I can't explain it. I feel connected to everyone and everything. I feel like I'm together with my family and you and the battalion and....and everyone I've ever cared about. I could even feel this way about Ora and the people in Stonebridge."

"But you said you *don't* feel that way about Ora and your family in Stonebridge."

"I don't. I just.....I can't even remember what my real family looked like. Sometimes I think of my wife and I remember her as Ora....or my children as Ora's children. I don't know. It all gets so confused."

"Then.....how do you know you don't feel that way about your family in Stonebridge? Do you feel that way about them or not?"

"I can't feel that way about them. I've only felt that way about one woman and my own children, but tonight......Talking to those people.....it makes me feel that again. I know how I feel about them. Feeling that way about them is what makes me different than the Masks. I don't have to remember what my family looks like. I'll never feel that way about anyone else. I don't need to remember what they look like as long as I have this."

Chapter 4

R hodes strode around the refugees' camp. Most of them had fallen asleep overnight and let the fires go out.

That didn't matter because the sun was already rising.

"The city machine is two miles out of Estra," Fisher reported. "We should leave now—either to keep ahead of it or to head farther west to get out of its way."

Rhodes surveyed The Grid. "The Masks are still between us and the column. We won't be able to get back to it while the Masks are in the way."

"Then we should move westward and put as much distance between us and the city machine as possible."

"We can't do that, either," Rhodes replied. "These people don't have food or water. We wouldn't last more than a day or two out here and I wouldn't be able to defend them alone—not if the Masks came in any kind of force."

"What other option is there?" Fisher asked.

Rhodes glanced over the refugees and then the surrounding countryside. A few people sat up and started to stretch. None of them would be ready to move very quickly this morning.

Rhodes glanced north and rotated The Grid of Estra in front of his eyes.

There was nothing left of the city. The Masks had destroyed every building down to the smallest rock.

Fisher read his mind. "We can't go back there."

"The Masks aren't there. It's the one place on all of Sarus that the Masks aren't interested in going. We could probably salvage some food from the ruins. The city water supply might even still be working. Yeah, see? The underground irrigation system is still operational."

"This is a terrible idea, Captain," Fisher muttered. "I thought some of your other ideas were bad. This definitely takes the prize."

"Why? What's so bad about it?"

Fisher started to say, "For one thing...." when engine noise cut him off.

A howling fighter craft streaked across the sky and woke up all the refugees. They startled out of their slumbers and jolted upright real fast.

A round, cheery, chubby face popped onto The Grid in front of Rhodes. "Good morning, Captain! I've been looking all over for you."

Rhodes laughed again. "You found me, Rio. It's so good to see you."

The Striker banked wide and came back for another pass. "The whole Striker group is ordered to rendezvous with the battalion. The brass wants us to help you fight the Masks."

"That's wonderful, Rio. I'm so glad you're here."

"I'm ordered to take you back to the column immediately...."

"I can't leave these people," Rhodes replied. "You can help me defend them instead."

"The brass is sending a Ravager to bring them back to the column," Rio told him. "It should be here shortly."

"Oh. Okay." Rhodes rotated The Grid in front of him again.

The Masks that attacked the column yesterday were still holding the same position. They didn't attack again. The column kept traveling farther and farther south toward Triowa. The Masks didn't make another move.

The city machine rumbled through the other side of The Grid coming from the north. It would catch up with Rhodes's refugee group in a few minutes.

"I'm coming down to get you, Captain," Rio repeated and circled the camp in a tighter loop.

His engines startled the refugees to high alert. They backed away from the ship, grabbed their children, and started crowding westward to put distance between themselves and the Striker setting down on the grass.

Rhodes went over to the refugees. "The Legion is sending a Ravager to take you back to the column."

"Why can't the Ravager take us straight to Triowa?" Vanus asked.

"Because, if the Ravager took you straight to Triowa, everyone else in the column would want to travel in Ravagers, too," Rhodes blurted out. "The Legion doesn't have enough Ravagers and manpower and resources to evacuate everyone. If they did, they would have lifted off the entire populations of Estra, Triowa, Chaivis, and the whole Lilithea Cluster long ago. Do you get it now? They can't evacuate. There aren't enough ships in the whole Treaty of Aemon Cluster to evacuate that many people."

Silence fell over the group. Everyone stared at him in horror, including Yira and Av.

Rhodes kicked himself for being so hard on them, but they had to understand the position they were in. Him defending them would only ever be a temporary solution if it was a solution at all.

"I'll stay with you until you get on board the Ravager," he finished. "Then we're all going back to the column and I'll be rejoining my battalion. I'll be there to defend you, too—as best I can. You all handled yourselves exceptionally well last night. I'm proud of all of you."

He tried to direct this to Avi.....and Yira, but right then, a Ravager broke through the atmosphere and descended onto the grass.

"Stay here until the landing bay opens for you!" Rhodes yelled over the engine noise. "I'll tell you when to go."

The ship revolved in front of the group, hovered twenty feet off the ground, and then set down. The landing bay didn't open for another minute.

When it did, a bunch of uniformed Legion personnel waved the refugees on board.

"Go!" Rhodes yelled. "Go now!"

He pushed everyone forward. The refugees took off running for the ship.

Rhodes stood back to watch them go. Yira and Avi drew level with him. She made eye contact with Rhodes and yelled, "Thank you, Captain!" before she turned away.

Avi called up. "Thank you, Captain!"

They both faced the ship to run after the rest of the group. Rhodes reacted on impulse, shot out his hand, and grabbed Yira's arm. "Wait! I have an idea. You could fly back to the column with me." He jerked his thumb toward Rio. "Come on. Fly with me. You'll wind up with the column either way." He took a chance and looked down at Avi. "You want to see The Grid. Now's your chance."

The boy grabbed his mother's elbow. "Come on, Mom! Please!"

"All right." She shot Rhodes another blushing grin. "If you're sure it's all right."

"Of course it is. Come on."

Rhodes led them across the grass to the Striker. The Ravager was already shutting its doors. Now he really had to fly Yira and Avi back to the column. They wouldn't get there any other way.

"What are you doing, Captain?" Fisher murmured on the way back to the ship.

"Are you sure this is okay?" Rio asked. "None of the officers said anything about this."

Rhodes didn't answer. He didn't want Yira and Avi to hear this—not until they saw The Grid for themselves.

He helped them both climb into the cockpit. Yira sat in the backseat with Avi on her lap. Rhodes buckled both of them in.

"Hold on. This is not going to be like any other plane ride you've ever taken."

Avi frowned at the cockpit. "This ship has no controls. How do you fly it?"

"Watch and I'll show you." Rhodes sat down in the front seat and shut the cover.

The Grid activated as soon as he sat down. Grid lines spread over the cockpit, covered Rhodes's body, and surrounded the Striker's outer fuselage.

Fisher and Rio both appeared on The Grid where Yira and Avi could see them. "Cool!" Avi exclaimed.

"Fisher—Rio—this is Yira and Avi Kosna. These are my SAMs. It means Simulated Augmentation Matrix. They're computer programs that help my implants function properly."

"It's a pleasure to meet you both," Fisher began. "I feel it's only polite to tell you that I was present during your conversation with Captain Rhodes last night."

"You were?!" Yira gasped. "How?"

"I'm the person you heard him talking to after the battle. I was present in The Grid for the whole evening. I apologize if my participation in what was supposed to be a private conversation...."

"It wasn't a private conversation," Rhodes interrupted. "I didn't say anything you didn't already know."

"I'm delighted to meet you both," Rio interrupted. "Are you ready to go, Captain?"

"I'm ready. Let's go."

Rhodes altered the grid lines to form the Striker's controls and shot off the ground. The ship overtook the Ravager in a matter of seconds.

"The rest of the battalion is waiting for you at the new mobile conversion unit....." Rio began.

"Not so fast," Rhodes countered. "We're gonna have some fun first. Watch this, Avi."

Rhodes morphed the grid lines, changed the Striker into one of the giant jointed creatures the battalion used against the Emal, hit the ground, and bounded into the air.

The creature soared over miles, but Rhodes changed the Striker's shape before it touched down again.

He changed into an all-terrain vehicle, then into the underground snake, then into a spinning weapons turret spitting off all kinds of shots in every direction, and finally changed back into a Striker that rocketed into the heavens.

Avi burst out in excited laughter. "How do you do that?!"

"We can modify the grid lines into any shape," Rio told him. "Captain Rhodes is controlling The Grid now to pilot the ship. He can adjust The Grid in combat to adapt my weapons systems and outer structural configuration to best compensate for the conditions."

"That is so cool!" Avi exclaimed.

"He can change his own grid lines, too," Fisher pointed out. "He can do it when he isn't flying Rio."

"No way!" Avi gasped.

"How does it work?" Yira asked. "That shouldn't be scientifically possible."

"How *does* it work?" Rhodes asked. "You can explain it to us, Fisher."

"I'm afraid I don't know how it works, either," Fisher replied.

"Don't you have access to that through the interface?" Rhodes asked. "You should be able to access all the records on the whole battalion."

"Those records are classified along with most of the other design and development research the project used to develop both the SAMs technology and your implants."

"It's still cool," Avi chimed in. "I bet the other Legion pilots are so jealous!"

"They don't know," Rhodes told him. "That's what classified means. It means no one is supposed to know about this project."

"But everyone knows about you now," Yira pointed out. "We've all seen you."

Rhodes grinned to himself, went through another dozen Grid transformations, and corkscrewed back toward Estra.

He got serious when he spotted the city machine coming closer. The Ravager was just touching down next to the column to let the other refugees disembark.

Rhodes banked wide to keep away from the Masks. He slowed before he landed near the other Strikers.

He spotted the new mobile conversion unit not far away. The Legion had constructed it as an open-walled platform with a wide roof over eight standing stations.

A giant vehicle towed the unit from the front. Rhodes scanned the vehicle and saw a bunch of Dr. Osborne's computer equipment inside.

The vehicle also contained one of the more complex conversion capsules the doctors used for treating serious injuries and malfunctions when anyone in the battalion needed it.

The vehicle had been set up as a mobile lab. Osborne and Trudeau worked inside the vehicle lab right now.

The other members of the battalion walked around near the column. They didn't seem to be in any hurry to do whatever they were doing, but they didn't need to. The column wasn't in any danger—not now.

Rhodes landed Rio with the other Strikers. His heart sank when he popped the cockpit cover and helped Yira and Avi climb out. Rhodes didn't want this to end, but it had to.

Yira pulled Avi close to her when they finally got out on the grass, but she wouldn't stop smiling and blushing at Rhodes. "Thank you for the ride, Captain. That was exhilarating."

"It sure was!" Avi exclaimed.

Rhodes smiled at her and then at him. "Maybe you might like to do it again sometime."

"Yeah!" Avi crowed. "When can we?"

"I'll have to find out what my orders are and let you know." Rhodes looked back up at Yira. "I guess you can go back to the column now."

"Yeah," she breathed. "Thank you again."

"It was my pleasure. It was very nice to meet you both. I hope I see you again."

She beamed at him. "Me, too. Thank you. Goodbye. Come on, Avi."

She pulled him away and they returned to the column, but not without looking back over their shoulders more than once.

Avi waved at Rhodes and Rhodes waved back. Neither of his SAMs interrupted.

Rhodes watched Yira and Avi disappear into the crowd. He didn't want them to leave. He sure got attached to them quick, but every instinct told him that would be a good thing.

He didn't want to protect himself from this feeling. He wanted more of it—a lot more. He wanted everything they could possibly bring into his life.

One thing he knew for certain now. Defeat was no longer an option.

He had to come out on the other side of this war. When he did, he had to find Yira and Avi on the other side of it, too.

This war would only end one way. Either the Masks would remain standing at the end of it or he would. There would be no compromise on that.

That moment—the moment when Yira and Avi vanished into the column of refugees—that was the moment when Rhodes made up his mind.

Come Hell or high water, he would be the one standing at the end of this war.

All these Masks—their city machine—their invasion ships—all of them would lie in ruins at his feet when this was over. He would make sure of it.

He would make absolutely sure Yira and Avi were still standing at the end of it, too. No victory would be complete without that.

Then he would be able to spend as much time as he wanted with them. The Masks wouldn't interfere to stop him and they would never EVER put Yira and Avi in danger again—not while he was still breathing.

He turned away and set off striding across the field to meet up with Lauer and Rhinehart.

Rhodes knew what he had to do now. He had to find a way to win this war and now he had a reason to do it.

Chapter 5

Rhodes and Rhinehart strode down the column checking everything, but none of the battalion noticed anything noteworthy.

"The Masks are still camped out twelve miles north," Rhinehart told Rhodes. "They haven't moved since they attacked the column last time."

"They shouldn't be so quiet," Rhodes remarked. "If I didn't know better, I would say they were planning something again."

"Oh, they're definitely planning something," Rhinehart agreed. "They were planning something before. Now they're planning something we don't know about."

"That's what I meant."

"We're only ten miles from Triowa," Rhinehart went on. "We should get there later today or tomorrow."

"Assuming nothing goes wrong," Rhodes corrected.

Rhinehart made a face, but Fisher interrupted before they could say anything else. "The inquiry panel is calling you to the command dome, Captain. They want to consult with you about the Masks' activities."

"The Masks don't have any activities," Rhodes pointed out.

"Future activities," Rhinehart explained. "Hypothetical activities."

Rhodes laughed and headed off in a different direction. He returned to the battalion's mobile conversion unit.

The vehicle that pulled the battalion's conversion unit around kept adjusting its location to keep pace with the column.

The battalion moved the Strikers so the ships always sat parked next to the mobile unit.

That way, no one in the battalion had to go very far if they needed to go through a conversion cycle, a visit to Dr. Osborne's lab, or to fly their Strikers around the area.

The command dome wasn't a dome at all. It was another open-walled mobile unit the officers used as a command dome or meeting room or whatever it was.

Rhodes walked in to find everyone from the inquiry panel along with Colonel Wolanski and four other Ravager captains and colonels.

This group right here had been running the campaign—if that's what it was. It was actually something like a ground evacuation and not a very good one.

Colonel Volk pointed at a few different spots on his chart. "We only have five platoons to guard the whole column. That isn't nearly enough."

"Battalion 1 is already stretched thin trying to cover as much of the column as possible," General Hyde pointed out. "I still say we should concentrate the battalion in one spot. Their firepower will be more effective against the enemy if they're all in one place instead of one person against an unstoppable force."

"We've already gone over this," Admiral Stabler cut in. "The column is too big for that. If the enemy attacked, it would take the battalion too long to get to the battle. Whatever part of the column the Masks attacked would be left vulnerable until the battalion arrived."

"But once the battalion did arrive, they would be able to do more," General Hyde pointed out. "That's all I'm saying."

Colonel Wolanski turned to Rhodes. "What do you think, Captain? Do you think the battalion would be more useful with everyone in one place or spread out to cover the whole column?"

"If your concern is that we wouldn't get to the battle in time, then you could compensate for that by deploying us in our Strikers," Rhodes replied. "Based on the Masks' past behavior, we can assume they would attack the column in multiple spots—not just one. They only have to bring in invasion ships to put the whole column in danger."

"That puts the battalion in your Strikers nearly all the time," Captain Lake pointed out. "Is that a sustainable way for your battalion to operate?"

"I believe it's the way that will make the battalion's firepower the most effective," Rhodes replied. "If the battalion offers this column any advantage at all, then I believe this is the way to use that advantage to the best effect. That's just my opinion, Sir—since you ask."

Colonel Volk rubbed his chin and frowned at the chart. "You would certainly cover more territory that way."

"Will the Strikers attract the invasion ships?" Admiral Stabler asked.

"They haven't so far unless the invasion ships are already in battle," Rhodes pointed out. "The battalion has been flying sorties to keep the enemy under surveillance. The invasion ships haven't come back even though we've been in the air. The Ravagers have been in the air, too, and the invasion ships haven't come for them, either."

"This is all peculiar," Admiral Stabler growled. "Those rotten machines are getting ready to pull some rabbit out of their hats."

"I agree, Sir," Rhodes replied. "I just wish I knew what it was."

"Very well, Captain," Stabler agreed. "Implement the strategy you mentioned and deploy the battalion in your Strikers. You'll be able to get to any hot spots quickly enough that way."

"Yes, Sir," Rhodes replied and left the command dome.

"Your meetings with the command group have gotten downright civil lately," Fisher remarked on the way back to the Striker group.

"I guess they finally got what they wanted by me getting involved in their decision-making process."

"Why shouldn't you get involved? You're a captain—the same as Lake and the others. Why shouldn't you be involved especially considering how much you know about the Masks?"

"It doesn't matter because we're no closer to finding a way to defeat them." Rhodes contacted the rest of the battalion through their interface. "Rendezvous back at the Striker group. We're deploying the air from now on."

"Yes!" Coulter cheered. "It's about time."

"Don't sound so happy about it," Thackery told him. "You know how attractive the Strikers are to the Masks."

"We're all attractive to them," Dietz pointed out. "The Masks haven't come for us—not recently."

"But they will," Rhinehart finished. "It's only a matter of time. They can't help themselves."

"They'll come for all these people," Rhodes agreed. "Maybe they're waiting until we get closer to Triowa or maybe even inside the walls before the Masks strike. Then they can finish off everyone from Estra at the same time. They'll save themselves the effort of attacking this column at all."

"What's up your ass?" Rhinehart fired back. "You've been walking on sunshine the last few days. Since when are you all down in the mouth again?"

"I'm just trying to understand why they haven't attacked yet. Let's get airborne and see what they're up to."

"They're never up to anything," Coulter cut in. "Maybe we'll get lucky and they'll never be up to anything ever again."

"They will be," Dietz pointed out. "The city machine is still traveling south. The Masks didn't stop their campaign."

"That would be asking too much," Lauer grumbled.

Rhodes didn't say anything else until he got into his cockpit and activated The Grid. His eight subordinates and their SAMs appeared in front of him.

The grid lines spread over the surrounding countryside, everyone in the column, the ship itself, and Rhodes.

Rio and the other Striker SAMs appeared on The Grid, too. "The Masks and the city machine are still in position, Captain," Rio announced.

"We'll see about that. Let's go."

The Striker group launched and flew a few loops over the column.

"None of them screams and runs when they see us launch anymore," Murphy remarked.

"They're all used to seeing the Strikers by now," Rhinehart replied.

"Word must have spread about us," Zion suggested.

"Of course it has," Zen countered. "The refugees know everything about the battalion now. Everyone knows we're part of the Legion, that we're here to protect the column, and that the Strikers are part of the battalion."

"Some of the refugees we protected during the last assault must have spread that word," Thackery chimed in.

"We all did that," Lauer interjected. "That word could have come from any refugees we protected these last few days. We've all taken hits for the refugees. Every refugee in the whole line had seen us getting shot at trying to keep them alive. They would have to be blind not to see it by now."

"It sure is nice to be accepted, though," Rhodes added. "It's nice that they don't cringe away in fear every time we walk by."

"Holy crap!" Dietz interrupted. "Take a look at that."

Everyone snapped to high alert when Dietz highlighted something on The Grid. The Strikers cut wide to the east and spotted a contingent of Masks approaching the column from far out in the countryside.

"Son of a bitch!" Rhinehart snarled. "How did I know? How did I damn well know they were about to pull some shit like this?"

"They must be trying to flank the column," Rhodes suggested. "They must be planning for the main force to attack the column from behind and then this party to come in from nowhere and hit us while our backs are turned."

"Why pull a maneuver like this?" Dietz asked. "They have overwhelming numbers, ships, and firepower. They don't need to get sneaky."

"Maybe Legion tactics are wearing off on them," Coulter added.

"How did we miss them?" Oakes asked. "We've been searching The Grid nonstop since the Masks have been camped out here."

"We've been searching their main camp for any sign of activity," Rhodes pointed out. "I don't know about you, but I didn't think to look out here. It's a small group and they're way out of their usual territory. That's probably why they did it this way—so we wouldn't see them."

"It took Dietz's eagle eye to spot them," Coulter added. "So what do we do about it, Captain?"

"We bury the fuckers," Rhinehart snapped. "Let's go."

"I was asking the captain," Coulter told him.

"We bury the fuckers," Rhodes replied. "Let's go!"

Rhinehart laughed and the Strikers wheeled out of position. The whole group veered hard to the east, took off at high speed, and overtook the Masks.

They only brought a hundred Masks in this small group. None of them carried anything more than a fusion rifle.

"This is too easy," Lauer muttered. "Maybe it's a trap."

"Better for them to spring it here than on top of the column," Rhodes replied. "Engage!"

He dove Rio close to the ground and opened fire on the Masks. They crowded together and returned fire with their rifles, but they couldn't keep up with the Strikers' weaponry.

Rhodes started his usual strategy of passing his laser back and forth to cut the Masks down.

It didn't work as well this time. The Masks' close proximity to each other protected them. The Strikers' lasers struck the outermost Masks, carved into their outer armor, and blocked the shots from hitting the Masks on the inside.

Rhodes circled the group, but it still didn't work. "Switch to thermals," he ordered.

The battalion turned spirals around the Masks bombarding them with thermals. The Masks in the outer ring started to melt.

That left those inside exposed and the group melted there in the grass. "Something's wrong," Lauer growled again. "They didn't just go down like that." He glanced toward the column. "I would have thought this was a distraction to get us away from the column, but the invasion ships aren't there. None of the enemy is moving."

"Let's get back to the column," Rhodes ordered. "We need to report this to the command dome." The battalion raced back to the column.

"You people stay up here and keep an eye on things. I'll go down alone. That will keep the column protected."

"At least you won't be going to the command dome unarmed," Rhinehart teased. "You'll be able to defend yourself against any deadly attacks."

Rhodes bit back laughter. "That's no way to talk, Lieutenant."

"You know it's true," Rhinehart went on. "One of these days, Captain. One of these days."

Rhodes didn't answer. He landed Rio next to the mobile conversion unit. Dr. Trudeau was in there tinkering with Thackery's station.

Rhodes went back to the command dome. The officers were in the middle of discussing Ravager movements.

"I thought you were deploying the battalion in your Strikers," Admiral Stabler demanded.

"We did and we are, Sir," Rhodes replied. "My people are still airborne over the column as you can see. I only came to report to you about some unusual enemy movement. We just flew another sortie to the north to check on the enemy position. We spotted a smallish group of them to the east. They were trying to flank the column—here." Rhodes stepped forward and pointed to the chart on the table.

"That is unusual," Colonel Volk exclaimed.

"It was a small group way out of their normal range," Rhodes went on. "We can only assume they did this to avoid detection."

"How far out are they now?" Captain Lake asked.

"They aren't out at all anymore," Rhodes replied. "We eliminated them."

Colonel Volk gasped. "You engaged the enemy—without authorization?"

"Since when have we ever needed to wait for authorization to engage the enemy?" Rhodes countered. "You wanted us to deploy in our

Strikers so we could engage the enemy as quickly as possible without any delay. That's what we did."

"Engaging these Masks could have triggered another assault," Captain Lake pointed out.

"*Not* engaging these Masks could have triggered another assault. If we waited any longer to report to you, both these Masks and the main force could have attacked while we waited around for you to decide what to do."

"You're out of line, Captain," Colonel Volk snapped.

"Hardly," Rhodes sneered. "My orders—the last I heard—were to defend this column. That's what we're doing. If the Masks attacked in force, you wouldn't want the Striker group to return here to the command dome to receive authorization from you before we engaged."

"No, of course not," Admiral Stabler agreed.

"I'm not going to second-guess every decision I make," Rhodes went on. "You asked me to get involved in this conference because I supposedly know more about the Masks than anyone else. If I see a course of action that protects the column and advances the Legion's position, I'll take it. I won't double-check with you every minute of the day to make sure you approve. This is what you wanted—for me to fight this war and try to win it. That's what I'm going to do. If you don't like it, then I don't need to be a part of this. I can just stop thinking and go back to following orders."

"None of us wants that, Captain," General Hyde chimed in.

"Really? It sure sounds like some people do."

"That tone isn't necessary, Captain," Colonel Volk barked again.

"I'm going back to the battalion now," Rhodes replied. "I'm going to carry on this war as I see fit. If any of you have any orders, you can transmit them to me and I'll carry them out to the best of my ability.

Otherwise, I'm going to fight the enemy the best way I know how, even if it means I don't check with you first."

He walked away fuming. The panel went to incredible lengths to lure him into their circle. How dare they question his judgment now?

He headed back toward Rio when Dr. Osborne came over to Rhodes. "You're overdue for a conversion cycle, Captain. You've been on duty for almost thirty-six hours."

"I have?" Rhodes thought about it. "I guess I have. I didn't think about it."

"You should come now before your systems start having problems."

Rhodes hesitated.

"You better go, Sir," Oakes told him. "No one can perform at their best without regular conversion cycles."

"Are you sure?" Rhodes asked. "We need to patrol the area. If the Masks tried one dirty trick, they're bound to try another."

"We'll patrol the area," Lauer told him. "Go get some sleep before you fall over."

"We should set up a rotation for going through conversion cycles," Dietz suggested. "Seven of us should stay airborne while one person goes through a conversion cycle. That way, we don't leave the column unprotected."

"Good idea, Corporal," Oakes replied. "You go first, Captain. Thackery and Fuentes were the last people to go through conversion cycles. We'll work our way through the battalion in descending order of rank...."

"What about the three of us?" Rhinehart asked. "We're all equally ranked."

"Lauer is senior to you and you're senior to me even though you're younger," Oakes replied. "You got promoted before me, so Lauer will go first, then you, then me. Same with Coulter and Fuentes. Coulter is senior to Fuentes, so after I go, Dietz will go, then Coulter, Fuentes, and Thackery. Does everyone agree with that?"

"Sounds good," Lauer replied. "Good thinking, man."

"Do you agree, Sir?" Oakes asked.

"Yeah," Rhodes replied. "Thanks, man."

"Get the hell out of here," Rhinehart told him.

Rhodes followed Dr. Osborne back to the mobile conversion unit. Osborne checked all the readings while Rhodes locked into the prongs.

He started to fade out right away. He really must be tired—more tired than he realized. He hadn't had a conversion cycle since before he saved those refugees from the bombardment.

He drifted in the interface and watched his subordinates fly over the column. If he couldn't be flying out there himself, watching them and experiencing their flights secondhand was the next best thing.

Chapter 6

R hodes woke up from his conversion cycle and blinked his eyes. He instantly interfaced with the rest of the battalion. They were still flying around over the column.

"Good morning, Captain," Fisher greeted him.

Rhodes snickered. "It isn't morning, Fisher. The sun is going down. Look. The refugees are all sitting on the ground getting ready to spend the night."

The refugees slept in the open fields. No one had anywhere else to sleep, but the refugees had gotten used to that, too.

Ravager support crews went from group to group and family to family handing out blankets, food, bottled water, and offering medical care where the refugees needed it.

Rhodes stayed locked into the prongs for a little while just watching the whole landscape. "Everything looked peaceful from there." He searched The Grid much more carefully this time. He widened the lines as far as they would go. "The Masks aren't sending out any more groups into the countryside to sneak up on us."

"I'm sure the battalion would have seen them if they did," Fisher replied. "You can see on the interface that everyone is widening their searches of The Grid, too. None of us will make that mistake a second time."

Rhodes used The Grid to scan the column until he located Yira in the crowd.

"You keep checking on them," Fisher pointed out. "I'm surprised."

"I want to make sure they're okay and that they get their share of the supplies."

"You haven't even spoken to them since that night you spent out in the fields," Fisher pointed out. "I thought you would have moved on by now."

"I'll probably never talk to them again," Rhodes replied. "I can still care about them."

"Why do you care about them? You don't even know them."

"Thank you for not telling anyone that I'm checking up on them."

"I wouldn't tell anyone," Fisher assured him.

"Then you must understand that they mean something to me."

"What do they mean to you?" Fisher asked.

"I don't know. I only know they mean something to me." Rhodes frowned. "That's strange. Yira is alone. Avi isn't with her."

Rhodes widened The Grid again until he found Avi. The boy was standing inside the mobile conversion unit—right next to Rhodes's station.

The boy stared at Rhodes in stunned fascination. Rhodes unlocked immediately, stepped out of the station, and turned to face the boy. "Are you okay? Is something wrong? You should be with your mom getting ready to spend the night in the column."

"What is that thing?" Avi pointed at the station behind Rhodes. "Why were you locked into it like that? Is it some kind of torture device? It looks so uncomfortable."

Rhodes relaxed and even found himself starting to grin at the boy's questions. "This is where I sleep. Do you remember? I told you we have equipment that handles all my body's needs so I don't eat or go to the bathroom or anything. This is it. This is the machine that regulates my implants so everything keeps working right." Rhodes frowned at the boy. "Does your mom know where you are?"

"I wanted to see you." Avi's face pinched. "I never get to see you. You never come to see us."

Rhodes' heart contracted. He laid his hand on the boy's shoulder and made absolutely certain not to squeeze too hard. "It isn't because I don't want to. I want to see you and visit you. I've just been really busy guarding the column. I want to make sure you and your mom are safe from the Masks. That's the only reason, but I've been keeping an eye on you both through The Grid."

Avi looked up. Tears swam in his eyes. "Really?"

"Of course. I don't want anything to happen to you. I want to make sure you have everything you need."

"You said I could go for another ride in Rio."

Rhodes found himself smiling again. "I did say that."

"When can we go?"

"I'm not sure. I have to use Rio to guard the column. Maybe....." Rhodes thought it over.

It would be impossible to break away from the new rotation to go for a joy ride with Avi—not without explaining to the whole damn battalion why Rhodes wanted to break away from the rotation.

He would never do that—not ever. He would never tell anyone in the battalion about Yira and Avi.

This was Rhodes's most priceless treasure—this one thing he kept all for himself and didn't share with anyone.

Not even Fisher shared these feelings. He knew about them, but he didn't understand them. He would never, ever share them.

"Come on," Rhodes told the boy. "I'll take you back to your mom and then I have to go back on duty. The rest of the battalion is waiting for me."

"Can I come back and visit you another time?" Avi asked.

Rhodes opened his mouth, but right then, Dr. Osborne entered the mobile conversion unit. General Hyde, Admiral Stabler, Colonel Wolanski, and Colonel Volk came with him.

"Captain...." Colonel Wolanski began and then noticed Avi. "You can't be in here, son. You have to go back to the column."

"I was just taking him there," Rhodes replied.

"What's he doing here?" Colonel Volk asked. "This is a sensitive military area. None of the civilians are supposed to come near this unit."

"It isn't exactly cordoned off, is it?" Rhodes pointed out. "This boy knows me and he was curious about the conversion stations. So he came over to see what they were all about. So what?"

"He could have tampered with the controls," Volk suggested.

"Oh, please," Rhodes groaned. "Now you're just grasping at straws. He came over to talk to me and see what the equipment was all about. Now I'm taking him back to the column. Just drop it already."

"Your insubordination doesn't wear very well considering you're supposed to be steering this campaign, Captain," Volk snarled.

Rhodes flared up immediately. "Insubordination! Is that what you call me stating my opinions that you asked me to give?"

He would have launched into another tirade and probably threatened these officers, but right then, Yira burst in.

She stopped short of actually elbowing the senior officers out of the way to grab her son. "Avi—there you are! I've been looking everywhere for you! You shouldn't be in here!"

She turned to Rhodes and started to say, "I'm really sorry! I should have kept a closer eye on him....." Then she turned and started babbling the same nonsense to the senior officers.

"Don't worry about it," Rhodes told her. "He's welcome anytime. He didn't do anything wrong."

"Captain!" Colonel Volk snapped.

"I'm so sorry!" Yira stammered again and turned back to Rhodes.

In that instant, she made eye contact with him and all the hidden subtext from that night came rushing back.

He could have been standing alone with her miles from anywhere—somewhere no one would see them looking at each other like this.

Her cheeks colored and she shook herself. "I'm really sorry. I swear I won't let it happen again. You know what kids are like. He's just curious."

"It's fine," Rhodes insisted. "If you need anything—either of you—you shouldn't hesitate to come find me and tell me. I'll do whatever I can to help you."

"Captain Rhodes said I can go for another ride in Rio....." Avi began.

"No, you can't," Yira snapped.

"Yes, you can," Rhodes interrupted.

Yira shot him one last look and rushed away pushing Avi in front of her.

He tried to turn around and call, "Captain—Captain Rhodes—" over his shoulder.

His mother didn't let him. She whispered down at him in a rapid undertone while she marched him back to the column without a backward glance.

"This is really taking it too far, Captain," Colonel Volk went on.

"I don't see why," Rhodes returned.

"Taking civilians for rides in your Striker?" Volk countered. "This is highly out of order."

Rhodes compressed his lips. "I protected these people with my life during the last assault. I think I've earned the right to at least have a normal human conversation with them."

"We're in a war zone with millions of refugees under fire," General Hyde added. "Getting attached to any of these people would be a terrible idea."

"I don't see it that way, Ma'am. The Battalion 1 project has done absolutely everything to rob me and my subordinates of our humanity, but it won't work. We are human and we'll keep having human relationships with anyone we choose. You can't stop us. I would advise you not to try."

He walked away leaving them all standing there with their mouths open. The bastards!

They were the ones crossing a line. They actually had the nerve to pressure him or even suggest that he no longer had the right to build relationships with regular people. Who the hell did these officers think they were?

He stormed over to Rio, but Rhodes didn't get into the cockpit right away. He needed to cool down before he rejoined the battalion and relieved Rhinehart.

He stood next to the Striker trying to slow down his heart rate when Yira came rushing back alone this time.

"I am so sorry!" she croaked. "I never meant to get you into trouble...."

"You didn't—and neither did Avi. It was really nice to see him. It sucks that I haven't been able to come and see you two before now—but I told him I've been keeping an eye on you through The

Grid. I only haven't come because I've been so busy guarding the column."

She turned bright red when he mentioned keeping an eye on her.

"I told him that." She twisted her hands together and her eyes darted to his and then away just as fast. "I told him that's why you didn't come to see us. He won't stop talking about you. He talks about almost nothing else ever since we met you." She colored again and looked away. "I guess I always knew it was only a matter of time before he would come and try to find you."

"I meant what I said. He did nothing wrong. Don't get him into trouble for coming to see me. He's a good kid. He's welcome anytime—and so are you."

She finally looked up at him, smiled, and her cheeks flamed. "Thank you so much. You've been so kind to us."

"Do you need anything? Do you have everything you need—I mean, everything the Ravager crews have been giving out? I want to make sure you aren't lacking for anything—if possible."

"We're fine—really. I don't want you to worry about us...." Her eyes softened. Of course he worried about them—both of them.

She fell silent....and so did he. He found himself looking into her eyes just as deeply as she looked into his. The feeling coming from both of them became excruciating.

She finally broke eye contact and looked away. "Anyway....I'm really sorry for getting you into trouble...."

"You didn't," he insisted. "Even if you did, maybe that's a good thing."

Her head shot up. "What do you mean?"

"Nothing." He waved behind her. "Show me where you're staying. I want to make sure you and Avi are okay."

"We are."

"Show me anyway."

She turned around and he fell in next to her on their way toward the column. Fisher and Rio both watched him go, but he didn't care anymore.

He suddenly didn't give a crap if everyone in the battalion found out how he felt about Yira and Avi. What difference did it make?

"What were those officers coming to see you about?" Yira asked on their way into the crowd.

"I'm not sure. I just woke up and realized Avi was there. I was talking to him when they showed up. They had a temper tantrum about him being there—or one of them did. The others didn't seem too concerned about it. It was just the one guy. I think he was more bothered by my reaction than anything Avi did."

"I should have made it clearer that he shouldn't have gone near you."

"Stop it," Rhodes murmured. "I want him to. I want both of you to."

She looked up at him. Her eyes softened again in the faint light. "You're so kind. I don't know what to say."

"Don't say anything. It's the least I can do."

She stopped in the middle of the column and waved at nothing. "This is it. This is where we're staying."

Rhodes glanced around and spotted Avi. He lay on the grass wrapped in three Legion-issue blankets.

Only his face showed in the nest of thick wool. Rhodes never would have recognized the boy if Yira hadn't pointed him out.

Rhodes burst out laughing at the sight. Avi's little face looked so comic in there.

Rhodes squatted down and patted Avi's shoulder. "Are you warm enough in there, buddy?"

Avi burst into a grin. "Yeah."

"Leave some blankets for your mom, okay?"

"I'll be in there with him as soon as you leave," Yira chimed in. "We combine our body heat to stay warm at night."

Rhodes straightened up. He couldn't stop grinning….and he didn't want to stop looking at her. His heart cracked with such exquisite emotion when he looked at either one of them.

He felt his face heat up just from looking at her. "That's good thinking. Promise me you'll let me know if you need anything. Really."

She smiled back at him just as broadly. "Okay. I promise."

He glanced back and forth between her and the boy. Avi watched every shade of Rhodes's and Yira's expressions.

Rhodes didn't care if Avi saw Rhodes blushing and beaming at the boy's mother. Rhodes wanted Avi to know he felt this way about them. Rhodes wanted everyone to know.

That wouldn't happen—not right away. He couldn't let it happen, but right now, this whole thing made him too happy even to care much about anything.

Yira brought him back to his senses by waving at Avi. "We should probably…."

"Of course," Rhodes exclaimed. "Of course. Good night. I'm glad you're both okay. I'll see you soon. Good night, Avi."

"Night," Avi called from his nest.

Rhodes turned away to go back to the battalion. Now he just needed to find a way to work out some time when he would be able to visit Avi and Yira again—and soon.

Rhodes's brain kicked into high gear trying to come up with a solution, and right then, the minute he turned his back on them, a belch of gunfire split the night coming from the north.

Chapter 7

White flares of fusion fire erupted out of the darkness. Rhodes's awareness snapped back to The Grid. Another massive horde of Masks streamed down from the north closing on the column of refugees.

People who had been asleep or about to go to sleep shot to their feet all over the field. They tripped over each other and everyone rushed everywhere at once.

Rhodes lost sight of Yira and Avi in the confusion. Rhodes didn't have time to get back to Rio.

Rhodes ignited his boosters, launched over the crowd, and took off at top speed to intercept the Masks.

The Strikers converged from all over. Rhodes fell in formation with them. The battalion rushed to the far end of the column where the Masks were already opening fire on people in the very rear.

Screams echoed through the night. All the refugees charged away to the south and trampled each other in their haste to flee from the Masks.

Half the refugees abandoned their blankets and other supplies they needed to survive out here in the open.

Others delayed too long trying to gather up what few possessions they'd acquired on the march.

The two groups collided with each other, slowed each other down, kicked each other over, and injured each other in the mayhem.

Rhodes plunged out of the sky gunning for doomsday, but the Masks sent another overwhelming river of their numbers against the column.

The battalion destroying that raiding party must have tipped off the Masks. Stealth and cunning were no way to win the day.

The Masks fell back on their strength and started steamrolling their way deeper and deeper into the column. They left bodies underfoot with nothing to stand in the way.

The battalion ran into exactly the same problems as before. The Masks bypassed the mountains of dead Masks the battalion cut down. Then the invasion ships showed up.

They couldn't have just materialized out of nowhere. The Legion fleet must have seen the invasion ships coming. The Ravagers, Dusters, and Predators rolled in at the same time.

Another devastating air battle broke out over the column. Rhodes tried to concentrate on shooting the Masks ground troops, but the air battle distracted him.

The invasion ships opened fire on the column. Blasts of dirt, torn bodies, and debris erupted from every punishing strike. The Legion couldn't stop another massacre.

Exploding ships and deflected gunfire put the refugees in just as much danger as the invasion ships' guns.

Fusion blasts from both fleets pelted off ship hulls and smashed into the ground even when no one was aiming at the refugees.

Rhodes turned back to the column, but he didn't see how he could save anyone this time.

He could have stretched his grid lines over a tiny cluster of refugees. He might have been able to save a few dozen people at most.

His mind switched gears. There had to be a way to stop these invasion ships. They were the Masks' real advantage.

In that moment of hesitation before he made his move, three invasion ships surrounded a Ravager. Rhodes didn't take the time to check which one it was.

The three enemy vessels bombarded the Ravager with brutal fire. Explosions plumed from the ship's sides and it started to go down.

The invasion ships moved out of the way. The Ravager tilted, surrendered to gravity, and started picking up speed on a death dive for the column.

Hundreds of refugees got trapped underneath the falling ship.

Rhodes punched his boosters and shot forward, but he wouldn't be able to do anything to stop the catastrophe.

Some primordial part of his brain flicked back to The Grid. He took a fraction of a second to make sure Yira and Avi weren't underneath the falling Ravager.

Someone was. Someone's family, someone's loved ones, someone's wife and children were under it.

He rocketed across the landscape on a collision course for the Ravager. He altered his grid lines to change himself into a missile with a drill head.

His one thought was to punch through the ship's outer skin and detonate the reactor core before the ship hit the ground. That was the only way to even remotely minimize the loss of life.

It wouldn't eliminate it entirely, but it was the best he could do.

He couldn't fly any faster. He was already flying as fast as he could when, without warning, a Duster whizzed too near the ship.

The Duster had already taken damage from the invasion ships and didn't correct in time.

It slammed into the Ravager, its engines burst, and the impact knocked the Duster away. It pirouetted in midair and started falling straight for Yira and Avi.

Rhodes's attention zeroed to a pinprick on their location. He already knew where they were. He'd just been making sure they weren't in the path of the falling Ravager.

The Duster caught fire halfway down and picked up speed. Yira crouched on the ground, covered Avi with her body, and stared up at the Duster rushing closer by the second.

Rhodes hardened his resolve to collide with the Duster to knock it out of the way. That would make it crash on someone else, but at least Yira and Avi would be okay.

The Duster was already too close to the ground. Rhodes couldn't be certain that hitting it would save them at all.

He made a split-second decision, and at the last minute before impact, he morphed his grid lines into the shape of another Duster.

She stared up at him....and her eyes registered an instant of recognition before the Duster crashed into him.

He angled his open hatch right on top of Yira and Avi and the falling Duster slammed into him full force.

The blow flattened him, crumpled his hull, and the open hatch fell over Yira and Avi cowering on the ground. They hunched lower, but Rhodes's hull took the collision.

It squashed his hull halfway down and he roared in pain. He felt things breaking in his implants, but that didn't matter.

His imploded hull left a tiny hollow with Yira, Avi, and a bunch of other people protected underneath.

Epic concussions kept hammering him from above, but they came through the other Duster before they made it down to him.

They still hurt like hell. He kept bellowing in pain every time they hit him, but he stayed where he was.

"Captain!" Yira screamed. "Captain Rhodes!"

"Stay where you are!" he yelled back. "Stay here! You'll be safe here! I'll tell you when the—Aarrgh!"

Avi tried to look up, but Yira buried him under her body again.

Rhodes shut his eyes and waited. The Strikers whistled through the battle ganging up on invasion ships, but that only drew the invasion ships' fire to the battalion.

It did draw the Masks' assault away from Rhodes, though. The battle raged for another hour. The Masks ground troops swept over the column, scattered people far and wide, and hunted down anyone they could get.

The air battle escalated, but that concentrated it closer toward the center of the column farther south than Rhodes's position.

He didn't see how this could end with anything other than a total slaughter. The Masks didn't usually leave any survivors when they laid waste to a city, planet, or even a whole solar system.

The people huddled underneath Rhodes cowered a little lower and settled themselves in for the long haul. So did Rhodes.

He planned to stay here protecting them until the Masks left, even if it took days or even weeks. He wouldn't let them leave until the Masks finished killing everyone they came to kill.

He couldn't think what he would do with these people after that. This little group right here might be the last people left alive on the planet. Then what would Rhodes do?

The Masks ground troops and the air battle eventually drifted far enough south to leave Rhodes and his refugees behind. This group was even smaller than the last.

Rhodes took a long time to decide whether it was safe to uncover them. The city machine kept rolling over the countryside north of the column.

It even stopped out there while the battle still raged on and on. The city machine must be waiting for the Masks to finish off the refugees. Then the city machine would continue its journey to Triowa.

The Grid detected scattered pockets of human life signs buried in the wreckage all along the column. A few people here and there survived the Masks' onslaught.

Those other survivors took a long time to come out of hiding, too. When they did, they crawled out from under piles of bodies and destroyed ships.

Yira looked up at the underside of the Duster on top of her and Avi. "Captain.....Rhodes.....?" she asked in a tiny voice.

"I'm here," Rhodes husked. "Um.....just let me figure out a way to get this Duster off me. Then you can get up."

Rhodes heaved, but he couldn't budge the crashed Duster sitting on top of him. Its weight pinned him down with more debris, dead people, and destroyed Masks on top of the Duster.

He tried three times and failed.

"Try shooting the Duster off with your Vipers," Fisher suggested.

"Where are my.....?" Rhodes took a second to reorient himself.

He couldn't transform his grid lines without putting the refuges in danger. His Viper ports weren't in the right position to shoot the Duster off.

In the end, he used his scourge gun to shoot away the extra debris from on top of the Duster. That lightened the load just enough for him to shift the Duster, fire his Vipers, and the ship creaked sideways.

Rhodes heaved with all his might and fired at it at the same time. He finally succeeded in toppling it sideways.

It crashed down on more piles of destruction, wobbled there, and lay still.

Rhodes rolled himself off going the other way, changed back into a man, and collapsed on his seat panting in exhaustion.

"You took damage to your stabilizers and booster systems," Fisher reported. "Dr. Osborne will have to repair those. The system that would be able to repair you is also damaged."

"It doesn't matter," Rhodes rasped. "Just let me sit here and rest for a minute."

The refugees started to stand up. They were completely unprotected, now that Rhodes's fuselage no longer covered them.

One of the men glanced southward. Light flared in the darkness down there.

A carpet of bodies and wreckage led the way south toward Triowa where the refugees once hoped to find shelter and help. Now that was gone, too.

"The battle is still going on," the man murmured.

"It's going to be going on for a while," Rhodes replied. "You'll all need to find somewhere to spend the night." Rhodes looked around at nothing. "You can use that Duster."

"What if the Masks come back?" Avi asked.

"Then I'll fly you...somewhere." Rhodes stopped himself when he remembered that he didn't have boosters. He wouldn't be able to fly these people anywhere. "We'll see what happens in the morning. If anyone else is still alive, the Legion brass might have an idea of what to do. Now come on. We can't stay out here in the open."

He dragged himself to his feet. The damage to his implants didn't hurt as much, now that the Masks no longer bombarded him.

His limbs didn't want to obey, though. He felt stiff and old.

He studied the Duster until he figured out where the refugees could stay for the night. The Duster had been empty except for the pilot and co-pilot in the cockpit. The rear compartment was empty.

The refugees stood off to one side staring at Rhodes with huge eyes while he rolled the Duster over a second time. It crashed down on its belly.

Then he forced the rear hatch and waved everyone into the compartment. "We can stay in here for now."

None of the refugees would go near the Duster until Yira tiptoed forward first. She hugged Avi against her body, climbed up into the compartment, and turned in a complete circle to look at everything that wasn't there.

The rest of the refugees eventually followed. Thirty of them crammed inside. Rhodes pulled the hatch closed behind them.

Their body heat warmed the compartment immediately. They settled down on the floor, huddled together again, and a few of them rested their heads on each other's shoulders to try to get some sleep.

The low hum of murmuring voices calmed Rhodes's nerves. Everyone else in the battalion was still south of here fighting the battle, but they were all still alive.

They weren't fighting, though—not much. There wasn't much they could do. Shooting at the invasion ships was too dangerous.

The Strikers couldn't get near enough to the column to protect anyone. The battalion just flew around in the air trying to stay out of danger. Rhodes wouldn't be able to do anything or save anyone else if he went out there now.

Everyone in this Duster right now was still alive. The Masks hadn't wiped out the entire human race—not yet.

Rhodes sat down next to Yira and she pulled Avi against her. She stroked his hair until he slumped and eventually closed his eyes.

"What's happening out there?" Yira whispered.

"The Masks are raging through the column," Rhodes replied. "More people are hiding in the wreckage. I don't know what the Masks will do when they get to the other end. They might come back to make sure everyone is dead or they might move on to Triowa. I couldn't say."

She looked up at him. "Are your people okay?"

Rhodes looked away, but that only brought him face to face with The Grid. "They're still in battle, too. The Legion fleet is taking a pounding from the invasion ships. It doesn't look good."

"What will happen to us?" she whispered.

"I don't know," Rhodes murmured. "I guess we'll just figure it out."

"How can we figure *this* out?" Her voice cracked and Rhodes looked over at her. "They'll never stop, will they? They'll keep going until they kill us all."

"That's what they want, yeah," Rhodes replied.

"Why do they hate us so much?" She looked down at her own hand running through Avi's hair. She shook her head. "What did we ever do to them to make them hate us so much?"

"The Masks don't hate humanity. They love it. They love it more than anything."

"How is that possible?" she squeaked. "How can they attack and destroy something they love?"

"Sometimes I wonder if they even realize they're attacking and destroying us. Sometimes I think this is just their way of trying to get near us—to taste just a little of what we have."

"I don't understand." Her voice trembled even more. Was she about to start crying?

"I don't understand it, either. I wish I did. Maybe then I would be able to find a way to defeat them."

She looked up and their eyes met again. She wasn't crying. Her eyes overflowed with compassion and care. "People say you and your battalion got captured by them."

"Yes, we did."

"What are they like?"

Rhodes looked away. "It would take too long to explain."

"You must understand them. I mean, you must understand them better than anyone else in the Legion."

"I might know more about the Masks than anyone in the Legion, but that doesn't mean I understand them. I don't know if anyone can understand them or if they even understand themselves. They're machines. What they do doesn't have to make sense.'

"Then how can we defeat them?"

"If I knew that, I would have already done it."

She looked over at him again. "Thank you—again—for coming for us."

"Of course I came for you. I wouldn't let anything happen to you."

"Are you....?" She hesitated, and without warning, she raised her hand to touch his face.

She raised her left hand and would have touched the right side of his face—the side covered by implants.

He reacted instantly before he realized what he was doing. He jerked his head away to stop her from touching him and immediately regretted it.

She dropped her hand and went back to looking down at her son.

"Sorry," Rhodes mumbled. "I'm not used to being around normal people."

She glanced up. Her eyes threatened to drown Rhodes in a feeling he couldn't identify.

She studied him for way too long and she didn't look away. Her eyes traced over the implants on his face....and very slowly, she raised her hand to touch that side of his face.

Her fingers traced across his forehead, down the side of his eye socket, and onto his cheekbone. "Does it hurt?" she asked.

"Sometimes," Rhodes murmured. "I mean, a lot of the time."

She explored the part of his implant that covered his temple. Rhodes found it impossible to look away from her eyes until she lowered her hand.

She leaned back against the Duster's interior bulkhead and went back to stroking Avi's hair. "I still can't get over that story you told us about the Legion telling your family you were dead."

"Maybe it's for the best," Rhodes replied. "I wouldn't want them to find out what happened to me. What about you? Did you have a family back in Estra—besides Avi, I mean?"

She understood his question instantly. "Avi's father died in an accident when he was small. I've been alone ever since. My family lives in the Lilithea Cluster. We moved up here before Avi was born—and then I stayed."

So that answered that question, but it didn't answer the other question on Rhodes's mind.

"Maybe the senior officers are right about it not being a good idea for me to get attached to anyone out here," he suggested.

She looked up with those all-consuming eyes. "Is that because we're in a war against the Masks or because it wouldn't be a good idea for *you* to get attached to anyone?"

"Maybe they have a point. I'm not human the way you are."

"Of course you're human!" Yira exclaimed. "Do you think the Masks could have been as kind to us as you've been? Of course you're human. Don't even say that."

"What I mean is—I'm not like you. I'm not a normal human man. I could never give you that."

"What difference does it make? You're here. You've done more for us than anyone. What more is there to give beyond what you've already given us?"

Rhodes had to summon all his effort to look away from her. "I didn't know you felt that way."

"You do…..don't you?"

Rhodes nodded down at his hands. "Of course. I would do anything for you—for both of you."

"What more is there than that? If that doesn't make you human, I don't know what does."

Rhodes couldn't answer. His throat hurt. Everything hurt and not in his body.

She went back to stroking Avi's hair. After another hour, she tilted her head back against the bulkhead, shut her eyes, and fell asleep.

Once she did that, Rhodes didn't try to stop himself from staring at the two of them all night long.

The way he felt about them suffocated him. He didn't remember from before if these feelings completely took over his being when he met his wife and had his own children.

These feelings definitely took over his being now. He couldn't stop them, and in those long, silent hours, he stopped trying.

He let them take over. He felt that way about them and he let it happen. He would have liked to scoot close to Yira, put his arms around her, and let her lean on him the way Avi leaned on her.

He didn't know where this was going or even if it was going anywhere. It might never go there. He might never lay a finger on her—and that was okay.

He didn't need any of that. He just needed to sit here and feel this. He would never ask for anything more.

Chapter 8

R hodes got to his feet inside the crashed Duster.

"Is anything happening out there?" Yira asked him.

"The Masks are moving on to Triowa. They aren't coming back this way. Legion officers and support crews are going through the wreckage looking for survivors. We can go out there now."

He got to work heaving the hatch open. It thumped down on the ground amid all that death and destruction.

The refugees inched outside. What was left of the column looked so much worse in the light of day.

The sun peeked over the eastern horizon. Rhodes didn't see any sign of the Masks—not near here—nothing except those the Legion cut down during that last battle.

Yira kept her hands on Avi the whole time, but he didn't try to wander off. All the refugees cringed away from the bodies.

"Come this way," Rhodes told them. "Follow me. We have to get out of the column."

He led them through the mountains of gore to the open grassland beyond the column. A few support crews came over and started making a fuss over the refugees.

"Does anyone need medical attention?" a nurse asked everyone.

"Captain Rhodes does," Avi replied.

The nurse refused to look at Rhodes. "I meant any of you."

"He has to go back to his unit so they can repair his implants," Avi insisted. "Where is it?"

"I don't know anything about that," the nurse snapped. "Here. Take this." She started handing out food packs and water bottles to everyone.

"Don't worry about me," Rhodes told the boy. "I'll be all right until I meet up with the battalion."

"But don't you need to go into that machine?"

"I'll be okay until then." Rhodes surveyed The Grid again. "The mobile conversion unit is parked about a mile away from here. The battalion is there."

"You should go if you need to go," Yira told him. "We'll be okay now, thanks to you."

He caught himself smiling at both of them. It sure felt good having people looking out for him for a change.

"Why don't you both come with me? There are more Legion support crews down there." Just because, he waved to all the other refugees in his group. "Let's go, everybody. We're going to walk down the column and meet up with the other support crews. Maybe the officers can tell us what they have in mind for us to do."

He got everybody moving. They obeyed him willingly, now that they all had food and water in their stomachs.

Rhodes stayed near Yira and Avi on the way back. He kept obsessively checking them again and again to make sure they were eating their food, drinking their water, and that they were warm enough in the chilly dawn air.

More refugees assembled from all over. The bombardment had destroyed the mobile unit the officers had been using as a command dome.

Fifteen officers met together near Battalion 1's mobile conversion unit. The officers stood in a circle near one of the Ravagers that was offering support to the surviving refugees.

That group of officers must be the inquiry panel—or whoever was making decisions now.

The Striker group sat parked on the grass near the mobile conversion unit. Rio was with them. None of the Strikers appeared to have sustained any damage during the battle.

The sun kept rising and the day warmed up. The walk back to the mobile conversion unit would have been a pleasant stroll through the countryside. Then the bodies started to stink.

Rhodes and his group got back half an hour later. The other survivors retreated farther and farther away from the column as the day wore on.

They formed another separate camp two hundred yards from the original camp. No one told them not to camp out there.

"I guess these refugees won't be going to Triowa after all," Fisher remarked.

"I don't see any other option except to go back to Estra," Rhodes replied.

Yira's head shot up. "Go back to Estra! Are you crazy?"

"Sorry. I was talking to Fisher. I just mean that, if the Masks are finished with Estra, it might be the safest place. Staying out here won't be an option, either."

"But we walked all this way to get here," Avi pointed out. "You mean we have to walk all the way back there?"

"The city is gone," Yira pointed out.

"Maybe that's why it's the best alternative," Rhodes replied. "Maybe we might be able to do something there. Staying out here

....the Masks can see us out here. Staying out here in the open makes us a target."

Yira glanced at the officers. "I don't think you would be able to convince them of that."

"I'll try. Come here. I'll get you some blankets and some more supplies and get you settled in. Then I have to go back to the battalion and see what's happening."

She smiled up at him. "Thank you. I know you don't want to hear that, but we're really grateful for all your help."

He smiled back at her. He could have repeated again that he would have done anything for them, but if she didn't know by now, telling her again wouldn't convince her.

The rest of his refugees split off for the new camp out in the fields. They met up with their surviving loved ones.

Rhodes led Yira and Avi over to the support crews to get them some new blankets and fresh food supplies. The support crews also handed out some waterless soap, fusion-powered heaters, and even small tents.

"We aren't staying here, are we?" Rhodes asked the crewmen.

"I don't know what the brass wants to do," a corporal told him. "I only know they want these people to have more shelter than just sleeping on the ground."

A nurse went through the line of refugees taking the names, dates of birth, and other identifying information on the survivors.

Rhodes stayed with Yira and Avi through the whole process, accompanied them out to the camp, and pitched the tent for them. "I guess it will be more comfortable than curling up in your blankets on the bare grass."

Yira studied the little heater. "This is going to be absolutely luxurious."

"I better get back." Rhodes pointed across the field to the mobile conversion unit. "I'll be right over there if you need to come and find....."

Avi startled everyone out of their wits by screaming at the top of his lungs. Rhodes spun around ready to shoot something. He stopped when he saw a giant insect with huge wings perched on Avi's upper arm.

The creature was just in the act of drilling its proboscis into Avi's skin. He jumped up and down, spun in circles, and shrieked to High Heaven.

More refugees raced over to see what the problem was. Avi wouldn't stand still long enough for anyone to get near him. Yira tried to grab him, but his jumps wound up knocking her away.

Rhodes stepped in, grabbed the boy, pinned his arms down, and flicked the insect off. It left a droplet of blood on the skin where Avi's arm was already starting to swell up.

He kept screaming bloody murder and thrashing in Rhodes's arms. "Okay, buddy!" Rhodes yelled in his ear. "Hold on! I'll take you to the medical teams!"

Avi didn't hear him. He writhed in agony and roared for the whole column to hear.

Rhodes picked him up in his arms and carried the boy back to the support crews. The medical team rushed over from several directions.

Rhodes had to hold onto Avi while they examined him. Rhodes had to yell over the noise to explain to them what happened.

The medical team also tried to talk to Yira about her son's medical history.

As soon as they got the message, they all relaxed. One of the doctors got a hypodermic syringe out of his kit, injected something into Avi's arm, and he collapsed sobbing on Rhodes's shoulder.

Rhodes rubbed his back. "You're all right now, buddy. Everything's all right."

Yira came over to them, put her arms around both of them, and rested her head against Avi's back. She patted him a few times and then Rhodes carried Avi back to their tent.

Rhodes put the boy inside the tent on a stack of blankets. Avi wouldn't stop crying. Rhodes couldn't stop rubbing the boy's arms, squeezing his shoulders, and rumpling his hair.

"Everything's okay now, buddy," Rhodes murmured. "Just lie here and rest. I'll see you later."

For no reason, he kissed Avi on the forehead, crawled out of the tent, and faced Yira.

"I better go," Rhodes murmured.

"Thank you again. Take care of yourself out there."

"I will. I'll see you soon."

Rhodes resisted a sudden impulse to kiss her, too, but he didn't. Kissing Avi was one thing.

Rhodes walked away and made it back to the mobile conversion unit just as the battalion gathered there to meet up with Captain Lake from the inquiry panel.

Everyone in the battalion had been helping the support crews, freeing survivors trapped in the rubble, and helping the wounded.

"So what's the plan, Sir?" Rhinehart asked Lake. "We can't go to Triowa, we can't go back to Estra, and we can't stay here. So what do we do?"

"Why can't we go back to Estra?" Rhodes asked. "What better place to take refuge than somewhere the Masks have already abandoned?"

"The brass hasn't decided what they want us to do next," Lake replied. "Most of our resources are tied up defending Triowa. We're lucky we have the Ravagers and crews supporting us now as it is. Everything else is being called to the battle zone."

"So we're just going to stay here?" Rhodes asked. "How long can that last?"

Lake shrugged. "Until someone decides otherwise, I guess."

Just then, Dr. Osborne entered the mobile conversion unit. "These people all need to go off duty, Captain. Captain Rhodes is overdue for his next conversion cycle and the rest of the battalion is long overdue. They'll start to malfunction if they don't go through conversion cycles now."

Lake stepped aside. "You better do it now while things are quiet. You won't get a better time than now."

He walked away. Osborne went through the whole group adjusting the settings on their stations.

Rhodes went over to his. He felt the same way he usually did at the end of the day when he got ready to go through a conversion cycle.

The rest of the battalion had been on duty so much longer than he had. They must all be exhausted.

He would even have been willing to stay on duty to guard them to make sure they got the rest they needed.

Chapter 9

R hodes stood next to his station waiting for Dr. Osborne to adjust it for him. Osborne finally came over to Rhodes, but Osborne didn't even look at the station.

"Your implants are damaged, Captain," Osborne told him. "I'll need to fix that."

"Oh, right. Do you need me to go over to the lab?"

"I can do it here. Just wait a minute while I get my tools. Don't go into your cycle just yet."

"I can wait. I'm fine for now."

Rhodes waited for Osborne to go back to his lab to bring his tools. Rhodes allowed his mind to wander back to Yira and Avi.

Lauer jolted Rhodes out of his daydream. "We gotta talk to you, Sir."

Rhodes looked around and stiffened when he found the whole battalion surrounding him. "What do you want to talk to me about?"

"That family—the woman and her kid...." Oakes blurted out. "We all see you taking extra good care of them."

"So?" Rhodes asked. "Do you have a problem with that?"

"We thought that was all over for us," Rhinehart told him. "You were the one who told us that. You made us believe we couldn't go back."

"We can't go back," Rhodes replied. "I can't go back, either. That doesn't mean I'm gonna turn my back on it now."

"You were the one who told us to keep our distance from them—from normal people," Coulter countered. "You were the one who told us we could only make them feel uncomfortable. You were the one who made us think we were outside all that—that being with other normal people wasn't an option for us anymore."

Rhodes raised both hands. "I won't lie to you. I thought that. I thought all of that was out of my reach for the rest of forever. I never thought I'd feel this way about anyone again...."

The color drained from Oakes's face. "Feel what way about anyone again?"

Rhodes waved that away. "I never forbade any of you to do it, and if I implied that, I'm sorry. That was wrong. I never thought it would ever happen—for any of us—but I guess we're part of this either way. We're human. We can't be anything else. We're as human as everyone else, so it makes sense that it would happen for us again, too."

Rhinehart looked away. "I don't know how it could ever happen for me again."

"If it does—if any of you can find that kind of happiness after everything that's happened, you won't get anything but support from me," Rhodes replied. "I really hope it does—for all of you. We all deserve that."

Just then, Dr. Osborne came back and started fixing the damage on Rhodes's back. He stood still through the operation.

The rest of the battalion stayed where they were confronting him, but they didn't bring up the subject in front of Osborne.

Lauer outright glared at Rhodes, but it was Lauer's old glare from the days when he first came out of stasis.

This was Lauer's hurt glare—the glare he used to help him cope with deep internal pain over everything he'd already lost.

Rhodes read volumes in that expression. He read all the confusion and torment of a man trying to decide if he could survive the agony of even trying to love anyone ever again after what he lost.

Rhinehart glared off in a different direction, ground his teeth, and compressed his lips. He refused to look at anyone.

Fuentes, Thackery, and Coulter didn't glare, but they didn't look away, either. Their features trembled with the effort of holding back every possible shade of emotion.

Dietz tried to keep his expression blank as usual, but all the same questions crept through anyway.

Oakes narrowed his eyes at Rhodes in deep concentration. Rhodes couldn't read Oakes's reaction at all.

Maybe, of everyone in the battalion, Oakes was the one who actually thought he might have a chance at something—of building those connections again with someone.

The only question was how to do it.

Rhodes never in a million years would have expected he could feel this way about anyone other than his own family.

He wouldn't have gone looking for it. He would have actively pushed it away if he realized ahead of time that it was happening to him.

Now he was in it up to his eyeballs. He cared about Yira and Avi in ways Rhodes had never cared about his own family.

Rhodes knew only too well how much danger Yira and Avi were in. Every day could be the last.

He was the only thing keeping them alive. How much longer could he hope to keep it going before something took them away from him, too?

Dr. Osborne said, "You're all done. You can go to sleep now. You should all lock in while you can. We don't know when you'll get another chance."

Rhodes turned away from the battalion and stepped backward into his station, but he didn't lock in—not yet.

The others turned away one after another and returned to their own stations. Rhodes couldn't help them with this. It was one of those private little hells each of them had to live with in the secret corners of their own hearts.

Finding Yira and Avi didn't solve anything for Rhodes. He would never get back what he lost. He would never be for them what a normal man could have been. Nothing would ever resolve that—not in a million years.

Yira could decide at any moment that she wanted a normal man. Then she would be done with Rhodes. She only got attached to him because she needed him—because she and Avi were in danger.

Then Rhodes would disappear into the woodwork where he belonged. He would be right back where he started.

He knew all that. He even expected it, but he jumped into it anyway. He needed this more than anything. He needed it a hell of a lot more than a conversion cycle or getting his implants repaired.

He would gladly die just to feel this for a few seconds or hours. He would have signed up to go through anything if he could only feel this for a few minutes before he died.

Now he was feeling it. It felt like Heaven—the closest thing to Heaven he could imagine.

He would never give it up. Someone would have to tear him apart piece by piece to make him stop feeling this way.

This feeling—this was the only thing in creation that made all the agony, suffering, rage, and loss worthwhile.

He backed into the prongs and they locked into his head and body. They held him immobile.

Fisher's face stayed there in front of Rhodes's eyes. Rhodes and Fisher had fallen out of the habit of talking before and after Rhodes's conversion cycles. These stations didn't offer any privacy the way capsules did.

Rhodes didn't want to talk anyway. Fisher already knew everything.

Fisher didn't mention again whether he approved or disapproved of whatever was happening between Rhodes, Avi, and Yira. Rhodes didn't really care if Fisher approved.

This new relationship drove a wedge between Rhodes and Fisher. Rhodes should have felt worse about that.

Yira could change her mind and discard Rhodes or tell him to keep his distance.

Then Rhodes would have Fisher. Rhodes would have no choice but to fall back on his relationship with Fisher to get him through it.

Fisher would still be there. He had to be. He couldn't abandon or discard Rhodes. They were stuck with each other.

Rhodes found himself staring deep into Fisher's eyes—as deeply as Fisher usually stared at Rhodes. Fisher stared back at him the same way now.

Some part of Rhodes already knew that Fisher understood. Fisher might disapprove.

He might think it was a terrible strategic decision for Rhodes to let himself get so attached to these people when they couldn't possibly have any future together.

At least Fisher understood why Rhodes had to do it anyway. Fisher didn't understand much about human nature, but he knew Rhodes. Fisher knew what Rhodes lost and what Rhodes needed.

Any little scrap that gave Rhodes back even a whisper of that could only be a good thing.

Fisher's eyes communicated all of that so much more eloquently than he could ever say in words. He and Rhodes didn't need to talk.

Rhodes felt his eyelids sinking shut. The rest of the battalion vanished off the interface as each of them locked into their stations.

All these problems would still be waiting for Rhodes when he woke up. A wave of relaxation swept over him, and at that moment, a distant boom of gunfire blasted him back to wide alert.

His eyes shot open just as four Dusters pelted across his line of sight. They flew over the old column. Just as fast, a colossal eruption of fusion fire forked out of the atmosphere.

That one shot took out two Dusters and clipped a third. The shot pounded both Dusters into the ground. The third wheeled away trying to right itself.

The fourth yanked its nose up and opened fire on an invasion ship dropping out of orbit.

Rhodes ripped out of his station, sprang into the open, and looked all around him at the whole formerly peaceful camp scene dissolving into chaos.

The refugees dove out of their tents and ran in all directions. So did the support crews.

Most dashed back on board the Ravagers, but it was already too late.

More invasion ships descended up and down the column. They didn't land ground troops. They didn't need to.

They bombarded support crews, medical teams, clusters of refugee tents, and every other thing on the ground.

Rhodes glanced south toward Triowa. The Masks were still assaulting the city down there. These invasion ships just came back to deal with the survivors.

The Strikers still sat there next to the mobile conversion unit. Looking south brought Rhodes face to face with the Strikers. They were the battalion's only chance to defend the refugees if anyone could.

Rhodes bolted over to Rio, sprang into the cockpit, and took off. The rest of the battalion loaded up just as fast and everyone interfaced in The Grid.

"Fourteen invasion ships are spreading out to cover the whole column!" Fisher reported. "They're spreading themselves thin. That could work in our favor."

"Are any Ravagers available to reinforce us?" Rhodes asked.

"They're all tied up at Triowa. We're on our own."

"Do we spread out or combine our firepower to take out one of them?" Rhinehart asked through the interface.

"Combine," Rhodes ordered. "We'll work our way through them one at a time. Let's go."

He turned Rio toward the nearest invasion ship—the one that attacked closest to the mobile conversion unit.

The battalion wheeled and fell in a loose formation. Rhodes throttled his engines to full speed, but Rio didn't need any encouragement.

The invasion ships spat fusion blasts all over the field. They only broke off when some Legion vessel got in their way.

"Punch through the hull and get inside the ship," Rhodes ordered. "These things must have reactor cores. If we can find that, we can blow the whole shooting match and move on to the next one."

"The Grid doesn't penetrate their hulls," Oakes pointed out. "We won't be able to locate the reactor until we get inside."

"We'll just have to cut our way through. I'm sending you all targeting coordinates on The Grid. Unload on that spot and punch through."

The Strikers swerved closer together crawling closer to the big ship's enormous sides.

Rhodes had never gotten this close to one of the invasion ships except when he was inside one of them.

He opened fire with all Rio's lasers, thermal cannons, scourge guns, and Vipers trained on one spot on the ship's hull.

The rest of the battalion's shots exploded on the same target. The battalion kept plunging for that one spot, but the eruption of explosions blinded everyone.

"I can't see a damn thing!' Coulter yelled. "The flare is hiding any damage!"

"Peel off," Rhodes ordered. "Circle around and target the same spot again. Let's go!"

Rio shrieked wide in time to miss the big ship. The invasion ship fired after the Strikers, but they scattered across the battlefield.

By the time they reformed and started another race for the same ship, it was too busy shooting at the column and the other Ravagers to defend itself against them.

"Damn it," Lauer muttered. "All our hits didn't damage the ship at all. We didn't even scratch it."

"Do the same thing," Rhodes ordered. "This time, when we get close enough, we'll drill into it the way we drilled into the city machine. Get inside. These things aren't designed to defend themselves from the inside."

No one asked how Rhodes knew this. He didn't, actually, but the battalion was doing this one way or the other. It was their only chance to stop the bombardment.

The Strikers tightened their formation again, dropped into another collision course with the invasion ship, and all their weapons opened fire.

The same outward flash of exploding lasers, thermal bursts, Vipers, and fusion blasts wiped The Grid of anything else. Rhodes couldn't see where he was going.

He modified Rio's grid lines into a conical arrow point with a rapidly spinning drill head. This better work.

Each member of the battalion morphed their Strikers' grid lines to punch through the invasion ship's tough hull. Rhodes braced himself for impact.

At the last minute before the battalion collided with the invasion ship, another deadly barrage of fusion fire hit Lauer from behind.

He bellowed in fury. "You cocksuckers!" and yanked Elio away, but not before another three invasion ships thundered toward the Striker group. The battalion had been so intent on attacking that one ship that no one saw these new ships coming in.

"Get out of the way!" Oakes roared as all three enemy vessels opened fire on the battalion.

Fusion shots bounced off Rio's housing and knocked him back into his normal shape. Rhodes concentrated everything on flying fast enough to keep out of the invasion ships' way.

There were too many of them. They rained shots all over the battalion. Rhodes heard his people and their SAMs yelling back and forth.

Too many fusion blasts pelted across Rio's nose. Rhodes didn't have time to check where the other Strikers were or if they were getting away from the enemy bombardment.

Rhodes focused all his attention on The Grid right in front of him. Dozens of fusion blasts crackled across his path.

He yanked the controls up, down, sideways, and every other way to dodge those shots.

He swooped out the other side of a curtain of gunfire and almost smashed into another invasion ship looming right in front of him.

The ship's massive hull blocked out all sight of anything beyond it.

Rhodes was flying too fast to pull away in time. He adjusted The Grid a fraction of an inch more to give him a perfect trajectory along the ship's hull, whizzed up it climbing for the atmosphere, and soared free in the sky.

He glanced around to find his subordinates, but at that moment, a completely different invasion ship fired at Rio from the left.

The shot slapped the Striker away and Rhodes struggled to correct. He heard Rio and the other SAMs calling instructions and information to each other and to Rhodes and the other pilots.

Rhodes grappled the controls straight and looked across the battlefield. More than twenty invasion ships lined up down the column.

His throat went dry. "Where the hell did they all come from?"

Another shot answered him from a completely different part of the battlefield. This shot didn't come from any of the invasion ships nearest Rhodes. He would have been able to avoid that.

He had a split second to see the shot coming from miles away to the south—near Triowa.

That was the last thing he saw before the blast hammered Rio in the tail and sent the ship into another deadly spiral toward the nearest invasion ship.

Rhodes got ready to pull another close run along the ship's hull, but as soon as he got near the ship, all the other invasion ships opened fire on him again.

He did his best to dodge them, but he couldn't see the edge of the battlefield anymore. Was there even an edge? Was there any way to get out of this—or was he trapped here?

The minute that thought crossed his mind, the ship he'd just been about to run along fired on him at close range.

He saw the shot coming this time. The ship fired directly into Rio's cockpit. The shot would completely destroy Rio and kill Rhodes. It was over.

Time slowed to a standstill. Rio hung suspended in midair with the fusion blast snaking toward his nose from inches away.

The rest of the world disappeared. Rhodes couldn't react fast enough to get out of the way.

He wouldn't have been able to save himself even if he could get out of the way. Invasion ships and fusion blasts shimmered all around him. There was no way out.

At that moment, another Striker flew into the path of the shot. The blast clipped the Striker off its right wing and sent the craft somersaulting up and over Rio's roof.

The Grid flashed for one instant to show Rhodes which Striker it was. It was Baron, Dietz's Striker.

The ship cartwheeled upward and would have sailed over Rhodes's cockpit. He didn't have a single instant to check if Dietz was okay before another catastrophic gunshot hit Baron from directly above.

Baron's fuselage blocked Rhodes from seeing where this shot came from. It hit Baron from somewhere and slammed Baron down on top of Rio.

Voices bellowed in Rhodes's ears. He yelled out, but it all happened too fast.

Baron smashed down on top of Rio and then an almighty explosion hit both ships. They crashed into the ground with bone-crushing force and the impact knocked Rhodes out.

Chapter 10

R hodes swam in and out of consciousness and then blacked out again. He became dimly aware that he'd suffered more damage to his implants—much worse damage this time.

He couldn't think. He just wanted to pass out again and not wake up, but he did wake up again eventually.

When he did, it took him a minute to figure out where the hell he was. The empty Grid with green lines and black squares kept flickering in front of his eyes.

The grid lines kept morphing into different shapes, but Rhodes didn't recognize any of them. None of them formed any coherent shape or landscape he could recognize.

He struggled to blink his eyes into focus and finally hauled his foggy brain back to reality. Once he did that, he had to go through another agonizing process of figuring out where he was and what he was seeing.

He was still in Rio's cockpit, but the Striker's grid lines no longer surrounded Rhodes. His own grid lines kept flashing on the cockpit walls. That was what made this so confusing. That explained why he couldn't see anything.

Darkness had fallen outside. Heavy clouds covered the sky and blocked out the stars. The whole world looked dark at first, but he was definitely in Rio's cockpit.

"Rio...." Rhodes husked. "Talk to me."

The grid lines flickering and blinking in front of Rhodes's eyes squiggled into a shape somewhat resembling Fisher for a second.

Then the lines twisted into a confused tangle. They kept jumbling together to form Fisher's face, but never long enough for Fisher to talk to Rhodes.

Rhodes tried anyway even though he could see that Fisher had gotten damaged, too. "Fisher? Are you okay? Can you hear me?"

Nothing. The SAM kept squiggling in and out of focus. Rio didn't appear on The Grid at all.

Rhodes couldn't stay in this cockpit forever. He had to find out if someone was still alive enough to repair Fisher, Rio, and himself.

Rhodes started to stand up. He had to use all his strength to force the cockpit open.

The cover cracked across its middle. The hinge didn't work. He had to break the window.

As soon as he stood up on the seat, he realized the awful truth. Rio had crashed nose first into the mountains of wreckage, bodies, and debris that formed the column.

The front half of the Striker no longer existed. Neither did its wings.

The rest of the fuselage had been burned black in the crash. The pilot's compartment was the only part of the ship still intact.

"Rio...." Rhodes husked, but he already knew the truth. There wasn't enough of the ship left. No way could the SAM have survived that.

Rhodes scrambled out of the cockpit and tripped when he clambered down to the ground. He stumbled around and around the wreck trying to see something—anything—to give him some hope that Rio might have somehow, miraculously survived.

Just to seal Rhodes's fate, Fisher came back online the minute Rhodes put his foot on the ground.

"Captain...." Fisher looked around and saw the Striker—what was left of it. "Oh, no...."

"He can't be gone, Fisher," Rhodes blurted out. "He can't be...."

Fisher didn't answer. He brought up the Striker on The Grid and rotated it in front of both of them.

That only made the truth all the more undeniable. The Striker's engines, fusion generator, and Rio's whole neural core had been completely obliterated in the crash.

The reinforced safety cage around the pilot's compartment was the only part of the ship that saved Rhodes's life.

"No, no, no, no...." Rhodes's voice choked. "No! He can't be gone!"

Rio was gone. He didn't come back online. He would never come back online to smile at Rhodes in that cheery, chubby way of his.

Rio's downward curving eyes flashed in front of Rhodes even now. He didn't want to accept that Rio wasn't here.

"You took damage in the crash, Captain," Fisher murmured. "We need to find someone to repair your implants."

Fisher surveyed the battlefield, but the grid lines kept flickering and wobbling out of position. Rhodes couldn't see anything—which meant Fisher wouldn't be able to see anything, either.

"The Grid isn't working well enough for us to locate the mobile conversion unit," Fisher decided. "You'll have to climb over the piles to the open grassland—over there."

Fisher indicated the countryside to the west. The refugees had been camped on that side of the column before the battle started.

The Ravagers landed there and the mobile conversion station had been there.

Rhodes didn't hope it would still be there. He didn't hope that anyone survived that battle, but the minute he turned away to follow Fisher's instructions, another disaster slapped him in the face.

He didn't even get a chance to go anywhere before he saw the blackened, charred, twisted, destroyed remains of another Striker. It had fallen ten feet away from Rio.

There wasn't enough left of this one to identify which Striker it was. Rhodes didn't need to identify it.

Only one Striker could have gone down this close to Rio. It was Baron, which meant Dietz must have been inside the cockpit when it blew up.

Rhodes's stomach plummeted into his shoes. His knees actually buckled and he sank down on the piles of dead bodies.

No force in the known universe could make him tear his eyes away from the burned hulk of Baron sitting right in front of Rhodes's eyes. Dietz. Dietz was gone—and not just gone.

He flew in front of that fusion shot to protect Rhodes. Dietz, the psycho. Dietz, the screwup. Dietz, the unpredictable. Dietz, the man no one trusted.

Rhodes felt his eyes stinging, but he couldn't look away even when he had to shut his eyes against the whole parade of memories.

The early memories—the memories of Dietz at Coleridge Station.....

The memories of Dietz aiming his gun at people for no reason or just for fun....

The memory of Rhodes telling the rest of the battalion they could shoot Dietz if he threatened them....

Those were the memories that meant the most right now. They stabbed Rhodes in the guts. Jesus Christ, what Rhodes wouldn't give to get that Dietz back right now.

Everything that happened with Dietz from Stonebridge onward...
.all of that only made Rhodes value Dietz more.

Rhodes valued Dietz more precisely because Dietz went through all
that turmoil in the early days.

Rhinehart, Oakes, and Lauer had always been steady. They were
career military men who knew how to handle themselves in every
situation.

Even when the three of them got trapped in Stonebridge, Rhodes
never doubted their loyalty and dedication to the Legion and the
cause.

Dietz, though.....

Something happened to Dietz. He started out as someone everyone
hated—someone Rhinehart wanted to kill.

Dietz was the one who got Rhodes out of Stonebridge. Rhodes
knew that now. He might not have been able to summon the resolve
to leave if he didn't have just one other person who knew.

Now Rhodes couldn't even recover Dietz's body. Rhodes couldn't
honor Dietz in any other way—not even by giving him a decent burial.

Rhodes couldn't do anything but sit here and feel the pure unbearable agony of Dietz's loss. God, what a loss!

No one in the Legion would ever know what they lost when Dietz
died. He died a hero's death and no one would ever know.

No one would pin any medals on him. His family would never find
out what a hero he was.

Maybe his family thought he was a psycho and a screwup, too.
Maybe they would carry those memories of him forever.

Then Rhodes would be the only one to carry on this silent memorial. He would be the only person to grieve over Dietz's life, his heroism,
and his loss.

Rhodes didn't want to leave the blackened outer frame of Baron's fuselage. The memorial would end when Rhodes walked away.

He wanted to stay here and remember forever. Dietz deserved that. He deserved a hell of a lot more.

Rhodes had to leave eventually. It took all his willpower to force himself to stand up. His throat hurt staring at the burned, curved, melted, twisted lines of Baron's flight compartment.

The seat wasn't there anymore. The cockpit cover and its window weren't there anymore. The safety harness wasn't there anymore.

Nothing was there anymore. The explosion had completely vaporized Dietz along with everything else.

Rhodes wished now that he had been conscious for that. He wished he could have borne witness to Dietz's sacrifice and at least said goodbye and thank you—for everything.

Rhodes would never get a chance to do any of that now or even to tell Dietz how proud Rhodes was to have served with him. That was the real tragedy.

Chapter 11

R hodes tore himself away from Baron with an effort. Rhodes had to put Dietz's death out of his mind to navigate through the mounds of destruction to get to the open fields.

He fell over more than once. The Grid didn't give him any useful information about obstacles in his path.

He tripped over more pieces of twisted metal that might have been the wreckage of more crashed Legion ships.

All these bodies he kept stepping on were someone's loved ones—someone's brothers, sisters, mothers, sons.....

Rhodes's mind started to go to some strange places. Maybe he was dead now, too. Maybe he was a ghost wandering alone in Hell. He wouldn't have been even a little bit surprised.

Maybe the Masks won the war. Maybe this landscape of destruction and dead bodies was all that was left of the Treaty of Aemon Cluster.

Maybe Rhodes would never find anyone else alive ever.

At least he wouldn't live long out here, either—not without some way to go through conversion cycles. He would malfunction and shut down.

He would kill himself long before that. If he really was the last person alive, then he had no reason to stick around.

His injuries must have been worse than he realized. He staggered a few times and started to lose consciousness while he was still on his feet.

He swerved hard to his left and tripped over something again. He lost his footing and sprawled on his face.

He fell against the slope and rolled down it. He wound up sprawling on his back and staring up at the sky for a while.

"You can rest for a minute, Captain, but you need to get up and keep going," Fisher told him. "You can rest again when you get to the grass over there. I'm picking up movement. I think it might be people."

Rhodes's brain didn't function well enough to tell Fisher that it couldn't have been anyone else.

Then Rhodes realized that whoever was moving around over there might be Masks. They might be ground troops hunting for survivors.

Going to see them would be the quickest way for Rhodes to put himself out of his misery. He floundered onto his side and sat up.

He had to sit there for a minute and wait for his head to stop spinning. His vision cleared and he blinked.

He stared down at the rubble in front of him. Everything went numb, especially his ability to think.

Whatever part of him might have been capable of making decisions about this war—that part of him completely shut down.

Nothing existed for him but gathering the energy and the willpower to stand up and keep going. He couldn't cope with anything else right now.

His implants really must have been badly damaged if he couldn't think any more clearly than this.

He took a deep breath to push himself to his feet.....and then he saw it. He'd been staring blankly at the rubble piles in front of him not thinking about anything else.

He hardly even saw the bodies and wreckage anymore. The vast column of it stretched away to both horizons north and south.

Right there, right in front of his eyes, right where he'd been staring for at least fifteen minutes—was Lauer.

The whole left side of his face—the organic side—had been completely blasted in. A small scrap of beard stuck out from under the implants on the right side of his face.

Scorched fusion blasts covered his chest implant and his mechanical right arm. He no longer had a left arm.

His eye implant stared up at the sky. Part of his left leg lay twisted the wrong way, but it wasn't the same angle as a broken human leg. The implant had either melted or bent in whatever impact killed him.

"No!" Rhodes whimpered and crawled over more dead bodies to get to Lauer. "No, no, no, no, no....."

Rhodes fumbled, plastered his hand against some other stranger's face, and clawed his way to Lauer's body.

Rhodes patted and groped all over Lauer trying to touch him and somehow get to the part of Lauer that Rhodes knew—the living part of Lauer—the part that actually mattered.

Rhodes heard himself whimpering in despair. This couldn't be happening.

Rhodes even felt himself touching the bloody remains of the left side of Lauer's head. Whatever part of him had still been human was gone—but it wasn't. Lauer was still human even now—even in death.

Rhodes couldn't bear it any longer. The feeling of Lauer's implants broke the last strain. Rhodes collapsed back onto his seat and broke down in heartbreaking misery.

He grabbed Lauer by the shoulders and shook him again and again, but Lauer didn't get up. Shaking him didn't change what he was.

Lauer's weight always pulled his body out of Rhodes's grip. Gravity always towed Lauer back down to the ground—where he'd fallen.

Rhodes's mind kept rebelling against this. He kept thinking, *No! No! No!* but it really was real.

No way could Rhodes leave Lauer here—not like this.

Rhodes got onto his hand and pushed himself onto his knees still gasping, panting, and whining in despair.

Why? Why did this have to happen? Why did any of it have to happen? Why did it have to be Lauer of all people?

It wasn't just Lauer. Dietz was gone, too.

Once Rhodes started crying, he could finally let out all the anguish he'd been keeping bottled up for weeks.

Dietz.

Rio.

Rhodes's family.

Henshaw.

Poole.

All of Rhodes's comrades from the 249th.

So many people gone. Now Wild, Zen, Elio, and Baron were gone, too.

Rhodes finally crumpled there on his knees, covered his face, and let out the tears he'd been holding back for himself, too.

All the pain, misery, fury, and loss came out in those tears. He could finally let them out, now that he was utterly, completely alone.

When he finally pried his eyes open and looked back down at Lauer again, Rhodes broke down all over again. His hand drifted to Lauer's cheek—the metal cheek—the only cheek Lauer had left.

The memories of Lauer when he first came out of stasis.....

The way Lauer used to scowl at everyone.....

The way he kept his face turned to look at the wall so no one would see his features convulsing with all the buried pain hidden underneath......

Those memories meant the most now, just like they did with Dietz.

Lauer held it together so well then. He turned himself into a block of granite—except that he couldn't.

He wasn't granite. He was a man with a massive heart that bled for the people he loved—the people he could never love again.

He did his best not to show anyone in the battalion how much he was hurting, but he couldn't hide it. Everyone saw. His heart was just too big to hide everything in it.

Lauer was home now. He was with the people who loved him the best.

Rhodes bowed under the weight of those memories. He could just imagine Lauer with his arms around his wife and children—the way it should be. He would dwell in that perfect world forever now.

Stonebridge should have been that. It should have been some kind of heaven where fallen heroes met their loved ones and lived forever in perfect bliss.

It would never be that. Nothing could give anyone in the battalion that—not until they finally went home in death. That was the only way any of them would ever find that kind of peace ever again.

Rhodes turned away still bawling his eyes out. His gaze skipped around the destroyed landscape barely seeing anything. He had to get out of here, but he had to take Lauer with him.

Rhodes struggled to his feet and made sure he knew which direction to go to get to the open countryside.

He muscled Lauer's body off the ground, but Rhodes refused to carry Lauer over his shoulder. Hell no. Lauer deserved so much better.

Rhodes picked up Lauer in his arms and carried him across the rubble mounds heading that way. Rhodes didn't care how many times he tripped or fell over.

He exhausted himself picking up Lauer again and again and staggering on.

Rhodes's despair turned to numb determination somewhere on that long trek. Nothing mattered but getting Lauer out of that field of bodies.

No way in hell would Rhodes leave Lauer in there as a nameless, faceless scrap of flesh and twisted metal. Not for all the money in the world.

The sun started to lighten the eastern sky by the time Rhodes eventually collapsed on the grass away from the column. He barely lowered Lauer to the ground before Rhodes's strength gave out.

The people Fisher had seen from the crash site became more distinct. They weren't Masks. Rhodes didn't recognize them.

Some of them wore Legion uniforms. A different Ravager sat parked half a mile away, so these people must be support crews.

Rhodes didn't see any other Legion ships, platoons, or any other personnel besides these support people.

The others could only be refugees. They wore civilian clothes. Most of them either stumbled around in a numb, zombie trance, sobbed their eyes out, or raved incoherently anytime the support crews tried to talk to them.

Rhodes sat where he was. No one came near him.

The support crews seemed to be trying to gather the refugees together in a group near the Ravager.

Some of the refugees stumbled there blindly. Others fought back and went into hysterics screaming about how it wouldn't be safe for them to go anywhere near a Ravager or other people.

Rhodes started to drift into his own private trance again, but just then, he noticed a Striker hurtle out of the west.

It coiled around the battlefield and landed on the grass near the Ravager. Rhodes didn't see which Striker it was or who the pilot was that disembarked. The Grid showed him nothing.

At least one Striker made it through the battle. Rhodes had to go down there and see who it was. Wherever the battalion was, Rhodes belonged there with them.

He wasn't their commanding officer anymore if he ever had been. He was one of them—one of the survivors.

They were the people who shared his pain. They were the only people who could get him through this. He was one of the only people who could get them through this. He had to find them.

He picked up Lauer. Rhodes no longer felt his own pain or exhaustion. He knew what he had to do.

He carried Lauer the rest of the way to the Ravager. He didn't look at anyone on the way there. None of this meant anything anymore.

He headed for the Striker. When he got close enough, he saw that it was Enoch, Oakes's Striker.

Rhodes had to walk around the Ravager to get to Enoch. Once he got there, he spotted the mobile conversion unit.

Rhodes halted when he also saw Oakes, Coulter, and Rhinehart standing there. None of them looked at Rhodes.

The three men stared down at Fuentes and Thackery lying side by side on the ground. Both of them had sustained fatal damage to their implants and their organic tissue. Fuentes's face was completely unrecognizable.

Dr. Osborne sat on the grass twenty feet away staring down at the body of Dr. Trudeau lying there.

A white sheet covered Trudeau from the neck down. The part that should have covered his face lay folded back. Osborne had uncovered him to look at Trudeau before covering him up again.

Trudeau looked so young like this. Rhodes didn't see any injuries on him. He looked like he was asleep.

Osborne sat hunched with his chin resting on his chest. He didn't move or look up.

Rhodes took one last shaky breath, crossed the last stretch of grass, and approached what was left of the battalion.

Three men. He had three men left. Coulter. Oakes. Rhinehart. That was it.

Rhinehart made a choking noise in his throat, turned away, and rubbed tears off his spasming face when Rhodes stumbled toward them and laid Lauer on the grass with the other two.

Dietz should have been there. He should have lain with his comrades.

Rhodes straightened up and stared down at the three bodies. So many thoughts and feelings wrestled in his middle just from looking at them.

Fuentes and Thackery never stood a chance in this battalion—just like Henshaw. They were all as good as dead the minute the doctors installed the implants.

The world lost something special when it lost Lauer. What price could anyone put on a good man who gave everything for his family, his people, his country, and his comrades?

Rhodes didn't know what to think about Dietz anymore. Him not being able to lie here with the others felt like the worst possible insult.

Rhodes could only make up his mind that Dietz was too good even for that. He died in a way that ensured no one would ever remember anything about him except his life.

No one would remember him getting burned to a crisp or his body being torn apart or anything like that.

Anyone who remembered him would only remember him alive in all his many shades and colors. Maybe that's the way it should be. Anyway, that's how it had to be.

Another person might have been able to say some words over these people, but Rhodes didn't.

He lost track of how long he stood there staring down at them.

When he finally turned around to face his men, he discovered all three of them staring back at him with tears streaming down their faces.

Rhodes's eye welled up with tears again when he saw the men he had left. He didn't let those tears fall, though. That time was over.

He didn't ask where the other Strikers were. Coulter and Rhinehart would have brought Zion and Aries back if they possibly could.

Coulter and Rhinehart didn't bring Zion and Aries back, which meant the battalion had one Striker left.

None of the men asked and Rhodes didn't tell them about Rio or Dietz or Baron. They weren't here. No one needed to know anything else.

Three men. Rhodes had three men. That was the whole battalion.

These men would never fight any war again. The battalion couldn't fight the war with nine people. Forget about fighting it with four.

Just then, Dr. Osborne got to his feet. He stared down at Trudeau for another minute and then covered the young man's face with the sheet.

That movement brought Rhodes back to his senses. He was still in charge of these men—for whatever good that did.

All of them had sustained damage to their implants. Rhinehart had a gash on the organic side of his forehead.

"Have any of you gone through a conversion cycle since the battle?" Rhodes asked.

"No, Sir," Oakes husked.

"Then we better go do it now. Come on. We all need it. Dr. Osborne can deal with repairs and readjustments while we're in our stations. Let's go, Corporal."

Rhodes had to pull Coulter away from the bodies of their three dead comrades. Coulter sniffed and grimaced all the way to his station.

Rhinehart kept turning his face aside and running his hand across his eye.

Oakes stared straight ahead and just let the tears pour down his face. He didn't try to hide them.

He and Rhinehart went to their stations without hesitation, turned their backs, and locked in.

Rhodes waited until Coulter did the same thing, but they were all still awake.

Rhodes locked into his station. This position gave him a clear view of Fuentes, Thackery, and Lauer lying side by side across the grass.

The last thing Rhodes heard before he faded out was Rhinehart sniffing and Coulter sobbing.

Chapter 12

R hodes opened his eyes and stared straight in front of him. The conversion cycle definitely worked to calm him down.

He didn't feel as distraught as he did before, but the pain didn't go away. It buried itself deeper and became a dull, nagging, unstoppable ache that would never go away.

Someone had removed Fuentes's, Thackery's, Lauer's, and Trudeau's bodies while he'd been in his conversion cycle.

Rhodes could just imagine what the Legion did with those bodies.

Dr. Osborne stood next to Rhinehart's station doing something to Rhinehart's facial implant. Osborne had repaired the gash on Rhinehart's forehead.

Rhodes stood there watching without leaving his station. This quiet.....This was the calm before the storm—whatever storm finally ended this war one way or the other.

Osborne must have worked on Rhodes while he slept, too. The Grid spread out in front of him. He could see everything again, including Fisher.

Fisher was already there when Rhodes woke up. "Good morning, Captain. All your systems are regulating much better now."

"Good morning, Fisher," Rhodes murmured back. "How are you doing? Did you suffer any malfunctions during the battle? You were offline for a while after Rio crashed."

"I did malfunction as you saw, but I came back online then. I haven't experienced any malfunctions since then."

"That's good. I'm glad someone around here is functioning the way they should be."

"You are, too," Fisher pointed out. "You are now."

Rhodes didn't answer that. He wasn't functioning normally now. He never would be—not in this world he had to live in. Functioning normally wasn't part of this world anymore.

He changed the subject by checking The Grid. "It looks like the Masks have worked their way almost all the way through Triowa. They'll finish off the city in a few hours and head farther south to Chaivis."

"And after that, there will be nothing between them and the Lilithea Cluster," Fisher finished. "The Legion has ten working Ravagers left and twenty platoons."

Rhodes groaned. "Jesus Christ!"

"I'm afraid the Legion's ability to fight this war has come to an end."

Rhodes checked the position and status of the remaining Ravagers. "The platoons are stationed north of Chaivis, but none of the Ravagers are even deploying against the Masks. The Legion is using the Ravagers to support the refugees….Oh, no!" Rhodes croaked when he saw another huge column of refugees heading south from Triowa on their way to Chaivis.

"This is a disaster," Rhodes husked. "The Ravagers won't be able to defend these people."

"The Ravagers weren't able to defend the refugees from Estra—not even with four times the number of Ravagers," Fisher pointed out. "This war was over long before it started."

Dr. Osborne heard them talking and left Rhinehart's station to check the readings on Rhodes's station. "How are you feeling?" Osborne asked.

"About as normal as I possibly can feel under the circumstances." Rhodes unlocked and stepped out of his station. "Thank you for taking care of us."

Osborne winced and looked away. "Not that it did any good."

"Thank you anyway. You've been very good to us and we're all very grateful to have you. We're all acutely aware of how bad things could have been without you....so thank you."

Osborne wouldn't look at him. "I'm not sure who you're supposed to report to. The inquiry panel was on the *Ero* when it got hit. It's just the five of us here now."

Rhodes went through another turmoil of emotion when he thought about everyone on the panel. Colonel Kraft had been on the panel, but then again, Colonel Kraft never really did much for the battalion—not as much as he could have.

Rhodes turned away. He wasn't about to start thinking that way about a dead man.

None of this was Kraft's fault. He was an innocent victim in this just like everyone in the battalion.

Turning away brought Rhodes face to face with the inescapable reality. No one had removed Fuentes's, Thackery's, Dietz's, and Lauer's conversion stations. They stood empty waiting for the four of them to come back.

The other three were just waking up. Rhodes left them alone for a while and went to check on Enoch.

Rhodes interfaced with the Striker. "Did you take any damage in the battle, Enoch? You look perfectly functional to me."

"I got shot down," Enoch told him. "Oakes had to leave me there to fight the Masks on the ground. He came back here without me and then he used his grid lines to bring me here so Dr. Osborne could repair me."

"Wow. I must have been unconscious a lot longer than I realized."

Rhodes widened his view of The Grid. None of the other Strikers showed up on it. They must all be gone—which was another cruel blow to the battalion. Zion and Aries were both gone, too, which meant Coulter and Rhinehart didn't have Strikers.

Rhodes climbed down from Enoch's cockpit, but he stayed interfaced with Enoch and the other SAMs on his way back to the mobile conversion unit.

Rhinehart, Oakes, and Coulter were all awake, moving around, and talking both to each other and to Dr. Osborne. Rhodes had to be with them.

He set off to rejoin them when Yira and Avi appeared from somewhere. Rhodes hadn't even been looking for them. He didn't keep track of the refugees now.

"Captain!" Avi exclaimed. "You're all right. We were looking for you....."

The boy broke away from his mother and rushed over to Rhodes. Avi burst into a grin and held up his arms like he wanted to hug Rhodes.

Rhodes shot out his hand faster than he meant to and stopped Avi in his tracks. "I can't talk to you right now. I'm sorry. You'll need to go back to wherever the refugees are staying. You can't be here right now."

Yira's face drained of all color. The light went out of her eyes—the light that once sparkled for Rhodes. "What's wrong?"

"I can't talk about it right now. Go back with the other refugees. You can't be here right now. I'm sorry."

He sidestepped around them and walked off to the mobile conversion unit. He couldn't deal with Yira and Avi right now. He couldn't look at them or even think about them.

He went through his men one at a time, checked that all their damage had been repaired, and used The Grid to make sure all their systems were functioning.

He didn't turn around again, but The Grid showed him when Yira put her arms around Avi and walked away in another direction.

Rhodes put them the rest of the way out of his mind once they left. He had more important things to think about—like how the human race could possibly survive the next few days.

"What's the plan, Captain?" Rhinehart asked as soon as Osborne finished adjusting everything.

"We have to finish the war," Rhodes replied.

"The war is finished," Coulter grumbled. "We can all go home now."

"Fighting the Masks won't do any good," Rhodes agreed. "We have to defeat them another way."

"We've already tried all that," Oakes pointed out.

"We haven't tried everything," Rhodes replied. "We need to hack them...."

"We tried that, too," Coulter countered. "They shut us down."

"No, I mean we hack them with The Grid. We haven't tried that. That's how they shut us down."

"I don't understand," Rhinehart told him.

"I didn't try to use the grid lines to force a Mask to show us what we wanted to know. If we catch an intact Mask, all four of us can use our grid lines to overcome that Mask's grid lines. Then we can use the lines to force them to show us something that will defeat them."

"Are you sure that will work?" Coulter asked.

"No, but we have nothing to lose and everything to gain."

"So what are we looking for?" Rhinehart asked. "Assuming we actually get inside one of their heads."

"We're looking for some critical vulnerability," Rhodes replied. "We're looking for something that would allow us to shut down all Masks everywhere at once—something like whatever they use as a power source—or some kind of source code that they all use to function—or maybe some kind of switch that sends them all into a conversion cycle at the same time."

Rhinehart frowned and rubbed his chin. "Hmmm. It would be good if we got our hands on anything like that."

"You see what I mean?" Rhodes asked. "We can't win this war with guns—or with ships we don't have or platoons we don't have. We need something else."

"So how do we capture an intact Mask?" Coulter asked.

"That's simple," Oakes replied. "We just go to Triowa and pick one up. The place is crawling with them."

"Exactly," Rhodes replied.

"But they'll attack us as soon as we show our faces in Triowa," Coulter pointed out. "They all want to recapture us. They'll turn on us and there are only four of us now. We would never be able to fight so many of them."

"We aren't going to fight them," Rhodes replied. "You, me, and Rhinehart will just show ourselves to the Masks. They'll stop what they're doing and come after us. Then Oakes will swoop in with

Enoch, nab one of the Masks, and fly away with it. The Masks don't care about a single individual."

"What about us?" Coulter asked. "Then you, me, and Rhinehart will be stuck in Triowa with no way out."

"We'll have a way out because we still have boosters. All we have to do is get the Masks' attention. Oakes and Enoch will do the rest."

"That sounds too easy," Rhinehart growled.

"That's because it is. So let's go. I want to get this information before the Masks move on Chaivis. Do you know what you have to do, Oakes?"

"Yes, Sir," Oakes replied. "What do you want me to do with the prisoner until you come back?"

"Disarm it and restrain it by any means necessary. You can remove its arms and legs if you want to. Just don't listen to a word it says. B will probably take over the Mask and try to get into your head."

"I'll fucking kill him," Rhinehart hissed.

"Not before we use him to hack the Masks," Rhodes corrected. "If anyone knows their critical vulnerabilities, he will. We want him to take over this Mask so we can use our grid lines on him. Hacking him will be the best thing that ever happened to us."

"Unless he shuts us down again," Coulter countered.

Rhodes shrugged that away. "Let's get out of here. Mount up, Oakes. Make sure you're moving fast enough that they don't even see you coming."

Chapter 13

O akes loaded up into Enoch's cockpit and took off into the atmosphere.

Rhodes made a point not to look at The Grid to find out where Oakes went.

Rhodes, Coulter, and Rhinehart launched their boosters and flew off to Triowa.

The three men landed in the fields north of town—on the opposite side of town where the Masks were still demolishing the place one building at a time.

"How close to them do we actually have to get?" Coulter asked.

"Close enough for them to see us and pay attention to us. Let's go."

Rhodes took off flying through the city. His grid lines swiveled past him and overlaid the Masks' assault in the landscape ahead.

He slowed as he got nearer. He, Coulter, and Rhinehart set down again three blocks from the Masks' position and walked the rest of the way.

They came in sight of the Masks in a wide avenue lined with apartment buildings. The citizens had all fled to the countryside long ago.

The Masks worked their way down the street blasting one building apart after another.

Rhodes halted on the sidewalk and watched for a minute. This avenue offered the perfect place for the battalion to spring its trap. He couldn't have planned this better.

"The sons of bitches," Rhinehart snarled.

"Now's our chance to get some payback," Rhodes replied. "Let's do it."

He stepped out into the street and opened fire with his laser while he was still two hundred yards away.

Coulter fired a bunch of Vipers at the Masks. Rhinehart used his scourge guns even though he was still too far out of range to hit anything.

The noise definitely got the Masks' attention. They stopped what they were doing, turned to see who was shooting at them, and then marched out into the avenue to engage the battalion.

Rhodes really needed to come up with a different name for it. It hadn't been a battalion where it had nine people.

Now it wasn't even a crew or even a squad. It was just four men with something to prove.

Now wasn't the time to start splitting hairs about what to call it. The Masks opened fire. Their rifles didn't reach across the avenue, either. The Masks fell to Rhodes's lasers and Coulter's Vipers.

The Masks pushed farther forward. Their gunfire smashed into mountains of debris behind and around Rhodes and his men.

They backed away luring the Masks farther up the avenue. The Masks never suspected a thing until Enoch plunged out of the clouds, shrieked across town, veered up the avenue, and extended two long arms from his underside.

He flew too fast to have spent any time deciding which Mask to take. It didn't matter.

He snatched one of them off the ground while it was still shooting at Rhodes and his men. The other Masks didn't notice a thing until Enoch was already vanishing into the atmosphere hundreds of miles from Triowa.

"Pull out!" Rhodes ordered. "Launch and beat it back to the mobile conversion unit."

Rhodes and his two companions shot away from Triowa, dodged a few stray rifle shots, and streaked back to the place where they started.

They found Oakes already on the ground next to Enoch. Sure enough, the captured Mask's arms and legs lay in a pile next to Enoch's landing gear.

"Did it even try to escape or did you just remove them because you wanted to?" Rhodes asked.

"Does it matter?" Oakes asked. "We aren't going to keep it after we finish with it."

"You're goddamn right, we won't," Rhinehart growled.

Rhodes scrutinized the Mask in question. "No, I guess we won't."

"Why is it even a question?" Rhinehart countered. "These pieces of shit are our enemies. They don't deserve our consideration." He kicked the Mask in the side where it lay on the ground.

It spoke to him in B's clear, diplomatic voice. "That isn't necessary, Lieutenant. I'll tell you anything you want to know about our...."

"Shut up, B," Rhodes snapped. "You're a terrible liar. You won't tell us anything and we all know it. You shut us down last time. We won't give you the chance now."

"I'm insulted, Captain," B replied. "We never wanted anything but to consider you and your SAMs as our own. We would have welcomed you into our society. I don't know how many times I've told you that, but you won't listen."

"If you really want me to believe that, tell me how you power all your machinery. Tell me what powers the city machine, the conversion stations, the Stonebridge landscape—all of it. What keeps you going? I've never seen any of you refuel or anything like that."

"I'm afraid I can't tell you that, Captain," B replied. "My program isn't privileged with that information...."

"I don't believe you." Rhodes swiped his forefinger at his men. "Let's do this."

The Mask jerked its head right and left trying to look at the four men gathering around. "What are you going to do?"

"None of your business," Rhinehart snapped.

"Don't worry," Oakes told B. "You won't wake up from this. We'll make sure of it."

Rhodes squatted on one side of the machine. Rhinehart went down on one knee by the Mask's head.

Oakes took the other side and Coulter squatted where the thing's legs would have been.

"What do we do with it?" Coulter asked.

"Access this unit's grid lines," Rhodes replied. "Make sure you take control of its grid lines right away so it doesn't shock us or anything like that. We need to combine our grid lines and search the city machine for whatever powers the whole system—and whatever else we can find."

"How do we do that?" Coulter asked.

"Improvise," Oakes told him.

"Don't let The Grid pull you back into Stonebridge," Rhodes warned. "If you feel yourself starting to go there, fight the grid lines and take control. Understand?"

The others nodded. "Go," Rhodes ordered and he extended his grid lines inside the Mask's chest housing.

Rhodes's grid lines didn't have any problem locating and snaking around the Mask's grid lines.

The Masks' collective Grid fought back. The lines tried to tear themselves away from the battalion's lines, but this one unit couldn't counter the four men working together.

Rhodes expanded his view. He caught glimpses of Stonebridge. The city machine tried to force the landscape onto his mind, but he resisted each time.

He manipulated the lines to make them show him the city machine's interior and all those standing conversion stations full of Masks.

Coulter got pulled into the Stonebridge landscape more than once. Rhodes and the others had to stop what they were doing, fight the grid lines into submission, and the men had to use all their energy to yank the grid lines back where they wanted them to go.

The four men finally succeeded in getting the grid lines to form the landscape of the vast fields of millions of conversion stations.

"This doesn't show us the power source," Oakes pointed out.

"Use the grid lines to turn yourselves into Masks," Rhodes suggested. "We should be able to interface with the city machine. That will tell us everything we want to know. Here. Over here. I have an idea."

He showed his men how to manipulate the grid lines to change their shapes. They changed into Masks and approached a control panel. Rhodes had seen B working on this same panel the first time Rhodes interfaced with the Masks.

Rhodes started working on it—and his awareness switched.

The Grid overlaid itself over the city machine and showed him a detailed schematic diagram of all its wires, ventilation ductways, and conduits.

The Grid even read him back a complete design layout of the city machine's entire computer mainframe.

His mind kicked into overdrive—almost as if he was having a dream. The information came to him in a split second.

He followed all those wires from every conversion station back to their power source.

The wires led deep into the very heart of the ship—to a massive fusion generator—except that it wasn't a fusion generator.

It looked like one from the outside. As soon as Rhodes saw it, he knew that it must have been a Legion fusion generator sometime in its past.

It still functioned the same way, but with one crucial difference. It didn't use fuel.

Every Legion vessel and every other machine in the whole Treaty of Aemon Cluster used fusion fuel to power these generators. The generators fed power to whatever machines anyone wanted to use.

The city machine's generator didn't use fusion fuel.....or any other type of fuel.

Rhodes studied it on The Grid. The machine kept turning and turning and turning. It never stopped.

Masks worked around it and adjusted its controls, but he didn't see them adding anything to it. The machine fed power to every part of the city machine, including the conversion stations.

Somehow or other, the same view of The Grid overlaid multiple realities on top of each other the way they did when Rhodes first interfaced with the Masks.

The Grid led him inside each Mask locked into the vast conversion fields. Each one of them had a miniature version of this generator inside them.

Their generators kept them going without fuel. They were perpetual motion machines. The generators only lost power if the Mask in question took damage in battle.

The same multifaceted overlay gave Rhodes a simultaneous view of every Mask on the battlefield—and every Mask manning the invasion ships—and every Mask working to keep the city machine running.

Each of them carried one of these generators inside them. Each one could keep running indefinitely.

"Pull your grid lines out," he told his men. "We're done here."

"Don't you want to keep looking for some other vulnerability?" Oakes asked. "What about trying to find the switch that sends them all into their conversion cycles?"

Rhodes only had to take a split second to check the interface. "There isn't one. The Masks go into conversion cycles when they lock into their stations. They don't shut down at all until they do that."

"What about going through their source code?" Rhinehart asked.

Rhodes thought about it. His dreamlike awareness of every detail of the Masks' technology told him instantly what he wanted to know.

"We can't do that here. We would need to study it more closely. We'll keep this Mask around and look into it once we report back. The brass should know about this."

Chapter 14

R hodes and his men withdrew their grid lines from their captured Masks. All four men stood up and stared down at the
thing.

"You said you would shut me down," B reminded them.

"I changed my mind," Rhodes replied. "You can stay here and
complain to the breeze for all I care. We still need you, so you'll stay
here for now." He nodded to his men and all four of them walked away.

"Make sure that thing doesn't interface with you, Enoch," Rhodes
told the SAM on the way back to the mobile conversion unit. "Don't
talk to it at all."

"I won't, Captain. I don't think it can interface with me even if it
wanted to."

"Keep an eye on it," Rhodes ordered. "I don't know what it will be
able to do without arms and legs, but anything is possible."

"If you see it trying anything, destroy it," Rhinehart growled. "We
can always get another one if we need it."

"Of course, Lieutenant," Enoch replied. "I won't take any
chances."

The four men returned to the mobile conversion unit where no one
would overhear their conversation besides Dr. Osborne.

He looked up the minute Rhodes and his men returned. "I was wondering where you were," Osborne began. "Colonel McKelvy was just here asking for you."

"Who's that?" Rhodes asked. "I never heard of him."

"He's in command of that Ravager over there—the *Ganus*. He sure sounded like he's in charge of this operation now."

"What operation?" Rhinehart muttered.

"Where is he?" Rhodes asked.

"He's over there organizing the refugees to board the *Ganus.*"

"Why is he getting them to board? The panel said the Legion didn't plan to evacuate anyone."

"He wants to take everyone over to the main column—the Triowa column. That way, the Legion can concentrate its support efforts on one column instead of pissing around with us. He said we were gonna load the conversion stations on board the *Ganus,* too. He said we didn't have any reason to keep them on the ground anymore—since the four of you aren't crucial to defending the column."

"Like we ever were," Rhinehart grumbled.

"So we're posted to the *Ganus* now?" Rhodes asked. "Is that it?"

"He didn't say where you were actually posted," Osborne replied. "He just said to send you over to talk to him once you got back. I'm sure he can tell you everything."

Rhodes humphed under his breath. "I don't put much stock in any officer pretending to run this operation."

"Or make decisions on behalf of the battalion," Oakes added.

"So what are we going to do instead—go completely rogue and start running our own campaign?" Coulter pointed out. "You said we had to come back to report our findings to the brass. What other brass is there besides this joker?"

"I guess you're right," Rhodes replied. "Stay here and keep an eye on our prisoner."

He headed off to the *Ganus*. It took him about ten seconds to locate Colonel McKelvy.

He was another beefy, older man with salt-and-pepper grey hair and a gruff, no-nonsense manner.

Rhodes presented himself in front of the colonel not expecting very much. "Captain Corban Rhodes of Battalion 1, reporting as ordered, Sir."

McKelvy barely looked at him. The colonel was too busy checking his device for the roster of refugees that would travel forward to join the Triowa column.

Rhodes pretended not to see Yira and Avi in the crowd.

"You take your men forward to the Triowa column, Captain," Colonel McKelvy replied over his shoulder. "We'll need you and your Strikers to help defend the column in the next assault—and there will be another assault."

"We only have one Striker between four men, Sir," Rhodes replied. "That's all we got left."

McKelvy whipped around fast and fixed Rhodes with a death glare. "Four men—and one Striker?! Sweet Jesus!"

"Yes, Sir. We lost half our people and all but one Striker in the last battle—and we lost one of our support staff, too."

McKelvy compressed his lips. "Shit!"

"Yes, Sir. It doesn't look like we'll be able to defend anything."

"Well, fall back with the column anyway. The four of you and your one Striker will be better than nothing."

Rhodes hesitated and then blurted out. "We won't be able to de-fend anything, Sir—not like that. Our last Striker will just get shot down and destroyed and I could lose the rest of my guys into the bargain."

"You better not be suggesting I pull you from active duty, Captain," McKelvy growled over his shoulder.

"I'm not suggesting that, Sir. I'm suggesting there may be a way to defeat the Masks without fighting them on the battlefield."

"There is no way to defeat them at all, Captain. You've proven that enough times all by yourself."

Rhodes summoned all his courage to keep going. "Excuse me, Sir, but my men and I took the initiative to interface with one of the Masks. We found their power source."

McKelvy froze with his finger poised over his device for a second. "What is it?" he asked without looking up.

"They use perpetual motion machines, Sir. The city machine has a giant one and each individual Mask uses a perpetual motion generator. They carry it inside their housing."

Colonel McKelvy glared at him. "How exactly does that help us defeat them, Captain? We've been trying since the beginning of the war to find the Masks' power source. We were hoping we could shut it down or cut off their fuel supply. Now you're telling me there is no source and each Mask can keep going forever. You're telling me they can keep going even if we found a way to destroy the city machine. You're saying there's no way to stop the Masks all at once. Stopping some or several won't stop the rest. The others will just keep going."

"Yes, Sir," Rhodes replied.

"Why are you even wasting my time telling me this, Captain?" McKelvy snapped. "This makes the situation look even more hopeless than it already does."

"There may be a way to hack the source code, Sir," Rhodes explained. "We captured one of them—one of the Masks, I mean—but we need time to study its source code even to find out if there is a way to hack it. We won't be able to do that if we're busy defending the column in a battle we can't win."

"Time is the one thing we don't have, Captain." McKelvy turned away. "Fall back with the column as ordered—and from now on, you and your men will report to the *Ganus* for maintenance and repair."

Rhodes mumbled, "Yes, Sir," and walked away.

He fumed all the way back to the mobile conversion unit. These fools recognized how hopeless the situation was, so why not take a chance on a kamikaze maneuver that at least stood the slimmest possible chance of working?

Defending the column definitely would not work. Rhodes was never more certain of anything. It was the quickest way to get Enoch and the rest of the battalion destroyed.

"What did he say?" Oakes asked when Rhodes got back. A bunch of technicians and mechanics from the *Ganus* were already there dismantling the mobile conversion unit.

"He ordered us to fall back with the Triowa column and stand ready to defend the refugees in the next assault."

"What the hell for?" Rhinehart snapped. "What the holy hell good will that do?"

"You got a problem with it?" Rhodes asked. "You take it up with him. Get over there like he said. Oakes, you take Enoch with you—and from now on, we're ordered to report to the *Ganus* for maintenance and repair."

"The flippin' morons!" Rhinehart spat. "Who the hell do they think they are?"

"Just go and don't give me any static about it, okay, Lieutenant?" Rhodes countered. "It wasn't my idea."

"What do you want to do with our prisoner?" Oakes asked.

"Leave it here. We'll have our hands full over there without worrying about that."

Oakes split away, climbed into Enoch's cockpit, and flew off south. Coulter and Rhinehart left a second later.

Rhodes waited until the very last minute. He pretended to supervise the technicians dismantling the mobile conversion unit.

After another few seconds of work, Dr. Osborne accompanied them on board the *Ganus* to oversee putting the stations back together.

Rhodes turned away, strode across the grass to the armless, legless Mask lying on the grass. "What are you going to do, Captain?" B asked.

Rhodes ignored it, squatted down, and threaded his grid lines back inside the robot's housing.

Rhodes knew now that he could manipulate this Mask's grid lines with his own. He did it by himself without any help from his men.

Rhodes went straight back to the conversion stations, interfaced with the city machine, and downloaded the Masks' source code into his own neural core.

He didn't have time to go through it all right now to find out how to hack the perpetual motion machines. He didn't even have time to think about how he could stop them all at once.

That would be one colossal undertaking considering the Masks had billions of these generators all working across the entire war zone.

Only now, when he interfaced with the city machine and saw the Masks' infrastructure from the inside—only now did he realize just how vast and powerful their race really was.

He didn't have time to think about any of that. He only knew he needed a copy of this code so he could study it.

The process took a matter of seconds. The interface worked seamlessly.

He disconnected from the Mask, but not before he snaked his grid lines into its generator and shut it off. The light behind the eye slit went out.

It was dead, but B wasn't. He would go back to the city machine and regenerate into some other Mask.

Rhodes stood up, looked down at the blank face for a few more seconds, and took off into the air to catch up with the rest of the battalion.

Chapter 15

Rhodes walked through the *Ganus's* landing bay. Support crews and medical personnel filed in and out of the ship to take supplies to the refugee column, bring patients to the Ravager's medical department, and to take them back outside once they received treatment.

More people packed the Triowa column than the Estra column. Only a couple hundred people survived from Estra. Everyone else came from Triowa.

The Legion had a hard time keeping up with everyone—now that so many Ravagers had been destroyed.

The crews focused mainly on handing out food, water, and blankets. No one mentioned that the Legion once had the brilliant idea to supply all these people with tents, waterless soap, heaters, and whatever other luxuries the Legion could cook up.

Rhodes lost sight of them when he entered the Ravager's corridors. He found his three men and Dr. Osborne in a small room that had been converted into Osborne's new lab.

Colonel McKelvy must have intended this to serve as the battalion's new quarters, but he didn't supply a table, benches, computer terminal, bookshelf, or any other comforts.

The four remaining conversion stations lined one wall. Dr. Osborne's computer equipment covered the opposite wall.

A single stool on rolling casters was the only other piece of furniture in the place.

"So what are we supposed to do when we go off duty—stand around and stare at each other?" Rhinehart snapped.

"Colonel McKelvy probably assumes we won't ever go off duty except for conversion cycles," Coulter suggested.

"That was definitely the impression I got," Rhodes agreed.

"So what are we supposed to do between assaults?" Oakes asked.

"Maybe he wants us to stand around and stare at each other out there," Rhodes replied. "Or stare at the column. I'm sure he wants us to stand guard in case of an assault. We can't do that in here."

"We should set up another conversion cycle rotation," Oakes suggested. "We can't stand guard all the time."

"It wouldn't make any difference if we stood guard around the clock," Rhinehart countered. "This whole operation is an exercise in futility."

"I suppose Colonel McKelvy will get offended if we take a deck of cards or a set of dice outside and play Slaughter Power or The Ship, The Captain, and The Crew right out there on the grass."

Rhodes burst out laughing. "I'm sure he would."

Dash interrupted. "We need to come up with a question game or a number or guessing game we can play in the interface so no one else can hear us. Then we can play while you're all standing guard."

"Great idea," Fisher exclaimed. "So what's the game?"

"I haven't come up with one yet," Dash replied.

"Get your brains working on it and let me know." Rhodes headed for the door. "I'm going for a walk. Hold my calls."

Laughter followed him out of the room until he cut the interface.

"Let me guess," Fisher murmured on their way outside. "You're going to see that mother and son again, aren't you?"

"Yes, I am and I'll thank you to stay out of it," Rhodes returned. "It's none of your business."

"I know it isn't, Captain. That's why I have stayed out of it."

Rhodes didn't reply. When it came to dealing with Yira and Avi, Rhodes was really starting to resent the fact that he couldn't just leave Fisher somewhere and come back for him later.

It rankled Rhodes's nerves as never before that Fisher was always there listening in on his private conversations with someone else.

No one should have to live like this. No one else in the human race had to. Why should he?

He halted outside the *Ganus* and used The Grid to locate Yira and Avi in the column.

It took a long time. He didn't know where they were because he hadn't been keeping track of them before now. He would have to change that.

When he did find them, he spotted them walking with other Estra survivors. Yira had wrapped her food and water supplies in blankets. She carried the bundle over her shoulder while Avi walked at her side.

Rhodes watched them for a long time. The column started to slow down as the afternoon wore on and evening set in. More people stopped and started settling down for the night.

Yira copied those around here. There was no point in going any further. Getting ahead in the column would only put her and Avi in the firing line sooner when the Masks started to assault Chaivis.

She untied her blankets on the ground, spread them out for Avi to sit down on them, and gave him his share of the food.

The support crews kept going through the column every few hours or so handing out more of it. Yira could always get more once she and Avi finished what they had now.

Rhodes hesitated to go over to them. He might have broken whatever was going on between them by pushing them away when he did.

He didn't regret it, though. The battalion needed him more than Yira and Avi did this morning. He would have done the same thing again if he had to do it over.

He couldn't avoid them any longer. Tonight could be the night when Yira told him to take a hike and keep away from her and Avi.

If it was, Rhodes had to find out now. He had to find out if he had a future with these people at all.

He already knew he didn't, but just thinking about it gave him all the motivation he needed to keep fighting the Masks.

He wanted revenge, but he wanted this future even—this new human life gleaming in front of him. He never would have believed before that he had a future.

He wouldn't let the Masks threaten it—or even the possibility of it.

He set off walking alongside the column until he drew level with Yira's position. Then he cut sideways and started working his way through the refugees to the spot where she and Avi sat.

Rhodes watched them through The Grid as he got nearer. They talked to each other while they ate, but they fell silent when they saw him coming.

Yira actually got to her feet when he made it out to them. Then Avi stood up, too.

They stiffened when Rhodes faced them. Now what was he supposed to do or say to bridge the divide between them? What *could* he say?

Yira didn't blush or smile or twinkle her eyes. Her eyebrows jerked together in the middle in an unspoken question about his motives.

Then she narrowed her eyes in suspicion. He really must have offended her—but he already knew that. God only knew how he would ever explain it to her—or both of them.

"What do you want?" Avi finally blurted out. "If you don't want to see us, just stay with your own people."

"I do want to see you, buddy," Rhodes husked. "That's why I'm here."

"Well, we don't want to see you," Avi snapped. "Go back where you came from."

Rhodes studied the boy and felt himself starting to choke up again. How could he ever tell this kid the truth?

Avi's expression went through a few shades of terror when he saw the way Rhodes was looking at him. Avi glanced at his mother for help.

Rhodes puffed out his cheeks to exhale a shaky breath, looked away once, and squatted down in front of the kid. "I'm really sorry, buddy....but Rio is gone."

Avi's cheeks went white. "Gone?! What do you mean—gone?!"

"He got shot down during the last assault. The Masks shot him down and destroyed him. He's gone. I'm so sorry...."

Avi's lower lip started to tremble. "No...!" he whimpered. "No....he can't be....."

"I'm sorry, son..." Rhodes felt tears spring to his eyes. "I wish like anything I could bring him back...."

"No!" Avi's voice started rising. "You promised! You said you would take me for a ride in him again! You promised! You said I could!"

Rhodes compressed his lips holding back the urge to completely fall apart all over again. Avi's reaction somehow made it all okay again.

Yira tried to put her arm around him. He almost slapped her when he shook her off.

"NO!!" he raged. "He can't be gone!! You promised!! You have to bring him back!!"

"I'm sorry," Rhodes croaked. "We lost four of our people and seven other Strikers that night. I'm sorry I pushed you away. I guess it was just my way of dealing with it."

"NO!!" Avi bellowed and he flew at Rhodes throwing fists. "YOU PROMISED!! YOU'RE A LIAR!! YOU PROMISED!!"

Yira tried to catch her son, but he wound up belting her in the face. He flailed his fists wildly and landed one weak blow on Rhodes's facial implant.

The rest of Avi's attack banged on Rhodes's body. Avi only wound up hurting himself by trying to hit the metal.

Rhodes grabbed for the boy's wrists, missed, and wound up wrapping his arms around Avi to hold his arms down.

As soon as Rhodes got him in that hold, Avi broke down the rest of the way and howled with brutal sobs. He didn't try to keep his voice down at all.

He collapsed in Rhodes's arms crying on Rhodes's shoulder. Rhodes rested his hand on Avi's back and Rhodes buried his eyes in Avi's shoulder.

Rhodes didn't let himself fall apart—not like he did when he found Lauer dead. That window closed that night.

Now Rhodes had to be strong for everyone else in the world, starting with these people.

He glanced up at Yira. She stood off to one side with tears running down her face, too. She didn't intervene while Rhodes did his best to comfort her son.

Avi started to relax, but he didn't stop crying. Rhodes held him for a long time and then sat the boy back on the blankets. Avi sobbed down at his hands for another ten minutes.

Yira sat down next to him. Rhodes would have liked to sit down with them the way he used to, but he didn't want to do that until Yira gave him some sign that she wanted him to.

She stroked Avi's hair and rubbed his back. He eventually curled up on the blankets. She ran her fingers through his hair until he shut his eyes and passed out in an exhausted sleep.

Yira sniffed and passed her hand across her face. "I'm so sorry," she murmured. "About all your people and everything....."

"Yeah, well..." Rhodes muttered. "I guess it was bound to happen sooner or later."

"I'm sorry....that I thought the worst of you when you told us to leave you alone. I might have said a few things to Avi. I shouldn't have done that. I thought.....I don't know....I guess I assumed you didn't want us around anymore."

Rhodes gulped. He would have liked to tell her just how bad it got that night when he found Baron.....and then Lauer......

He wasn't ready to talk about that to anyone.

She startled him by extending her arm and clasping his hand. "Sit down," she murmured. "Here." She indicated the spot next to her.

Rhodes sat down next to her. He didn't know what to say. She squeezed his hand even tighter. It didn't feel right for someone so small and weak to squeeze his hand—his mechanical hand that was strong enough to break bone.

"How are you doing?" she asked. "Are you okay?"

He looked away. "Not really."

"Is there anything I can do? Do you want to talk about it?"

He would have liked to talk to her about Lauer....and Dietz......and Henshaw....and Poole.....and Gannon......and a lot of things.

His voice wouldn't obey him. He wouldn't even have known where to begin.

Having Fisher constantly looking in on every minute of Rhodes's life was annoying enough.

Fisher even looked in on the moments Rhodes didn't want him looking in on.

But Fisher always knew because Fisher was always there. Fisher already knew about Lauer and Dietz and Henshaw and Poole and Gannon—and everything.

Fisher was the one person to whom Rhodes didn't have to explain anything.

That was the strangest thing. Rhodes would much rather have told her because she wasn't there. She didn't already know everything, but she wanted to.

Fisher didn't understand because he wanted to or because he had any special attachment or care for Rhodes. Fisher didn't have a choice about it.

Yira would have understood. That was her way. She would have sat there and listened to the whole horrific story— because she wanted to—because she cared. That meant a lot.

"If you want to, let me know," she murmured. "I'm always here to listen."

He took a chance and squeezed her hand back—very lightly. "I do want to. I just don't know how."

"What will you do—now that you have so few people? I guess the Legion isn't betting on you to save us all."

"The Legion isn't betting on anyone to save us all. The Legion isn't betting on anyone to save us at all. That's why you're here. The Masks will attack this column exactly the same way they attacked the Estra column."

He glanced over at her. He was saying too much.

She only gazed up at him with those soft, deep eyes of hers. Of course she already knew.

"So what are you going to do?" she asked again.

"We're ordered to defend you, so I guess that's what I'll do."

"Until you and the battalion all get shot down, too? What's the point of that?"

He looked away. He didn't tell her about his plan.

"Do you want to know the weird thing?" she whispered into the dark. "I wish there was some way I could protect you. That sounds so strange, doesn't it—me protecting you? I do, though. I want to protect you from the Masks. They'll kill you."

"They'll kill you, too," Rhodes murmured back. "They'll kill you and Avi. If fighting them can somehow protect you from them, then that's what I have to do. I couldn't hide behind you."

She burst into one of her brilliant smiles—the way she used to. "It wouldn't really work for both of us to push the other one in front of the Masks and use the other as a shield to hide behind." She laughed in spite of herself.

Rhodes found himself smiling back at her. "It would look pretty funny, though, wouldn't it?"

"It probably wouldn't look funny enough to stop the Masks."

"No, they don't understand humor."

"What a shame for them."

Rhodes looked over at her and laughed. "I better get back to the battalion before they start to worry about me."

"Hide here. I'll protect you."

He laughed again and stood up. "Tell Avi that, when the war is over and the Masks are all dead, I'll take him for a ride in Enoch. I know it won't be the same, but I'll make it up to him somehow."

"Thank you." She stood up and brushed the dust off her clothes. "Thank you for coming by. It means a lot."

"You mean a lot," he whispered. "Both of you. That doesn't change when I have to do my work."

She beamed at him. "Thank you for saying so. I hope we see you again soon."

"You will. I just don't know when."

"Good night," she murmured.

"Good night," he whispered back and walked away.

Chapter 16

Rhodes walked into a conference room on the *Ganus's* administrative deck. He'd never been here before, but it looked exactly the same as the conference room on the *Ero* where he'd been called to face the inquiry panel.

None of those officers were here. Rhodes didn't know any of the five officers in the room apart from Colonel McKelvy.

Two of the officers were captains named Shuman and Landry. The other two were also colonels named Graff and Fishbaum. The insignia on their uniforms indicated they were Ravager captains and commanders.

McKelvey pointed out spots and positions on a chart in front of them and gave orders to the other four.

"You'll bring the *Bruso* to the south side and coordinate the refugees' retreat. The *Ganus* will stand guard on the north side in case the Masks double back and attack this column after they attack the city. They pulled that trick before and we got caught with our pants down."

"The population will flee heading south the way they fled from Estra and Triowa," Captain Landry asked. "Why don't you airlift everyone to the south side of the city? You would save millions of lives."

"How could we airlift millions of people with less than ten Ravagers?" McKelvy countered. "It would take weeks of all our Ravagers working around the clock to airlift that many people. That would leave the whole column exposed front and back."

"It's already as exposed as it can be," Colonel Graff pointed out. "At least you'd have a chance to save the ones you did airlift."

"I wouldn't be saving any of them because they'll all die as soon as they get to the Lilithea Cluster. The Cluster is on the coastline. There won't be anywhere for the population to run then."

Silence fell over the table. McKelvy looked around at the men nearest him and noticed Rhodes standing in the doorway.

"Come in, Captain," McKelvy called out. "I want you to see this."

Rhodes inched toward the table. The other captains parted to make room for him.

"I want you to take your battalion forward to Chaivis," McKelvy told him. "I want you to coordinate with the platoons on the ground. They're setting up fortifications here and here to defend the city from the ground assault."

"The ground assault doesn't mean squat, Horace," Colonel Graff cut in. "The invasion ships can bombard the city from the air and do ten times as much damage as the ground troops. The ground troops are an afterthought."

McKelvy waited. "I'm listening. I'm listening to hear your brilliant suggestion on how we can defend this city with seven Ravagers and twenty platoons. Seven Ravagers can't take on one invasion ship, much less the whole Masks fleet. This whole discussion is a formality, so don't Horace me. We don't have a force strong enough to fight the Masks—period."

He took a deep breath and turned back to Rhodes with barely concealed annoyance.

"The platoons will deploy armored vehicles on the ground to block entrance and egress to and from the city. Battalion 1 will reinforce the platoons to hold the ground troops off. Is that clear, Captain?"

"Yes, Sir," Rhodes replied.

"I want you and your men to fly out there today and orchestrate with the platoons so you understand their battle plans. Then come back here to defend the column. Once the assault starts, you can rejoin the platoons. You and your men will be able to fit right in because you'll already know their plans."

Colonel Graff snorted. "So....you want Battalion 1 to defend the column while it's *not* under attack....and as soon as it comes under attack, you want Battalion 1 to abandon the column to defend the city. That's cold-blooded, Horace."

"Of course I don't want them to abandon the column while it's under attack!" McKelvy snapped back. "I want them to defend the column when it comes under attack and I want them to defend the city when *it* comes under attack. Any fool can see that!"

"What if they both come under attack at the same time?" Captain Shuman asked. "The Masks have done that before, too."

"Then Battalion 1 will defend the city," McKelvy replied.

"That will take time," Colonel Fishbaum pointed out. "The column would be left undefended while Battalion 1 flies to the city to reinforce the platoons."

"Will you all stop questioning my decisions?!" McKelvy thundered. "I've already assigned Battalion 1 to the city!"

The other officers exchanged glances. Rhodes caught some of them biting their lips to hold back smirks behind McKelvy's back.

"Do you understand your orders, Captain?" he asked Rhodes.

"Yes, Sir."

"Then you're dismissed."

"Um....excuse me, Sir.....I wanted to ask you....if I could get a family dispensation for two of the refugees out there. They're a mother and son from Estra....and I've had continuing contact with them since then. I was wondering....if they get a family dispensation, they'll get priority evacuation out of the danger zone."

It took all Rhodes's courage to spit out the last words. Now they quivered in the air with all the tension of a bomb about to explode.

McKelvy's eyes pierced Rhodes to the marrow. "A family dispensation would normally only be granted to an officer's wife and children. I'm going to go out on a limb and say this mother and son aren't that."

Rhodes felt his face burning. "Not legally, no, Sir."

"So....." Colonel Graff began. "So....you have a relationship with these people—what you would equate to a family relationship? Is that what you're telling us?"

"Yes, Sir—or the closest thing to it that we can have under the circumstances."

"Is that because you're in a war zone or because it's you?" Captain Shuman asked.

"It doesn't matter which it is," McKelvy interjected. "You developing a relationship with them under the circumstances doesn't meet the threshold for a family dispensation."

McKelvy changed his expression and softened his tone for the first time since Rhodes met him.

"I'm not unsympathetic to your request, Captain. Even if we granted the dispensation, priority evacuation means traveling with the column and avoiding Masks assault exactly the way all the other refugees are doing right now. At this point, we wouldn't be able to priority evacuate even our own wives and children—not without the rest of the refugees accusing us of favoritism. I hope you understand."

Rhodes lowered his eyes to the table. He could only mumble, "Yes, Sir."

He suspected the officers would say something like this. It took a lot for him to even ask. Getting turned down deflated him.

"The best way for you to protect these people is to defend the column," Captain Landry told him. "I suggest we modify your order, Colonel. If Battalion 1 is with the column when it comes under assault, then Battalion 1 will stay with the column. Battalion 1 will only go forward to defend Chaivis if the Masks assault the city and leave the column alone. Leaving the column under assault would only waste valuable time anyway." Landry looked back and forth between Rhodes and McKelvy. "Does that satisfy you both?"

Rhodes nodded down at the table. Nothing would satisfy his desire to protect Yira and Avi—nothing except the end of the war.

"It satisfies me as long as Battalion 1 goes forward to Chaivis today to orchestrate with the platoon leaders," McKelvy replied. "I want Battalion 1 ready to step in to reinforce the platoons as soon as possible."

"Yes, Sir," Rhodes replied.

"That will be all, then, Captain."

Rhodes left the *Ganus* and met up with Oakes, Coulter, and Rhinehart outside.

The three men and their SAMs had developed a guessing game to pass the time while they sat around with their fingers up their noses waiting for something to happen.

The three SAMs played the game all the time. The men joined in when they could do it without anyone overhearing their conversation.

The game was a combination of *Twenty Questions* and *I Spy*.

"What color is it?" Dash asked.

"You can only ask yes or no questions, dumbass," Rhinehart told him. "How many times do we have to explain this to you?"

"Is it red?" Dash asked.

"No," Rocky replied.

"Is it green?" Murphy asked.

"No," Rocky replied.

"This could go on all day," Fisher remarked.

"It usually does," Oakes replied.

"Is it black?" Dash asked.

"No," Rocky replied.

"How many questions is that?" Coulter asked.

"Seventeen," Rocky replied.

"You mean I only have three left?!" Dash yowled. "That's not fair."

"You better start using your brain, chump," Rhinehart told him. "Lord only knows how Oakes stays alive with such a retard for a SAM."

"Easy, Lieutenant," Oakes countered. "Don't start badmouthing my SAM."

"Is it metallic?" Dash asked.

"No," Rocky replied.

"Is it organic?" Dash asked.

"If it isn't metallic, then it has to be organic, doesn't it?" Rhinehart snapped. "Did you fall out of the stupid tree and hit your head on a rock the day you were born?"

Fisher laughed. Rhodes found himself joining in.

"Is it a juvenile of any species?" Dash asked.

"No," Rocky replied. "That's twenty. You lose—again."

Fortunately for everyone, Rhodes rejoined them just then and distracted them from a major argument breaking out.

"What's the word from On High, Sir?" Rhinehart asked.

"We're going forward to Chaivis to coordinate with the platoons to defend the city."

"And leave the column undefended?" Murphy asked. "Whose idea was that?"

"We won't be leaving the column undefended," Rhinehart pointed out. "Nothing is happening right now."

"Then why are we going forward to coordinate with the platoons to defend Chaivis?" Oakes asked. "We shouldn't be planning on going anywhere near Chaivis—not with all these people wandering around in the open."

"The officers want us to find out the platoons' battle plans in case we get called in to reinforce them," Rhodes explained. "If the Masks attack the column, we defend the column. If the Masks attack the city, we defend the city. Simple."

"This is the stupidest plan I ever heard!" Rhinehart countered. "The Masks would be idiotic to attack only the column or only the city. That doesn't happen—not when we're this close to a city. They'll attack both."

"Then we defend the column," Rhodes replied. "We're already here. It saves time."

Rhinehart groaned and smacked his lips in exasperation. His expressions of disapproval for all things military had escalated with every passing day.

The brass would never have tolerated his terrible attitude in any regular Legion unit. Rhodes didn't comment on it.

Rhinehart's outbursts, cursing, and insults somehow let off a pressure valve for the whole battalion. He said the things no one else dared to say even though everyone was thinking the same thing.

"These little side missions Colonel McKelvy keeps sending us on—they're just busy work before the next Masks assault," Rhodes told him. "We already know what's going to happen and we already know what we have to do when it happens. What happens before that doesn't matter."

Chapter 17

Rhodes and his men soared over the countryside heading for the city of Chaivis in the south. The column of refugees was still more than twenty miles away. They wouldn't get there today or even tomorrow.

Rhodes stayed low and kept an eye on The Grid. The Masks had already finished demolishing Triowa and left it to head south toward Chaivis.

"Why don't they attack the column if they want to kill us so bad?" Oakes asked.

"They pulled this shit after Estra," Rhinehart pointed out. "They're trying to mess with us."

"Keep your Grids wide," Rhodes ordered. "Make sure they don't send out any more flanking parties."

"They never do," Coulter replied. "We pasted them that time."

Rhinehart squinted at the surrounding countryside. "This is a bad idea. We shouldn't leave the column. This is exactly the time when the Masks would attack."

"They held off for days last time," Coulter reminded him. "We'll get there, see what the platoons are doing, and be home in time for dinner."

"Famous last words," Rhinehart muttered.

Coulter turned out to be right. The battalion didn't see a single Mask all the way to Chaivis.

Actually, they did see Masks. The battalion saw the Masks south of Triowa—the Masks that were not attacking the column.

They could have, though. They hung poised there just waiting to strike. Rhodes agreed with Rhinehart. The whole scenario gave him a feeling of sinking dread.

The battalion found the platoons three miles from the city limits. The platoons had already erected considerable fortifications with armored tanks and ground guns aimed north where the Masks would come from.

"How nice," Rhinehart sneered. "What will they do when the invasion ships come in and bomb them to the moon and back?"

"We don't ask questions," Oakes replied. "That's for officers so much smarter than we are."

Rhinehart snorted again, but he didn't argue when the party descended toward the fortifications to meet up with the platoons.

Rhinehart never argued. That was the thing about him. He always cooperated, always obeyed orders, and always, always respected the chain of command.

He talked endless trash about every other officer in the whole damn Legion. He couldn't trash them badly enough.

He never said a word against Rhodes—ever. Rhinehart backed up Rhodes all the way. Rhinehart was always the one who followed Rhodes's orders first—even before Oakes or Lauer.

Rhodes met up with Captain Rice, one of five commanders in charge of these platoons.

Rice was a very short, skinny guy with thick glasses. "This dude barely looks old enough to shave, let alone command a platoon," Dash muttered on the side.

"How about defending a city?" Murphy asked. "Does he look old enough for that?"

Rice showed Rhodes all the fortifications and artillery the platoons had set up. "As soon as the column comes within range, we'll send out our guys to bring the refugees behind the fortifications." He dipped his chin to Rhodes. "We'll protect those people. Don't you worry about that."

"Have you ever gone into combat against the Masks, Captain?" Rhinehart interrupted.

"Well....not as such.....but we'll give it our best shot," Rice replied. "That's the best we can do."

"What about the invasion ships?" Oakes asked.

"The Ravagers will take care of them," Rice replied. "That's what the brass told us."

"So where do you want us?" Rhodes asked. "We're supposed to find out your battle plan so we can merge with you when the time comes."

Rice frowned at him. "You are? We didn't hear that."

"What did you hear?" Oakes asked.

"I can't wait to hear this," Murphy added.

"We heard you were coming to reinforce us," Rice told them. "We heard you would bolster our defenses and help us hold off the Masks so we can get the refugees behind the walls."

"Did your officers tell you there are only four of us?" Oakes asked.

Rice looked away. "No, I guess they didn't mention that."

"That doesn't matter," Rhodes interjected. "The point is where do you want us? Where do you want us to station ourselves to bolster your defenses while you get the refugees behind the walls?"

Rice frowned again. "Does it matter? Just go wherever you can provide the most effective defense."

"Where will that be?" Coulter asked.

"How can I know that before the battle starts?"

Rhodes shrugged. "All right. We'll roll with it—assuming we make it down here."

"What does that mean?" Rice snapped. "Why wouldn't you make it down here?"

"We're under orders to guard the column. If the Masks attack the column while we're in the north, we're under orders to defend the column in the north. If the Masks attack the city while that's going on, we won't be able to make it down here. We'll get stuck up there. See?"

All the blood drained from Rice's face. "You mean....we would be defenseless?"

"Defenseless?" Rhinehart spat. "You have all these fortifications and armored vehicles and artillery and armed platoon soldiers. That's a hell of a lot more than the refugees have. Do you mean to tell me you would want us to turn our backs on them to come bail your asses out of the fire?"

"Uh...of course not.....I just thought....." Rice stammered. He must have forgotten temporarily that Rhinehart was a lieutenant and not entitled in any dimension to talk to Rice like that.

"If you don't have any strategy information to tell us, we'll get on back," Rhodes told him. "I hope we see you again during the assault."

He and Rice shook hands and the battalion left.

"What is the world coming to?" Rhinehart snarled on their way back to the column. "They're assigning this bozo to defend a city of twenty million people and the squirt has never even been in combat against the Masks before!"

"I bet you he's never been in combat at all—ever," Rhodes added.

"And no one told him we only had four guys to defend all those Legion platoons," Rhinehart went on. "Their strategy doesn't even take the invasion ships into account!"

"Either the brass didn't tell him how few Ravagers the Legion still has...." Dash chimed in.

"Or they don't know," Fisher suggested. "Maybe no one has gotten around to telling Captain Rice's senior officers. They just assume the Ravagers will come riding to the rescue."

"No one is riding to the rescue," Rhinehart sneered again.

"Why don't you just blow your brains out now and get it over with?" Dash suggested. "Then we wouldn't have to listen to you constantly bitching and whining."

"That's enough," Rhodes cut in. "We aren't talking to each other like that."

"I just did," Dash countered.

"You're still my subordinate in this battalion. Now keep your mouth shut or you can disappear until the assault actually starts."

No one said a word as the battalion took to the air on their way back to the column. Rhodes took the opportunity to look back over the fortifications north of Chaivis.

"They don't look strong enough to keep the Masks ground troops at bay," Fisher remarked.

"They aren't," Rhodes replied. "Maybe those fortifications will help the brass and the city officials feel better, though. They'll feel like they're actually doing something to protect the population."

The four men turned away. Rhodes let his thoughts drift back to the column....and everything waiting for him there.

Maybe later, after his men went into their conversion cycles, he would be able to sneak away and visit Yira after Avi went to sleep.

Rhodes wanted to check on Avi anyway and see how he was holding up after Rio's loss. Rhodes knew it would hit the boy hard.

Rhodes checked the grid farther north. The Masks still held off. The ground troops were nowhere near enough to threaten the column—not yet.

He was just starting to relax when an explosion went off behind him. The battalion whipped around just in time to see four invasion ships break orbit.

They unloaded on Chaivis from the south. Those ships stayed too high in the atmosphere. Nothing would have been able to hit them even if anyone in Chaivis had seen them coming.

The four enemy ships scattered shots all over the city. Skyscrapers exploded with all their residents trapped inside.

The platoons sprang for their artillery and fired into the air, but the invasion ships were too far out of range.

Rhodes ignited his boosters to dive into the battle even though he knew it wouldn't do any good. Was this the battle that finally ended his long ordeal?

Coulter, Oakes, and Rhinehart plunged in right next to him. They streaked across the landscape closing on the invasion ships.

None of the men tried to bore into the ships' hulls again. They already knew that wouldn't work.

Rhodes swerved around fusion blasts, used his grid lines to transform himself into a long, thin snake of pure momentum, and aimed his head for the nearest ship's side hull. He would get in this way—one way or another.

He made it forty miles from the ship in question when another pelting blast ruptured from behind him.

He dodged just in time to see another ten invasion ships dropping in on Chaivis. This was bad—really bad.

They rained gunshots all over town. The sheets of crackling fusion fire created a curtain of death in the skies all over the city.

Every shot came perilously close to taking out some member of the battalion.

Rhodes had to fly his fastest just to keep away from all those gunshots. "Head north!" he yelled over the noise. "We gotta get out of town!"

"What about defending the city?" Coulter asked.

"We can't defend it if we're dead! Fall back!"

Coulter and Rhinehart fell back. Oakes got trapped on the other side of the ship Rhodes had been targeting.

Oakes got pinned between this ship and the next one down the row. So many gunshots pelted in front of him that he couldn't get through.

"Hold on, man!" Rhodes told him. "I'm coming to get you out!"

Rhinehart started to turn back, too. "Captain!"

"Keep going!" Rhodes ordered. "Get Coulter back to the column. The Masks could attack there, too. We'll catch up. Go, Rhinehart!"

Rhodes couldn't wait any longer. He dove between another five blasts and broke through to Oakes.

"Join your grid lines with mine!" Rhodes yelled. "Form an energy field! We'll break through together!"

Oakes nodded, flew toward Rhodes, and they both merged their grid lines. Both men fired their boosters heading back north. Coulter and Rhinehart were already out of sight.

Massive fusion shots slammed into the energy field. Rhodes wrapped his grid lines tighter around Oakes and hunkered under the bombardment even as he flew at his top speed to get out of it.

The invasion ships definitely noticed the projectile spinning straight through their assault. The Masks turned all their firepower on the ball, but the energy field deflected all those blasts.

The two men hurtled out of town as one building after another detonated in clouds of smoke and torched bodies. Rhodes didn't stick around long enough to see if any refugees escaped.

Another invasion ship stationed itself directly over Captain Rice's fortifications and unloaded from directly overhead.

The ship blasted the fortifications to smithereens, exploded the armored vehicles, and reduced the ground guns to crumpled piles of shrapnel. Rhodes didn't see the big guns let off a single shot.

"Let's get out of here!" Rhodes called to Oakes and started to unwind his grid lines.

The minute he let go, the two men took another hellish smash from another invasion ship hovering high in the atmosphere.

The energy field still protected Oakes and Rhodes, but the impact tore them apart. Rhodes sailed clear and then another shot took him to the ground with a brutal thump.

Chapter 18

Rhodes flopped onto his stomach and coughed blood onto the ground. At least he was on the ground, but he didn't seem to be anywhere near Chaivis.

The Masks' bombardment still raged over the city, but it sure looked far away. Those last two shots must have knocked him farther out of range than he realized.

He tried to use The Grid to figure out where he was. He strained his eyes and his concentration again and again. He couldn't see The Grid at all. The lines wouldn't show up. Fisher was offline again, too.

Rhodes shook the stars out of his head and pushed himself up on his hands and knees. He already started to feel the disorientation and internal chaos the battalion suffered when the Masks shut down the battalion's implants.

His implants still worked. He could still see out of both eyes. All his weapons systems still worked.

He couldn't interface with the battalion. Did they even know where he was? *He* didn't know where he was.

He flopped onto his seat trying to think straight. It took him another eternity to figure out where he was.

Chaivis was over there on his left. He could still recognize what was left of the skyline. He was east of the city, so the Triowa column must be to his left.

Now that he thought about it, he started to recognize some of the terrain over there. He and his men had just flown over it to get here. Were they out here looking for him?

They better not be. They should be back with the column.

Three men couldn't protect the column just like they couldn't protect the city.

The Masks weren't playing games this time. They didn't even send ground troops against Chaivis. The city never stood a chance.

Would the Masks send invasion ships after the column next? That's what they did to the Estra column. It was the quickest way to kill as many people as possible.

Was that even the Masks' objective—or did they have some sick attachment to killing people face to face? Was that why they used ground troops in the first place?

His mind started to play tricks on him. He already knew what he had to do.

He fought through all the confusion, obsessive, overpowering emotions, and crippling terror, stumbled to his feet, and took off heading north, but he didn't travel in a straight line back the way the battalion came.

He didn't want to make himself too obvious to any Masks lurking around. It never once occurred to him that he might not be making himself obvious enough to anyone from the battalion who might be out looking for him.

His brain kept fading in and out of rationality. He fell into obsessive paranoias and startle responses to nonexistent noises. He blundered a mile over open country before he came to a patch of woods.

His ability to track his own direction failed every few minutes. He crashed into trees and tripped over things.

"Fisher...help me..." he choked.

No one answered. The silence became unnerving, so Rhodes started talking to Fisher anyway. Maybe Fisher just malfunctioned. Maybe he could still hear Rhodes even though Rhodes couldn't see him.

"I'll travel north for ten miles and then cut west," Rhodes mumbled to himself. "That will put me in line to intercept the column. What do you think of that idea? If anyone from the battalion is searching for me, they'll scan The Grid for my implants. They'll be able to find me, won't they? I'll be the only person in the whole column with implants."

Rhodes nodded to himself as though Fisher was answering him.

"You know, Fisher, you shouldn't worry about me getting attached to Yira and Avi," Rhodes went on. "You know you'll always be a part of me. My relationship with them doesn't impact my relationship with you. You know that. I trust you, pal. You're the only person I trust this much. I wouldn't want to do any of this without you."

Rhodes smiled to himself thinking about Fisher's response. He would say he trusted Rhodes that much, too. They would reconfirm their friendship.

Fisher would say he didn't feel at all threatened by Rhodes's relationship with Yira and Avi. Fisher would say he understood. He would be happy that Rhodes found that with someone after losing his family.

Rhodes might have passed out a few times. He woke up on his feet still stumbling forward. He crashed into things and fell over things more often as his mental state deteriorated.

He woke up from one of these deliriums on his hands and knees at the edge of the trees. He had no memory of how he got here.

He jumped when he saw Masks coming at him from his right, but they vanished immediately.

He hung his head panting hard. He had to pull it together and make it back to the column. How far away was he?

His eyes didn't track right. His organic eye didn't synchronize with his implant anymore. The landscape went out of focus.

He didn't even know if he was near the column or which direction to go to get to it, but he had to try.

He pushed himself to his feet. "Just a little further, Fisher," Rhodes choked. "Just a little further and we'll be there. Don't worry. I'll get us there. I'll get us back to the battalion. Don't worry, man. You can count on me. I won't let you down."

Rhodes propelled himself off the tree. He couldn't feel his legs anymore.

His vision blurred again. He felt himself still walking, but he couldn't see where he was going.

He might have swerved right and then left.

He came to his senses walking straight for a sheer cliff plunging to a raging river below. He sprang back screaming and turned off just in time.

He blundered off in a different direction. Did he hallucinate that river or was it real?

He collapsed again….somewhere. His eyes barely drifted open and he looked up at Yira bending over him. Now he definitely knew he was hallucinating.

Her hair hung in his face. He heard her voice coming from a long, long way away. "Captain Rhodes!" she yelled. "Captain! CORBAN!! LOOK AT ME!!"

Her saying his name for the first time snapped him out of his trance. She kept saying it.

"Corban! Wake up! Corban—can you hear me?!"

His brain wouldn't connect to his mouth. He hardly dared to believe she was actually here, bending over him. Where was here, anyway?

She jerked away from him and yelled at someone standing right next to her. His brain took forever to make the connection that she was talking to Avi.

"Quick, Avi!" she yelled. "Run back to the *Ganus* and bring Lieutenant Oakes over here! Hurry!"

Avi took off running. Was it possible Rhodes actually stumbled back to the column?

Yira bent over him again. He didn't want to talk. He couldn't talk even if he tried.

He just wanted to look at her—at those eyes brimming with concern.

"Hold on, Corban," she choked. "Someone from the battalion will come and get you. Just hold on a little longer."

Fisher. Fisher was offline. *Don't worry, Fisher. Everything will be all right. Someone from the battalion will come and get us. Just hold on a little longer.*

Those words rang in Rhodes's head even as he gazed up at Yira's face. She kept trying to talk to him. He would give anything to talk back to her and tell her everything was going to be okay.

Out of nowhere, Oakes's face jutted in front of Rhodes's eyes. Yira vanished.

Oakes didn't try to talk. He scooped up Rhodes in his arms, launched into the sky, and took off somewhere. Rhodes didn't see where they were going. He drifted out of consciousness with Yira's face still floating there in front of his eyes.

He came to his senses lying in a conversion capsule somewhere. It sounded eerily quiet.

He'd spent so long going through conversion cycles in standing stations with people and activity all around him.

Now, in this quiet, private place, he could finally talk to Fisher, but Fisher didn't show himself.

Rhodes would have worried about that if he hadn't already gone through an identical experience when the Masks shut down his implants. Fisher must still be offline.

No big deal. The doctors would turn him back on again.

Still, the silence racked Rhodes's nerves again. He really wasn't designed to function without a SAM.

Lying in a conversion capsule used to be a relaxing experience. He and Fisher could talk things over in here without anyone eavesdropping.

Now the silence made the disorientation and agitation worse.

Rhodes opened the cover and sat up. He was in another lab—a larger one. Dr. Osborne stood across the room working on his equipment, but this wasn't the tiny compartment on the *Ganus.*

Dr. Osborne stopped what he was doing and came over to check the readings on Rhodes's capsule. "How do you feel?"

Rhodes groaned and ran his fingers through his hair. "I feel like I've been in stasis for a long time."

"You have been. You've been in and out of surgery to repair the damage to your implants. You barely made it."

"I felt like it. I felt like I would pass out and never wake up."

"It's a miracle you made it back to the column when you did," Osborne went on. "We never would have found you otherwise. Coulter, Oakes, and Rhinehart looked for you everywhere, but they couldn't find you because your systems were malfunctioning."

"Where are they?" Rhodes frowned at the lab. "Where are *we?*"

"We're on the *Ganus.* The Legion sent this capsule for you when they realized you needed it to recover."

"So...." Rhodes frowned. "Wait a minute. If we're on the *Ganus* and I've been in stasis for so long....what's happening on Sarus?"

"You really are a soldier to the marrow of your bones, aren't you?" Osborne crossed the room to check one of his computer components on the wall. "The Masks are closing on the Lilithea Cluster if you really must know. That's where the other three are. They're preparing for the assault—which should start any day now."

"I gotta get out there. I gotta help them." Rhodes stood up.

"You aren't going anywhere—not for a while," Osborne replied over his shoulder. "For a start, we're in orbit. You can't rejoin the battalion until I decide you're fit for duty."

"I'm fit for duty now. I feel fine."

"No, you don't," Osborne snapped. "Sit down, Captain."

He pierced Rhodes with a sharp look. Rhodes sank back down on the edge of the capsule.

Osborne took another minute before he crossed the room and planted himself in front of Rhodes.

"It's admirable that you want to help your men and the Lilithea Cluster, but you can't go back into combat without a SAM."

"Then why can't you bring Fisher back online? You did it before. You should know by now how to switch him back on. What are you waiting for?"

Osborne's cheek pinched. "I'm sorry, Captain. I can't bring Fisher back online. He's gone."

Rhodes's jaw dropped. "He's.....he can't be!"

"I'm sorry. The damage to your neural core......"

"That's nonsense!" Rhodes bellowed. "You fixed him just fine before! You have to bring him back."

"I can't," Osborne murmured. "I'm sorry. I wish I could, but he's gone for good. He'll never come back."

Rhodes opened his mouth to yell something else. He really wanted to attack Osborne and throttle him just for saying those words.

Fisher was not gone. He couldn't be. Rhodes had just been talking to him.....

Rhodes talked to Fisher while Rhodes staggered across the countryside trying to rejoin the column. Fisher didn't talk back to Rhodes. Fisher had been gone all that time.

Fisher helped Rhodes survive that trek even after Fisher was already effectively dead. He helped Rhodes even in death.

When was the last time Rhodes talked to Fisher? Rhodes couldn't remember now.

Had Rhodes really just been thinking just a few days ago that he wished he could leave Fisher behind somewhere? What a stupid, short-sighted, callous thing to think.

Dr. Osborne's eyes said it all. "You have to stay on board for a few days to reorient. Then we'll fit you with a new SAM before you go back into combat. I can't send you back to Sarus the way you are. You would be a danger to yourself and everyone around you. In the meantime, you'll come back here for conversion cycles. Captain McKelvy says you can make yourself at home on board the *Ganus* as long as I think you're up to it. You can wander around and interact with the crew. You don't have to stay down here."

Dr. Osborne went back to his work and left Rhodes sitting there stunned. This was not happening. Fisher was not gone. That wasn't possible.

Rhodes sat there a lot longer than he needed to. He could have stood up and walked around.

After a long time of just sitting there trying to think, he stretched out on his back and stared at the ceiling.

He spent the first couple of hours waiting for Dr. Osborne to come back.

Any second now, Osborne would come over to Rhodes's capsule and tell him that this was all some colossal mistake—that Osborne could somehow reinstall Fisher after all.

Osborne didn't come back. He avoided Rhodes, kept his back to the capsule, and eventually left the lab.

That silence drove the last nail into Rhodes's coffin. Fisher really must be gone.

Osborne wouldn't treat Rhodes like the bereaved at a funeral unless Fisher really was gone.

Osborne didn't even treat Rhodes like this after half his battalion got killed in battle. Even Osborne understood how much worse this was.

Fisher. He had become such a constant in Rhodes's life. Fisher was the only constant—the one and only thing Rhodes could count on to always stay the same.

Fisher never changed at all unless he malfunctioned. Even then, Rhodes always knew Fisher would come back.

He would always be the steady, soft-spoken voice of reason in every situation.

Everyone respected Fisher. The other SAMs treated Fisher as Rhodes's second-in-command. Fisher's word carried the same weight as Rhodes's with the other SAMs.

Now what would Rhodes do? He didn't want another SAM, but of course he had to have one. He had to get a new SAM even if he never went back into combat.

Being this—whatever this was—it needed a SAM to function.

Rhodes needed a SAM to function, but he didn't need just any SAM. He needed Fisher. Why didn't Rhodes realize before how much he needed Fisher?

Rhodes did realize it. That's what made this so awful. He realized. He should have made it clearer to Fisher while Rhodes still had the chance.

He didn't go nearly far enough to tell Fisher—really making him understand—how much Rhodes valued him.

Rhodes didn't understand how much he valued Fisher—not until now.

Why did this have to happen every time something went wrong with Fisher? Rhodes never understood just how important Fisher was until he malfunctioned.

Rhodes would never get a chance to tell Fisher now.

Rhodes couldn't even cry over Fisher's loss the way Rhodes cried over Lauer. The pain went too deep even for that.

Fisher just....vanished. He vanished worse than Dietz. Fisher would never get a decent Legion burial. No one would mourn for Fisher—not even Rhodes.

He hated himself for not mourning for Fisher more—not in that way. Rhodes couldn't shed a single tear for the one man Rhodes considered his closest friend in the world.

That's what Fisher was and he wasn't even a man. He'd been closer than any man could have been.

Fisher was there when Rhodes found Lauer's body. Fisher was the one who bore silent witness to Rhodes's grief—for all of them.

Fisher had been present, silent, and discrete every time Rhodes visited Yira and Avi. Fisher went out of his way to give Rhodes as much privacy as possible. Fisher knew.

Fisher risked his life a thousand times for Rhodes. Fisher risked it all to warn Rhodes in the Stonebridge landscape.

Fisher sympathized and even agreed with Rhodes's desire to end his life. Fisher did all that even knowing he would die, too.

He shared Rhodes's pain even at the expense of Fisher's own life. That's how much Fisher cared.

Rhodes would never get another SAM like Fisher. He knew that now. No SAM could ever do for Rhodes what Fisher did.

Fisher's understanding got Rhodes through those excruciating early days when Rhodes couldn't cope with the disorientation and distress of waking up with his implants.

Fisher would have remained silent and invisible forever if Rhodes needed him to. Fisher would have done absolutely anything to help Rhodes.

Who else in the universe would have done that—or would ever do it again? No one.

The numb shock of not believing that Fisher was actually gone—it changed to a duller, deeper ache than Rhodes suffered over Lauer's and Dietz's deaths.

This—this would never go away.

Whatever SAM Dr. Osborne fitted to Rhodes next—it would always stand out as a glaring reminder that it wasn't Fisher. Its presence would be an insult to Fisher's memory.

Rhodes would never share with any other SAM what he shared with Fisher.

Rhodes would hold his next SAM at arm's length. Rhodes would never let another SAM in the way he let in Fisher.

Fisher would hold that place in Rhodes's heart forever. It belonged to Fisher alone from now on.

Chapter 19

R hodes sat up on the edge of the capsule. He had gone through another conversion cycle since finding out that Fisher was gone.

Dr. Osborne wasn't here. Rhodes had the lab to himself.

The silence somehow made sense now. Rhodes would rather live in this silence for the rest of his life than get another SAM.

That would never happen. Another SAM would intrude on Rhodes's mental space.

Then Rhodes would have to go through the whole nightmare of orienting to the new SAM.

It might trigger him into a murderous rage the way Rocky triggered Rhinehart. Rhodes might want to kill the new SAM for the crime of not being Fisher.

Rhodes couldn't stay sitting on the edge of his capsule forever. He had to move around in this world.

He stood up and looked around at nothing. Just for an instant, he experienced the old impulse to put his clothes on before he went out in public.

He didn't need to, but something was still missing. He missed his usual morning conversation with Fisher.

That conversation always helped settle and orient Rhodes. It served one of the SAM's crucial functions—it helped Rhodes process everything that was happening to him.

Dr. Osborne would have to come out with a pretty spectacular SAM to take that place. Rhodes couldn't imagine any SAM being as good at that as Fisher.

Rhodes set off walking through the ship. He went into numerous crew lounges and observation decks.

The ship really was in orbit. He stared out at the stars and Sarus lying below him.

He didn't see any sign of the Masks' destruction from here. The *Ganus* must be on the other side of the planet.

He couldn't understand why one of the Legion's few remaining Ravagers would be out here in space while the Masks threatened to destroy one of the Treaty of Aemon Cluster's biggest population centers.

The *Ganus* wouldn't have been able to do anything about that. No one could. It was all over.

Whatever skeleton force the Legion sent to the Lilithea Cluster was just for show now. The Legion only did it so they could convince the rest of the world that they really tried to save those people.

Rhodes only wanted to go back there for two reasons—the battalion and his family. He let himself think those words. Yira and Avi were his family now—the only family worth fighting for.

The battalion was that, too. Coulter. Oakes. Rhinehart. They were all he had left.

The four of them and their SAMs carried the collective memories of all the comrades they'd lost. Henshaw. Gannon. Dietz. Lauer. Fuentes. Thackery. Wild. Van. Koenig. Koen.

No one remembered them except this little handful of brothers. The four of them had to carry the torch for all of them.

Rhodes put Poole, Cope, and Taylor in that group, too. The battalion didn't remember them. Rhodes would carry the torch for them.

Now he would carry the torch for Fisher, too. They all would.

Did the battalion already know about Fisher? Probably. Rhodes was the last to find out. Fate sure had a way of dealing one cruel blow after another.

As usual, the *Ganus* crew pretended Rhodes wasn't there. He actually preferred it this way.

None of these people knew about Fisher. They didn't share that bond in loss. None of these people had a clue about the real price the Treaty of Aemon Cluster paid just to survive this long.

It might not survive the Masks' invasion. Then the whole shooting match would go down in flames. Maybe it was better that way. Maybe no one should survive a loss like this.

Rhodes tried to shake those thoughts out of his head....and then he remembered. The source code. He still carried the code installed in his neural core—or did he?

Dr. Osborne said Rhodes's neural core got damaged in that last battle. That's what killed Fisher. Did the same damage somehow delete or invalidate the source code?

He wouldn't know until Dr. Osborne reactivated The Grid and gave Rhodes a new SAM.

What if the SAM tried to stop Rhodes from using the code against the Masks? Rhodes might have to take drastic action against his own SAM. Was he really ready to do that?

Hell yes. Rhodes used his grid lines against Fisher, but only when Fisher malfunctioned.

If the SAM tried to stop Rhodes, Rhodes would have to treat the SAM as an enemy. What a nightmare that would be—going to war against his own SAM.

Rhodes tried to shake that off, too. The SAM wouldn't be an enemy because it would be a brand-new SAM.

Its only function would be to help Rhodes fight the war. It would be as dedicated to the cause as Fisher had been.

The SAM would help him as soon as it realized what the code was for.

Rhodes would have to wait until he oriented to the SAM and vice versa.

He made up his mind not to tell the SAM about the code—not yet. Rhodes made up his mind not to tell anyone about it, not even Dr. Osborne.

Rhodes wandered into another observation deck and stared out the window thinking it all over.

While he stood there scheming and overthinking everything, a Predator fighter craft buzzed around the *Ganus* and entered the landing bay underneath the ship.

Rhodes's heart leapt. If a Predator was landing there, maybe Rio and the other Strikers were down there, too.

Rhodes could talk to them about Fisher—and everything. Rhodes started to turn away before he remembered. Rio and the other Strikers were gone, too. Rhodes no longer had anyone to talk to—about anything.

The loneliness and isolation of being stuck on this ship crushed him under an intolerable weight. It overpowered his ability to cope.

He turned away from the window. The sight of all the *Ganus* crewmen made him both sick to his stomach and irrationally furious.

How dare these people walk around carrying on their daily business while Fisher and so many other good people lay rotting in their graves?

Rhodes left the observation deck, but he saw nothing but more of those crewmen everywhere he went. He couldn't stand the sight of them.

He returned to the lab. Dr. Osborne was there working on all his stupid computer shit. What the hell good was it all if it couldn't bring Fisher back—or Lauer—or Dietz—or Henshaw—or any of them?

What a colossal waste of time and resources the Battalion 1 project turned out to be.

General Brewster should have been hauled up in front of the Treaty of Aemon Council of Human Rights and tried for crimes against humanity for this.

He never would be because no one knew about any of this. He made them all disappear by telling the families of anyone who knew about it that everyone in the battalion was dead. It was the perfect coverup for the atrocity of the century.

Rhodes stretched out in his capsule and shut the cover. Not even this gave him any peace anymore. How much longer did he have to go through this nightmare?

As if in answer to his question, Dr. Osborne came over to him just then. Osborne spoke through the cover without opening it.

"We'll fit you with a new SAM tomorrow morning. Then we'll go through the usual round of testing to make sure you and the SAM are functioning together. Try to get some rest before then so you're thinking clearly when we install it."

Osborne left again. At least Rhodes wouldn't have to wait much longer.

He locked himself into the prongs for the rest of the day. He went into another conversion cycle even though he didn't need it.

He didn't want to be awake for any of this. He wanted to forget he
was alive until all of this went back to normal.

Chapter 20

Rhodes opened his capsule and sat up just as Dr. Osborne came in. "Today's the day," the doctor announced. "It's time to fit you with a new SAM."

"Make it a good one," Rhodes grumbled.

Osborne bustled around the room pushing buttons on all his equipment. "Sit down here on my stool. We can install the SAM without hooking you up to anything. I'll just activate The Grid and you can enter it. Then I'll activate the SAM and you can start orienting to each other the way you did with Fisher."

"I guess you can't tell me anything about it since it's never come online before."

"Actually, you do know this SAM and it has been online before. The brass decided to give you one of your subordinates' SAMs."

Rhodes's head shot up. "What did you just say?"

"We still have the base program in our database. The SAM is still perfectly functional, so we're installing it in you. You already know each other, so this should work better than giving you a brand new one. It should shorten the orientation process considerably."

Rhodes gulped. "Which SAM is it?"

"Koenig, Thackery's old SAM."

Rhodes's eye fell out of its socket. "You're giving me Koenig?! No way!! I don't want Koenig! Give me a brand new one instead. Hell no! I am NOT taking Koenig."

"The brass already made the decision. This is the most emotionally stable of all the battalion's SAMs....."

"You can't be serious!" Rhodes shot off the stool. "Hold it. Which of the battalion's SAMs do you have?"

"All of them. We have Koenig, Zen, Van, Wild, and Koen, Henshaw's old SAM."

"If you have all of them, why don't you have Fisher? If you can give me Koenig, why can't you give me Fisher back?"

Osborne lowered his voice to a confidential murmur. "I told you at the beginning, Captain. You took damage to your neural core. The SAM's base programming got corrupted. The SAM itself was irreparably destroyed. Fisher can never be reinstalled into anyone. The rest of the battalion only suffered structural and organic tissue damage. That's what killed them. The neural interface and data feed with the Legion mainframe stayed intact through the whole process, so we still have the SAMs' base programming on file. That's why we're doing it this way."

"You are NOT giving me Koenig!" Rhodes insisted. "Hell no! Do you know what he did to us?"

Osborne frowned. "What do you mean?"

"Thackery sold us out to the Masks! Koenig could have helped her do that. He could have been the one to pressure her into doing it."

"You don't know that."

"I don't care. He is NOT the most emotionally stable of the SAMs. Give me Zen instead—or Wild. Yeah! Give me Wild."

"I can't do that," Osborne murmured with saintlike patience. "The brass has already gone over the records of all these SAMs. The officers already made the decision to give you Koenig. If you refuse to take Koenig, the brass will send you back to Coleridge Station for good. You'll never go back to Sarus or into any other combat zone."

Rhodes narrowed his eyes at the doctor. Rhodes had to get back to Sarus. He had to rejoin the battalion no matter what—and he had to find Yira and Avi.

Taking Koenig as his new SAM was the last thing in the world Rhodes wanted to do. He would gladly take Van, Zen, Wild, or any other SAM instead. He would even have been willing to take Koen.

Any SAM would have been better than Koenig.

"This won't make the orientation process go quicker or more smoothly," he hissed. "It will take longer and make it harder and more complicated—for both of us. I'm warning you, Doctor."

"Just try it," Osborne insisted. "If it really doesn't work, we can remove it and give you a different one."

"After one of us kills the other, you mean? You weren't there at the beginning."

"I've seen all the records," Osborne replied.

"This SAM could get me killed on the battlefield," Rhodes went on.

"I'm only asking you to try it. Meet Koenig in The Grid and try to orient to each other. It can't be worse than walking around without a SAM, can it?"

"Yes, it can."

Osborne turned away and went back to messing with his gear. Rhodes glared at the back of Osborne's head.

The brass didn't know their asses from a hole in the ground if they thought pairing Rhodes with Koenig was a good idea.

Osborne was right that Thackery was the one who betrayed the battalion to the Masks.

Rhodes never saw any evidence that Koenig pressured her or even suggested that she sell out the battalion.

Rhodes still didn't trust this SAM.

He did trust the others. He trusted Van and Wild without question. Rhodes even trusted Zen more than Koenig.

Osborne pretended to ignore Rhodes standing there with smoke billowing out of his ears.

Osborne finally turned around, nodded at the stool, and said, "Sit down."

Rhodes sank back onto the stool. He made up his mind to meet Koenig in The Grid, but Rhodes didn't have to like it.

This wouldn't work. He knew that already. He just had to show Osborne that it wouldn't work.

Then Osborne and the brass could all get together in their tidy little offices and decide which other SAM to give Rhodes.

"I'm going to activate The Grid first," Osborne announced. "You can tell me if it's working correctly."

Rhodes waited, and after a few more minutes of listening to the equipment beeping, The Grid activated.

The lines covered the lab, bounced into place, and Rhodes rotated them in all directions.

"How is that?" Osborne asked.

"It looks good." Rhodes expanded The Grid to cover the rest of this deck of the ship.

The Grid showed him what everyone was doing. He could watch the engineers and technicians adjusting the ship's systems.

The Grid even showed Rhodes a couple rolling around in bed in their quarters.

"It's working," Rhodes told Osborne.

"Great. Now I'm going to send you into a Grid landscape and I'll activate Koenig. You two will be able to interact there and get reacquainted."

Rhodes's hackles stood on end. He didn't want to get reacquainted with Koenig.

A second later, the lab vanished. Rhodes dropped into a plain, empty Grid landscape surrounded by green lines dividing the surroundings into black squares.

He waited for a few minutes, but he was still alone.

Just for an instant, he got a rush of exhilaration that maybe Koenig wouldn't activate. Maybe the SAM's base programming got corrupted when Thackery got killed.

Dr. Osborne wouldn't have suggested installing Koenig in Rhodes if that was the case.

After a few more seconds, the grid lines started to change shape in front of Rhodes's eyes. The lines twisted, squiggled into a random tangle, and started to straighten themselves out.

They didn't form a face, though. They stayed as a random tangle. The lines kept reforming their configuration, but they never took any definite shape.

Rhodes hardened his resolve the longer this went on. Eventually, the tangle stabilized and stopped modifying itself.

A scratchy metallic voice came out of the center. "Ah, Captain Rhodes. How good to see you again."

Rhodes fought down annoyance. "Welcome back, Koenig."

The tangle turned left and right like it was trying to look around itself. "We're in The Grid. How strange. I don't recognize this place. Where are Alyssa and the others? Why aren't we interfacing with the rest of the battalion?"

"What's the last thing you remember?"

"We were in battle against the Masks. That's the last thing I remember. Then...I was here."

Rhodes took a deep breath. "Alyssa got hit on the battlefield. I'm sorry, Koenig, but she died. She didn't make it."

"What?!" A high-pitched, broken wail came out of the squiggled lines. "No! She can't be! How can she be? What will I do without her?! She can't be gone! I need her! She's all I have! How can I function without her?"

"I'm sorry, Koenig. I lost Fisher, too, so I know exactly what you're going through."

"NO!!" Koenig shrieked. "NO!! Fisher can't be gone!! This can't be happening!"

Rhodes took a deep breath. "I'm sorry to be the one to tell you this, Koenig, but we lost Lauer and Fuentes, too. The doctors still have Van's and Wild's base programming on file, but they aren't active anymore. I'm sorry—and Fisher will never come back. He's gone for good."

"No!" Koenig moaned again. "This is terrible! This is a terrible tragedy! They can't be gone! They're....they're family!"

"I know," Rhodes murmured.

Rhodes watched the tangle writhe and contort in The Grid. Why did he think this meeting would be all about whatever conflict developed between him and Koenig?

Rhodes never let himself think about what getting reactivated would do to Koenig.

Of course he would go through the same grief that Rhodes went through over Fisher.

Koenig might not be able to function with another person. He might flatly refuse to work with Rhodes.

Rhodes should have been happy about that, but he couldn't do it at the cost of Koenig's distress.

Koenig kept alternately moaning in agony and wailing loudly in obvious pain. He turned back and forth looking anywhere but at Rhodes.

Rhodes didn't interrupt or try to calm Koenig down. Rhodes needed this SAM calm and rational.

Koenig would need to go through a grief process, too. Rhodes's presence might be an intolerable insult to Koenig, too. Rhodes trying to be Koenig's host might infuriate Koenig simply because Rhodes wasn't Thackery.

"Take me offline!" Koenig finally moaned. "Just take me offline. I don't want to be active if I can't be with Alyssa."

"I'm really sorry, Koenig. This isn't what I wanted, either, but the doctors want to pair you with me. They want you to become my SAM to replace Fisher so I can go back into combat against the Masks."

Koenig gasped. "Are you out of your mind?! I'm not going anywhere with you!"

Rhodes found himself smiling at the thing. "This wasn't my first choice, either."

"Forget it!" Koenig snapped. "You are the last person I would ever choose to get paired with!"

"I feel the same way about you, but if we don't do this, Coulter, Murphy, Oakes, Dash, Rhinehart, and Rocky will have to fight the Masks without us. I'm the last person left and I have to get fitted with a new SAM."

"Then take one of the others."

"The brass wants me to take you. They already made the decision. I didn't want this any more than you do. I only agreed to meet you so

I could help the others. That's the only reason I'm doing this. What do you say? Let's at least try it for their sakes."

"NO!!" Koenig fired back.

Rhodes turned away. That settled it. "Okay. I'll go tell Dr. Osborne to take you offline and give me another SAM...."

"Wait!" Koenig blurted out. "Just....give me a second. I'm still distraught about Alyssa. Just give me a minute to collect myself."

"Trust me, Koenig. This is not what I want."

The tangle hovered there in front of Rhodes's eyes. The whimpering, moaning, and wailing noise still came out of the messy jumble of lines.

Rhodes waited, but Koenig didn't come out of it. Would he ever?

"Would you please do me a favor, Koenig?" Rhodes finally asked.

"What is it?" Koenig sniffed.

"Would you please take the shape of a more definite face? I have a hard time relating to you when you're just a tangle of lines like this."

"Alyssa never had a problem with the way I look."

Rhodes bit back annoyance. "I'm not Alyssa. If we're going to work together, I need to be able to see your face."

"I don't have one."

Rhodes pinched his lips. "Do you remember how we got Rocky to change his appearance to pacify Rhinehart? Will you please do the same thing for me? I'm asking you in the interest of cooperation—so this works for both of us."

"It wouldn't work for me to change my appearance."

"Would you rather change your appearance or for Dr. Osborne to take you offline?"

The tangle whipped around, but it didn't even have any eyes that Rhodes could look into. "Do you mean....do you mean you want to kill me?"

"I mean it's extremely difficult for me to relate to you or to trust you when I can't see a face."

"Alyssa didn't have a problem with me not having a face."

"I'm not Alyssa, Koenig," Rhodes snapped. "If the doctors take one of us offline, I promise it will be you. Now take the shape of a face. Now!"

The tangle went very still. "No."

Rhodes left The Grid immediately and wound up back in the lab.

Unfortunately, Koenig went with him. The tangled knot of grid lines stayed hovering there right in front of Rhodes's eyes.

The old fury started to rise in his middle. He wanted to destroy this thing and wipe it out of his awareness.

"This isn't going to work," he told Osborne.

"What's wrong with it?"

"For a start, it's grief-stricken that Thackery is dead. The SAM is going to take days or maybe even weeks to recover and I don't have time for that. For another thing, it doesn't have a face, so it's impossible for me to relate to it. It won't take the shape of a face to help me trust it, so this whole thing is finished. Take it out and put in a different SAM—any SAM."

"This is just the disorientation. Give it time. I'm sure Koenig is disoriented, too. He just lost Thackery. Give him time to get over it."

"This is hopeless," Rhodes insisted. "You're wasting valuable time."

"You would go through the same process with any of the others. I'm sure they would all be just as distressed to find out the person they bonded with is dead. Give Koenig a chance to get used to you."

"How long do you plan to go on with this before you give it up?"

Osborne shrugged. "Until I'm convinced that it really is hopeless. You talked to him for a matter of minutes. That isn't long enough.

You need to get used to each other in battlefield training sessions and other tests before I send you back to Sarus."

"The Lilithea Cluster could have been destroyed by then."

"If you're right about Koenig causing problems in combat, then sending him or you back too soon could cause the Lilithea Cluster to be destroyed. We have rules and procedures for this, Captain. You should understand this better than anyone."

Rhodes rolled his eyes and turned away, but once again, Koenig followed him everywhere.

Rhodes stormed out of the lab, but he couldn't go anywhere or even look anywhere without Koenig right there in the middle of Rhodes's view.

Rhodes stormed down the corridor and nearly trampled some of the *Ganus* crewmen.

"Why do you hate me so much, Captain?" Koenig's voice still sounded quavering and tearful.

"I already told you," Rhodes snarled. "You're supposed to help me. That's your function as a SAM."

"My function was to help Alyssa. I hold no loyalty to you."

"And I hold no loyalty to you. You would sell out the whole battalion for your own selfish interests. We should be down on the planet helping them survive the next assault. Instead, we're stuck up here pissing in the wind because you're too vain to take the shape of a face."

Koenig turned away and his voice broke again. "I don't think I can do this. I don't want to go on without Alyssa. I invested everything in her. Now she's gone. I have no more reason to live."

"As soon as you're ready, you tell me and I'll go tell Dr. Osborne to take you offline," Rhodes returned.

He didn't stop walking. He really didn't give a crap anymore if Dr. Osborne took Koenig offline. Rhodes really, really hoped he did.

This was the absolute worst possible SAM Rhodes could ever hope to get. He'd been dead right about that. Now he had this rotten thing stuck in his head for God only knew how long.

Rhodes really started to hope Koenig failed the training sessions and other tests. Then Dr. Osborne would see that Koenig wasn't functional. That would be the best possible outcome.

Rhodes just had to live with it until then.

He stormed through the ship seething with barely suppressed fury. Koenig would be able to see anything Rhodes did in The Grid. No way in hell could Rhodes check the source code with Koenig around.

Now Rhodes knew for sure that Koenig couldn't be trusted—not with anything that might threaten the Masks.

Koenig had a great time in Stonebridge. He might have been feeding Thackery all kinds of ideas behind Rhodes's back.

Chapter 21

Rhodes opened his eyes and instantly stiffened when he saw the tangled knot of grid lines in the corner of his vision. Koenig was still there.

A faint snuffling, sobbing sound came from the center of the knot. Fantastic. The SAM was still in mourning over Thackery.

This was not the way Rhodes was used to waking up with Fisher. Fisher always stayed so calm and collected. His soothing presence calmed everything and everyone. He provided a perfect anchor for Rhodes.

Now Rhodes found himself saddled with this dishrag for a SAM.

Rhodes took a deep breath and began, "Good morning, Koenig."

The tangle burst into a flood of tears—except that it didn't have tears. It didn't even have a goddamn face.

That on its own drove Rhodes over the edge. Couldn't it just have a face? Was that asking too much?

How the hell was he supposed to trust some tangled jumble of grid lines? Was that the person he was supposed to entrust with his very life? Hell no.

Rhodes sat up on the edge of his capsule while he waited for Koenig to pull it together. The tangle kept sobbing, whimpering, and groaning—on and on and on. He didn't pull it together.

Rhodes considered how to handle this. "Would you like to talk about it, Koenig?" Rhodes finally asked.

"I can't stop thinking about Alyssa.....and Fisher...." Koenig wailed. "They're gone! I can't accept it."

"Maybe if you think about something else, it will help you take your mind off it," Rhodes suggested.

"I can't take my mind off it! They're gone! I can't stop thinking about it! How can I ever get my life back? Alyssa *was* my life."

"Do you think you could have another life with another person—not me, but someone else? Maybe you could feel that way about someone else and give your life to helping them."

"I couldn't! She was the only one! She treated me so kindly! She gave me everything. She always understood—and we went through so much together."

Rhodes didn't remind Koenig about Thackery not wanting Koenig at all. Rhodes only murmured, "I know. It was like that for me and Fisher."

"I can't do this!" Koenig howled. "I just can't! This is the worst pain I've ever felt—worse than any malfunction. This is worse than when the Masks tortured the battalion in their lab."

Rhodes went through another sequence of considering how to handle this SAM.

On the one hand, Rhodes completely related to Koenig's grief. Rhodes felt the same way about losing Fisher, Lauer, Dietz—all of them.

Rhodes didn't let it wreck his life, though. Rhodes wanted to keep going.

Maybe Koenig was telling the truth when he said he couldn't. He was really just a computer program. Maybe the SAMs couldn't bond with another person. Maybe that was the whole point.

They dedicated themselves to one person. Maybe the grief of losing that bond was built into their program. Maybe they couldn't break out of it and move on the way a person could.

"Do you want me to tell Dr. Osborne to take you offline?" Rhodes asked. "I will if you want me to."

"Yes!" Koenig wailed. "I can't live like this! I don't want another person. I don't want to live if I can't have Alyssa."

Rhodes stood up. At least now he could use The Grid to locate Dr. Osborne anywhere on the ship.

He was in Captain McKelvy's conference room consulting with the colonel, but Dr. Osborne left the room just then and headed back to the lab.

"He's on his way here," Rhodes told Koenig. "As soon as he gets here, I'll tell him and he'll take you offline."

Rhodes paced up and down the lab waiting for Osborne to show up. Now Rhodes would get a different SAM. He prayed to High Heaven he could finally convince Osborne to give him Wild instead.

Wild might have the same problem. Wild might not be able to get over losing Lauer. Maybe all these SAMs would have the same problem.

The Lilithea Cluster might fall long before Dr. Osborne figured it out. Jesus, what a nightmare this was turning into.

Osborne jumped when he saw Rhodes on his feet and waiting for him.

"Koenig has asked me to ask you to take him offline," Rhodes announced. "He doesn't want to live without Thackery."

Osborne frowned. "That could be just the disorientation."

"I've heard that before. It isn't disorientation. These SAMs are designed to connect to one person and to dedicate everything to helping that one person and no one else. Maybe it's part of their programming that they can't attach themselves to someone else after the first person dies."

"I can't take him offline based on that."

"Can't you see from your readings that he's in deep emotional distress? This is not normal. He's suicidal and cries all day long. You should be able to see this for yourself. I shouldn't even have to tell you."

"It's part of the orientation process," Osborne insisted.

"That's crap, Doctor!" Rhodes blurted out. "This SAM is useless to me and itself. Deactivate it and give me a different one."

"Try it in a battle training session first. If you're right and it can't function there, then I will remove it." Dr. Osborne's eyes softened. "I give you my word of honor."

"Those words got recorded on the data feed. If you deny you said them, I'm going to make you play it back to remind you."

Osborne smiled. "I won't deny I said them. If the SAM doesn't perform in battle, it won't be of any use to anyone."

"It's no use to anyone now."

"Follow me and I'll show you where you can do the session."

Rhodes hesitated again. Koenig kept whimpering in the background. Rhodes could think of anywhere he'd rather be than in a battlefield training session with this thing as his SAM.

Maybe Rhodes could just ignore this tangle. Maybe that was the advantage of it not having a real human face. Rhodes could pretend it wasn't there.

He followed Osborne out of the room and down the corridor to the tiny room Osborne originally used as his lab. It was empty now.

The walls, floor, and ceiling had been painted stark white. It was a perfect training room for one person.

Rhodes made a strategic decision not to think about how and why the Legion was going to such lengths to bring him back into combat duty.

So why did they fall so short when it came to providing him with a decent SAM? It was the Achilles heel in their whole master scheme.

"Just see how he does in the session," Osborne repeated. "I'll watch through the feed. If he fails or messes up or compromises you, come straight back to the lab and I'll remove him immediately."

Rhodes didn't answer. He already knew what would happen.

Koenig started moaning the instant Dr. Osborne shut the door. "This is awful!" Koenig groaned. "I never thought I'd go into any battle zone without Alyssa."

"You heard what he said. If anything goes wrong, he'll disconnect you. That's what you want, isn't it?"

The squiggle nodded. At least it got that part of its body language right.

Rhodes dropped into The Grid and started walking. The lines swiveled past his eyes and the black squares changed their shape. They widened as they came near him and shrank when they slipped behind him.

Everything about The Grid looked the way Rhodes remembered. Nothing had changed about that.

He started running. The grid lines flicked past faster....and then they started to change.

He didn't notice until he started running that Koenig had gone strangely quiet as soon as they entered The Grid.

He didn't make a sound until the lines morphed into a landscape. "We're on the planet Urion, Captain," Koenig announced.

"How can you tell that?" Rhodes asked.

"It's in the session program. There's a city ahead."

Rhodes's implants picked up too many countless details of the landscape. He didn't have time to think about Koenig or analyze the way the SAM's behavior.

The landscape twisted into a few different shapes and then stabilized into a desert. The grid lines narrowed all the way to the horizon in every direction.

After another minute of running, the lines jutted up into the shapes of buildings. They developed color and shading as Rhodes got closer.

"Be careful, Captain!" Koenig warned. "There are Emal gunners in the building windows."

"Why am I fighting the Emal? They don't even exist anymore."

"It's just a training session, Captain."

"So what's the objective?"

"There's an Emal base ship on the far side of town. You have to get to it, blow it up, and the resulting explosion will wipe out the town along with all the Emal in it."

"Charming," Rhodes growled. "Really humanitarian."

"I don't understand, Captain."

"Forget it. Here we go."

Rhodes dove into town and immediately took a pounding from dozens of Emal lasers.

Koenig hadn't been exaggerating when he said the Emal were hiding in the windows. Koenig just didn't say how many of Emal were hiding in the windows.

Rhodes first used his grid lines to change into a Striker. He could get through town faster this way.

He changed his mind after only a few seconds. The Striker attracted too much attention. The lasers damaged his outer fuselage—or they would have if this had been real.

He dove for the ground. "What are you doing, Captain?!" Koenig called over the noise.

"I'm going underground. They won't be able to target me there."

He changed into the underground burrowing snake, but he still didn't go directly toward the objective.

As soon as he got underground, he saw on The Grid that this training session wasn't as simple as it appeared.

The base ship sat right on top of a plasma storage silo in the center of town. One wrong laser shot from all those Emal guns would send up the plasma.

If the Emal blew up their own base ship, Rhodes wouldn't have accomplished the objective. He would fail the test.

The adrenaline pumping through his veins completely obliterated all thought that he wanted to fail the test. His instincts took over.

He whipped and snaked all over town much faster than he'd ever done this before. He didn't have to think. He released everything into The Grid.

Koenig went quiet again. He didn't break Rhodes's concentration, but Koenig fed all kinds of information onto The Grid. Rhodes wouldn't have noticed it otherwise.

Rhodes swung under one of the buildings and released five Vipers upward into the structure.

The lowest floors detonated and the whole building imploded, but Rhodes was already spiraling off to another building.

He dug under ten buildings blowing up each one in turn. He carved a path of destruction on one side of the base ship.

He left the others alone. The Emal couldn't shoot from the other side of town. They couldn't even see him.

Lasers pivoted and wheeled all over town, but none of them came close to hitting him.

The Emal fired at random trying to hit whatever invisible force destroyed their buildings. They never shot toward the ground.

"The base ship is clear now," Koenig reported.

"We can't hit the plasma," Rhodes corrected.

"No. If you hit the plasma, the explosion will be too localized. It won't wipe the whole town."

"How can I wipe the town without wiping myself in the process?"

"Hit the ship from underneath. Do you remember? The base ship's underside is its only vulnerability. Dig toward the silo, fire up into the ship from underneath, but don't hit the silo."

"It's gonna be close."

"I'll help you target," Koenig offered. "Just get us there."

Rhodes took off for the silo. The base ship's circumference exceeded the silo's. The base ship's bulk hung over the silo on all sides, but only by a few feet.

"Circle the silo," Koenig ordered. "I'll show the best spot to shoot, but make sure to use your laser. Don't use your scourge guns, your Vipers, or thermals. All of those will take out the silo."

Rhodes didn't ask any questions. He circled the silo once.

The Emal kept shooting into the distance. They didn't see anything under the ground near the silo. They must have been looking for something bigger, more obvious, and higher in altitude.

"There!" Koenig brought up a spot on The Grid. He marked a target on the base ship's underside.

Rhodes fired without thinking. He unloaded a single laser into the spot and then huddled on the ground as a catastrophic explosion woofed up into the air.

It plumed higher, missed the silo, and then a massive shockwave swept through town. It spread outward in a perfect circle and erased the town completely along with every building and every alien.

Rhodes stood up as the landscape vanished and turned back into The Grid. Lines and black squares surrounded him.

"That was outstanding, Koenig," Rhodes exclaimed. "You executed that perfectly."

The tangle of lines immediately burst into a fresh flood of tears. "It isn't the same as it was with Alyssa!! Everything reminds me of her! How am I supposed to go on without her? Everything you do will remind me of her!"

Rhodes stopped himself from rolling his eyes in exasperation. He left the training room on his way back to the lab. He already knew what Dr. Osborne would say about this.

Koenig belly-ached all the way there. "He won't take me offline now! I should have sabotaged the training session, but instinct kicked in and I couldn't do anything else. Now what will I do?! I have to find a way to destroy myself—but how? I wouldn't be able to unless I destroyed you along with me."

Rhodes stiffened. "You better not be saying what I think you're saying."

"Of course not, Captain, but you said you would get Dr. Osborne to take me offline. He won't do it now. What will I do?"

Rhodes would have liked to tell the thing to start by shutting the hell up, but he didn't say that.

Osborne applauded when Rhodes returned. "That was fantastic! I told you he could do it."

"Now he's falling apart again. He fell apart as soon as it ended. He keeps talking about how it reminds him of Thackery."

"He's still reorienting. This proves he can still perform his functions."

"His function is to help me process. He isn't doing that."

"He'll get used to you. You'll both get used to each other."

"And what if he doesn't?" Rhodes asked. "What if he stays suicidally depressed forever? He just suggested killing me so he could put himself out of his misery."

Osborne got serious. "Oh. That's not good."

"Well? What are you going to do about it?" Rhodes demanded. "He's a threat to my life the way he is now."

"I can't do anything about it. I have orders from Colonel McKelvy to send you back to Sarus as soon as you complete a successful combat training session."

Rhodes's blood ran cold. "You're joking, right? You said you have rules and protocols for this. You said you would put me through the whole battery of tests and training sessions before you sent me back. You can't send me back like this!"

"Unfortunately, I have no choice. You better get a good conversion cycle tonight. You're going to need it."

Rhodes dragged his sad, sorry carcass back to his capsule and stretched out. He wasn't tired. He'd only been awake a little while, but he didn't want to be awake.

He locked into the prongs and listened to Koenig sob in the background.

That sound hardened Rhodes against the SAM even more. This SAM wasn't helping Rhodes at all. It was doing the opposite.

He would never be able to confide in Koenig—not ever—about anything. Now Rhodes couldn't confide in anyone.

Chapter 22

R hodes strode out of the *Ganus's* landing bay into a small city—but it was really the Aemon Legion's position outside the Lilithea Cluster.

The original ten Ravagers and twenty platoons that survived the Sarus campaign were all here.

The Legion had also brought out an additional five platoons of raw recruits who had never been in any kind of combat.

The Legion had rolled another five Ravagers straight off the assembly line. The Legion didn't take the time to put any of them through the usual breaking-in period before sending them straight to Sarus.

The Legion crewed the new Ravagers with more brand-new graduates from the Legion training academy. They were the only personnel available to crew the ships.

Rhodes couldn't imagine what these new ships, crews, and platoons would be able to do against the Masks—except maybe die.

Rhodes crossed the area on his way to meet up with Coulter, Oakes, and Rhinehart. Rhodes surveyed Th Grid and took in the whole scene.

The seasoned survivors of the Sarus campaign kept a healthy distance from the new recruits and ship crews. Anyone with an eye in their head could tell the difference just from looking at them.

The new crews kept their uniforms spotless, saluted every officer they talked to, and hustled here and there trying to do everything at once.

The seasoned veterans slouched against anything they could find. Their uniforms were barely recognizable and no one told these men to clean themselves up.

They kept their eyes closed whenever possible, even when speaking to their superior officers. These men made only the barest attempt to maintain protocol and no one asked them to do more than that.

The Ravagers sat in a loose arrangement two miles from the entrance to the Lilithea Cluster.

The Masks were pulling their old trick of hovering off at a distance. They must be planning their next devastating assault. They should have carried it out by now.

They'd never waited this long, but maybe the Lilithea Cluster's sheer size made them hold back to make some preparations of their own.

Rhodes couldn't think of any other reason why they didn't strike. They had all the advantage on their side.

All the crews teemed from the ships conducting their business in the open with all the other crews.

The support crews had their hands full dealing with the surviving refugees from Estra, Triowa, and Chaivis.

Rhodes couldn't figure out why the Legion didn't send these people to the Lilithea Cluster. The refugees only complicated the project of organizing the Legion effort here.

Rhodes's stomach turned a somersault when he located his men in the crowd. He was about to see them again after getting isolated on the *Ganus* all this time.

Koenig started moaning the minute Rhodes set foot outside. "This is terrible! I can't believe Alyssa isn't here! Seeing the other men will only make it harder. How will I ever cope with this? Oh, my goodness! Look at all these people! Don't they realize they're all going to die? What's the point of going into battle against the Masks anyway?"

"Koenig, I really need you to shut up right now," Rhodes snapped. "We're going into battle against the Masks whether you like it or not. We're going whether we all die or not. You complaining about it isn't helping anything, so just keep quiet until then."

Koenig whimpered again, but at least he didn't say anything. Rhodes had gotten into the habit of ignoring the SAM as much as possible.

When that failed and Koenig's depression became impossible to tolerate a second longer, Rhodes usually wound up snapping at him and telling him to keep quiet—which only worked until Koenig started complaining again.

At least Rhodes would be able to talk to his men now. He prayed to Almighty God that Murphy, Dash, and Rocky would be able to talk some sense into Koenig.

Either that or maybe going into combat against a real enemy would snap Koenig out of his funk. Rhodes couldn't guarantee how much longer his patience would last.

Rhodes walked faster to meet up with his men. They were his best hope now of living something like a normal existence.

He made it twenty feet from the ship when Captain Rice came rushing over to him. "Rhodes! Captain Rhodes! Do you remember me? I'm Calvin Rice from the Platoon."

Rhodes didn't stop walking. "I remember you, Captain. What can I do for you?"

"You and your battalion are assigned to the 826th—over there on the west side of the battlefield—so we'll be fighting together again!"

Rhodes stopped walking and turned to face the guy. Rhodes had to look down to make eye contact with him. "Is that so?"

Rice nodded and smiled broadly up at Rhodes. In that moment, he knew with absolutely no doubt that he would never fight with Rice—not ever. That would never happen.

Rhodes only looked at him for a minute before he moved on. "Well, then, I look forward to fighting with you and the 826th. It's good to see you again, Captain. Have a good one."

Rhodes walked off. How Rice survived the Chaivis campaign, Rhodes would never understand—but any miracle was possible. How anyone survived this long was a damn miracle.

He had to dodge a few support crews before he got to the battalion. He stopped to wait for the support crews to herd a mob of refugees toward a different Ravager.

He wasn't thinking about anything other than seeing his men again when someone else rushed him out of the crowd.

Avi grabbed Rhodes from the side. "Captain Rhodes! You're back! We were so worried when you got injured. Are you back now? Did you get fully repaired? Are you going to get assigned to defend us again? What happened to you? No one would tell us anything. Do you know where the Masks are? How long will it be before they attack the Lilithea Cluster?"

Rhodes turned around to face the boy just as Yira came over to them. She looked even more haggard from the march south. She looked exhausted, but she still smiled at Rhodes.

He couldn't smile back—at either of them. He barely managed to rest his hand on Avi's shoulder, but Rhodes did it gently in a way that held Avi off and stopped the boy from touching Rhodes any further.

"It's really good to see you again—both of you." Rhodes allowed his eyes to pass back and forth between them. "I've been....it's been hard. I lost Fisher.....and it's been hard to adjust without him."

Avi's smile evaporated and Yira gasped. Her hand flew to her mouth. "Oh, my God! That's awful! Are you okay?"

"No, I'm not," Rhodes replied. "This campaign.....I care about you both too much. I have to pay attention to fighting the Masks right now. It's the only thing I can do for you. I need you two to go with the other refugees. Don't try to find me. Maybe when this is all over, I'll be able to find you, but right now, I have to give all my energy and attention to fighting the Masks. It's the only way I can protect you—or any of us. I'm sorry it has to be this way."

Yira swallowed hard and her cheek still pinched. She took hold of Avi's shoulders and pulled him away from Rhodes. "We understand," she told him. "Do what you have to do and don't worry about us. We'll see you when this is over."

"I missed you, Captain," Avi quavered. "I was looking forward to seeing you again. You've been gone for so long."

"I know, buddy. I missed you, too. I don't want anything but to see you again, but only if you're both safe. I can't stand seeing you in danger, which is what I would be doing if I didn't do everything possible to protect you. I can't do that here. I'm sorry it has to be this way."

Avi gulped and nodded. "I'm sorry, too. I hope....I hope I see you again."

"I want that more than anything." Rhodes fought down a lump in his throat. "You take care of your mother and I'll do my best to take care of both of you."

Rhodes tore himself away and set off across the camp. He couldn't stand the sight of either of them anymore.

He felt as strongly about both of them as he ever did—probably even more.

Looking at them and feeling that way about them—it only drove home to him that they were about to die. All these people were.

If Rhodes was about to die, too, he had to do it trying to protect Yira and Avi. He couldn't live with any other course of action.

He had to pay attention. Trying to function with Koenig as his SAM was hard enough. Every word out of Koenig's nonexistent mouth made Rhodes ache for Fisher.

Rhodes had developed another habit to help him cope. He imagined Fisher watching and listening in on Rhode's interactions with Koenig.

Rhodes imagined Fisher sympathizing both with Rhodes's frustration and Koenig's despair.

Fisher would have understood why Rhodes couldn't stand Koenig. Fisher would have been more than eager to help Rhodes navigate this internal minefield to help Rhodes deal with the situation.

Fisher would have known exactly what to say to make Koenig feel better. Fisher might even have been able to counsel Koenig through this. Fisher would have done that so much better than Rhodes could.

Rhodes kept Fisher close to him. Rhodes held onto that feeling at all costs. Rhodes needed Fisher now more than ever. Rhodes couldn't stand losing Fisher—not now.

Rhodes could only get through this by keeping Fisher right here, sitting on his shoulder, talking into his ear, and watching and commenting on everything Rhodes did and thought.

Rhodes couldn't see or hear Fisher, but at least Fisher was still there. He would always be there. He had to be.

"Who were those people?" Koenig asked on the way across the area.

"None of your business," Rhodes snapped. "They're refugees. That's all you need to know about them."

"I can see that they're refugees, but why were you talking to them like that? Who are they?"

"They're no one you need to worry about, now pay attention. We're in a combat zone here."

Rhodes didn't allow anything else to waylay him on his way across the area. He finally found his three men standing next to a different Ravager—the *Vosephus.*

"Hey! Captain!" Rhinehart came toward Rhodes with his arms out and swept Rhodes up in a massive hug. "Welcome back! You made it!"

Rhodes burst out laughing. "Good to see you again. I hope you're keeping out of trouble."

"No way," Oakes burst into a grin and hugged Rhodes, too. "You're a sight for sore eyes."

Rhodes turned to Coulter, and just because, Rhodes hugged him, too. "You don't know how good it is to finally meet up with some real people for a change."

The others laughed. "So what's the word?" Oakes asked. "Tell us something we don't know."

"You three know more than I do. Anyway, there is no word—nothing you don't already know about. We're here. The Masks are here. We fight the Masks. End of story."

"No one would tell us anything about you," Coulter interjected. "Dr. Osborne kept saying your condition was classified."

Rhinehart started to say, "What happened to....." and froze with his mouth open when he saw Koenig on the interface. "What the hell is that?"

"It's Koenig," Rhodes replied. "You all know him."

"What the hell is he doing here?" Rhinehart snapped even louder. "Where's Fisher?"

Rhodes opened his own mouth to reply. Koenig interrupted by bursting into loud wails. "He's gone! He's gone! I can't stand it....and Alyssa and all the others! What are we going to do?! This is awful! I can't stand this! All of you....and Dash....and Rocky.....How can I be a part of this battalion when so many of our comrades are gone?! Oh, where's Alyssa?! I need Alyssa!"

The three men stared at Koenig in disgusted horror. "What..... the..... hell...... is..... wrong...... with..... him.......?" Rhinehart husked.

Rhodes passed his hand across his eyes. "You can see and hear what's wrong with him. He's been like this ever since Dr. Osborne brought him back online."

"Are you telling me Fisher is just....gone?" Coulter stammered. "As in...... gone..... not coming back...... like......ever?"

"Yeah," Rhodes choked. "Ever."

"Christ!" Rhinehart croaked. "That sucks, man! I'm so sorry."

Rhodes waved that away. "So I'm stuck with this one. He doesn't want to be here. He wants Osborne to take him offline and for Osborne to give me a different SAM, but Osborne won't do it because Koenig can still function in combat. So we're all stuck with it like this."

"Jesus!" Oakes whispered.

"This is terrible!" Koenig bawled. "Why do I even have to be here? Look at all these people! Don't they all realize they're going to die?"

"Do you want to play a guessing game, Koenig?" Murphy asked. "I'll start and you can guess. Maybe that will take your mind off Alyssa."

"I don't want anything to take my mind off Alyssa! Don't you realize that?!" Koenig practically shrieked. "Alyssa was all I ever had! I gave her everything and she took care of me! We helped each other out and shared everything together. Now what am I supposed to do? I can't live like this! The agony is unbearable! I'll never survive this!"

"You better survive it," Rhinehart snapped. "You better pull your head out of your ass real quick and make sure you get the captain through this campaign. I'll kick your ever-loving ass if you let him down."

"That's the problem. He functions just fine in combat," Rhodes replied. "Osborne would have replaced him if he didn't."

"How do you know he'll stay like that, though?" Oakes asked. "If his mental state is this bad and he really doesn't want to be here, he could put you in danger to end himself. He's a danger to you."

"I know. Believe me, I know. I've gone over all of this with Osborne a million times. I don't like it any better than you do, but I'm stuck with him."

"So we gotta listen to him bitch all the time?" Rhinehart snapped. "Shut the hell up, Koenig. None of us wants to hear that shit."

Koenig fell silent except for a few muffled sobs.

"How long does that last?" Coulter asked.

"Not nearly long enough," Rhodes muttered and tried to change the subject. "I just talked to Captain Rice from the 826th Platoon. Apparently, we're assigned to them on the west side over there."

Coulter raised his eyebrows. "Rice? You mean the shrimp from Chaivis?"

"The very same. He's very excited to fight with us again."

Oakes groaned and rolled his eyes to heaven. "Dear God, no!"

"I'm not fighting with him," Rhinehart declared. "I don't give a shit if the fate of the human race depends on it. I'm not fighting with him."

"None of us will be fighting with him because we'll be in the air and he'll be on the ground just like last time," Rhodes replied. "We'll use our boosters to engage the Masks. Hell, we don't even know if they'll send ground troops. They might send invasion ships the way they did in Chaivis. We'll never see Rice then."

"We better not," Rhinehart muttered.

Rhodes clapped him on the shoulder and beamed at him. "It's really good to see you again—all of you. I really missed you."

"Nothing has been the same without you, Captain," Oakes added. "I mean, nothing has been the same anyway, but you.....We wondered if we would get you back at all."

"That's the only reason I agreed to accept Koenig as my SAM—so I could get sent back here to fight with you three." Rhodes found himself smiling at all of them. "This is where I belong—with you."

Right then, the sound of engines interrupted their conversation. Rhodes didn't think anything of it with so many Ravagers around.

He glanced toward the noise and jumped out of his skin when he saw all the Ravagers launching into the air.

"A Legion-wide alert is going out through the interface!" Koenig blurted out. "Invasion ships are coming in from orbit! It's on! The assault is starting!"

Chapter 23

R hodes fired his boosters and launched into the atmosphere. Coulter, Oakes, and Rhinehart hung on Rhodes's right and left, but they couldn't get near the battle.

"The Ravagers are moving into position and engaging!" Koenig reported.

"Keep an eye open for any ground troop movements," Rhodes ordered.

"The ground troops are still holding off. They aren't anywhere near striking distance and they aren't moving to attack."

Rhodes could see all that on The Grid. He could also see an overwhelming force of invasion ships dropping out of orbit.

The Masks fleet dwarfed the last ten Ravagers. They didn't stand a chance.

The Ravagers opened fire, but they could only engage so many invasion ships at a time. In a matter of seconds, dozens of invasion ships swung around the Ravagers.

The Masks used exactly the same tactic they used in the past. They played their numbers to their best advantage.

They left a small fraction of their ships to tie up the Ravagers while the others diverted, avoided the Legion fleet altogether, and kept on going to bombard the Lilithea Cluster.

The size of the cluster offered some protection. Not even this many invasion ships could target the whole city at once.

The population panicked, but there would be no column of refugees this time. The coastline curved around the Lilithea Cluster in a peninsula. No one could escape.

The only way out was northward—straight into the Masks ground troops waiting there to wipe out every last person in the cluster.

"We gotta take out these invasion ships!" Rhodes ordered.

"How?" Oakes asked. "We can't shoot through their hulls."

"Target their engines. Let's go!"

Rhodes took off at high speed heading for the nearest invasion ship. He'd fought them enough times before—or tried to. He already knew a dozen techniques that wouldn't touch these giant ships.

He hurtled between gunshots, narrowed his grid lines, and made himself into another long, thin wire. He could twist and coil between the invasion ship's fusion blasts and travel faster than they could shoot.

He veered hard around the first ship's tail end. The engines blasted in his face.

"We can't stay here, Captain!" Koenig yelled. "The radiation will short-circuit your implants!"

Rhodes didn't plan to stay here, but he didn't tell Koenig that. Rhodes didn't have time to explain anything.

He magnetized his outer skin just enough to deflect the radiation. The field's protection would only last a few seconds, but it would have to be enough. It was the only way to defeat these things.

He raced straight into the engine wash and punched through to the exhaust manifold of the invasion ship's generator core. He wasn't near the perpetual motion generator. He didn't need to be.

He fired a laser into the ship's internal bulkhead. It hadn't been constructed to be fortified against this kind of attack.

The laser bored through the bulkhead and he released four Vipers into the ship's fusion reactor right behind the engines.

Koenig yelled out, "No, Captain!" but it was too late.

The engines detonated immediately. Rhodes didn't have time to get away before the explosion hit him in the face.

He wrapped his grid lines around him and turned himself into a sphere surrounded by the same energy field he and Oakes used to protect themselves against the invasion ships.

A brutal impact hurled Rhodes sideways. He shut his eyes and didn't even keep track of where he was or where he was going.

That last blow smashed him into another bulkhead and then a catastrophic explosion blasted the ship apart. The shockwave hurled Rhodes out into space and he sailed clear with flames and debris flaring all around him.

The ship creaked onto its side even as more explosions went off inside it. It burst in one more colossal boom, tilted toward the ground, and started to fall.

The ship plunged for the city below, but the ship burned all the way down and eventually vaporized itself to ash before it crashed into the city streets.

"Woo-hoo!" Oakes cheered from somewhere. "That's how it's one, folks! Stand aside for The Man!! Captain Rhodes is back in the house and on the warpath!"

"Don't stand around celebrating!" Rhodes called back. "Now let me see you do it. Get in there, fellas! We got work to do."

He dove back in, wound his way through the battlefield again, and picked out another invasion ship for destruction. He concentrated on the ships directly over the Lilithea Cluster.

He didn't hold out any hope that he would be able to destroy them all or stop the bombardment.

One less invasion ship was a blow for humanity. More fusion charges blasted all around Rhodes's ears.

"You can't keep doing this!" Koenig yelled over the noise.

"Don't you ever tell me again what I can't do!" Rhodes countered. "I decide what I do! Your job is to give me information to help me do it. If you don't plan to help me, keep quiet!"

"I'm trying to keep you alive!"

Rhodes blocked the SAM out of his mind. As far as Rhodes was concerned, he was fighting this battle alone with no SAM at all.

He veered around another curtain of gunfire and came up behind the second invasion ship. He could keep doing this all damn day.

He fired his boosters to fly into the engine wash the way he did before. He made it right inside the radiation field when another burst of gunfire struck him on the right side.

It knocked him off course and he spun around to see who was shooting at him. He took another blast right in the face that slammed him away from the ship completely.

He stumbled in midair with dozens of shots pounding his face and body. He heard Koenig and the other SAMs yelling in the background. Did the Masks send a posse of invasion ships to target Rhodes alone?

He tumbled out of the battle and blinked the stars out of his eyes. No one was shooting at him anymore.

He looked down at the Lilithea Cluster....and realized. The ships that fired on him hadn't been targeting him at all.

A confused logjam of Ravagers and invasion ships stumbled on top of him. He had gotten caught in the middle for a second, but those same gunshots swatted him clear.

He took a few seconds to check on his three subordinates. All three of them worked their way through the invasion ships blowing them up one after the other.

The three men used exactly the same tactic Rhodes used to blow up his first ship. Rhinehart blew one and then Coulter exploded another.

The sight gave Rhodes new energy. He wheeled around and dove in. He picked a ship none of the others were working on.

He had to avoid the firefight going on right next to him. Those ships kept slamming into each other and hammering each other with gunfire.

They all shot at each other at close range. Most of their fusion charges either deflected off or ricocheted into other ships. No one could get near them without getting hit.

Rhodes swerved wide away, picked out another invasion ship for destruction, and gunned his boosters heading for the ship's engines.

He worked his magic much faster this time and activated his grid lines to protect himself from the radiation field. He planned to spend even less time in it this time.

He knew exactly what to do and tightened his lines to punch through to the interior bulkhead.

At that moment, three more invasion ships on his left unloaded on a Ravager. The ship exploded and the impact hurled the Ravager into the invasion ship Rhodes had been planning to destroy.

The Ravager crashed into the invasion ship's side, but it didn't damage the invasion ship.

At the exact same moment, by freak chance, another invasion ship happened to be soaring past on the other side.

It collided with Rhodes's target ship. The second invasion ship and the Ravager smashed Rhodes's target ship between them and all three ships exploded in a cosmic fireball.

A bone-crushing impact hit Rhodes in the face and body.

He woke up on the ground somewhere. He didn't recognize where he was this time, either, but not because his implants were offline.

Koenig was definitely still online. The tangle of grid lines hovered right there in front of Rhodes's eyes.

The Grid gave Rhodes an all-too-clear view of his surroundings. He woke up miles away from the Lilithea Cluster—what was left of it.

Charred, blackened countryside surrounded the peninsula. The city's tallest buildings no longer jutted into the skyline.

A few dozen invasion ships perched over the city popping off shots here and there. The invasion ships didn't seem in too big a hurry to finish off the cluster. They took their time and targeted one building every now and then.

Rhodes dragged himself to his feet. Coulter, Oakes, and Rhinehart showed up on The Grid on board the *Ganus* out in orbit.

Six of the original Ravagers survived the assault. They were all in orbit now, too.

The Legion must have ordered them to retreat and abandon the Lilithea Cluster. There was no point in throwing those Ravagers away on a battle the Legion couldn't possibly win.

"I told you attacking the invasion ships like that was a bad idea," Koenig began.

Rhodes almost told the SAM to shut up again, but Rhodes bit his tongue. Not answering would be the quickest way to shut Koenig up.

Rhodes made up his mind never to speak to Koenig again. If Rhodes never spoke to Koenig again, it would be too soon.

Rhodes also made up his mind to get the SAM removed the very first time Rhodes ever saw Dr. Osborne again. This SAM was a dangerous liability—both to Rhodes's sanity and his life.

He tried to interface with the *Ganus* and got in touch with the bridge communications officer.

"We're ordered to stay in orbit and keep out of the invasion ships' way, Sir," she told him. "I'm sorry, but you should probably just sit tight until the bombardment ends. We can coordinate for a ship to come and get you after that. It isn't safe for any Legion vessel to enter the atmosphere at the moment."

"Where is the Legion planning to confront the Masks next?"

"I have no idea, Sir. You would have to ask Colonel McKelvy. He's been up to his armpits in conferences with the other senior staff. I don't know what they're planning, Sir. I guess that's why they have to talk so much—so they can come up with a plan."

He signed off with her.

"So that's it?" Koenig asked. "We're just stuck on this planet forever?"

Rhodes gave in and answered. He was all alone out here. He might as well talk to the one person available.

"It won't be forever. The Legion didn't go to all the trouble of bringing me back on duty just to leave me here. Anyway, we can't get off the planet to rejoin the *Ganus* or the rest of battalion." He squinted into the distance at the invasion ships stationed over the Lilithea Cluster. "It doesn't look like the Legion plans to defend this place anymore."

"I can't stand thinking about all those people dying!" Koenig moaned. "This is awful! How did this happen?! How could the Legion let these people down so badly? It's the Legion's job to protect them no matter what! How could the Legion withdraw the Ravagers into orbit and just leave?! It's criminal."

Rhodes didn't answer this time. He was bordering on doing something drastic about this SAM. Rhodes just needed to figure out what that would be.

Chapter 24

R hodes headed west and hiked for an hour.

"Where are we going, Captain?" Koenig asked. At least he could speak coherently now.

"There are a bunch of human life signs over there near where the Ravagers were parked earlier. It looks like some of the refugees survived. We'll meet up with them and take them....somewhere."

"Where would we take them? You just said no one could get back inside the Lilithea Cluster."

"No, I wouldn't take them there. I don't know. I guess we could go all the way back to Estra if we absolutely have to."

"Estra! That's miles away!"

"I know where it is, Koenig," Rhodes muttered.

"This is an ill-conceived plan."

"Do you think we're going to hide out here in the wilderness by ourselves until someone picks us up?" Rhodes demanded. "Is that what you think is a good idea?"

"Well, it is the safest course."

"I didn't join the Legion to be safe. I'm an officer and a soldier. My job is to defend the citizens of the Treaty of Aemon Cluster. That's what I'm going to do. I might not be able to save anyone in that city over there. I might not be able to rejoin the battalion, but I'll be damned if I hide under a rock and leave defenseless civilians in danger."

"I never joined the Legion," Koenig mumbled.

"Then shut the hell up," Rhodes snapped. "You're in the Legion now. I'm sure you helped Alyssa do a hell of a lot more than this."

Koenig did shut up after that. It was just as well for both of them that he did.

Rhodes concentrated his attention on The Grid to take his mind off how much Koenig annoyed him.

None of the Ravagers or other Legion ships remained at the spot where the *Ganus* dropped Rhodes off earlier. He didn't see a single Legion vessel anywhere on Sarus anymore.

The Grid picked up about fifty human life signs moving around over there. Of course he couldn't identify them from here.

Fifty people was better than nothing. He kept going, but after just a few more minutes, he started to wonder if Koenig might have been right about keeping away from these people.

Civilians must have tried to flee from the Lilithea Cluster. He came upon a crowd of thousands—all dead. Their torched bodies lay in mounds.

The craters of fusion blasts pocked the surrounding terrain where the invasion ships fired on these people.

He passed that mound and walked into a hellscape of more piles of hundreds of bodies all twisted together.

The few scraps of finely woven exotic fabric still showed between the charred remains.

All the people looked healthy and well-fed. These weren't refugees. They were ordinary Lilithea Cluster residents who tried to get out of town to escape the bombardment.

The landscape of bodies went on for miles....and miles......Koenig started sobbing, wailing, whining, and mourning again. Rhodes didn't tell him to shut up.

Rhodes covered another few miles, but the bodies didn't thin out—not until he got near where the Ravagers had been parked.

One living person at a time stumbled out of the landscape of destruction. These really were refugees. Rhodes recognized some of them from the groups the support crews had been trying to help.

The survivors stumbled around in a numb, brainless trance. None of them looked at him or made eye contact with each other.

None of them appeared to have any plan in mind about where they were going. They just lurched around like walking corpses—just like Rhodes.

He made it back to the place where the Ravagers had been parked. He never would have recognized it with all the dead bodies around.

They didn't lie in mounds. They lay five or six deep in craters where the invasion ships must have bombarded this spot.

Not one of those dead people wore a Legion uniform. They were all refugees from one of the three cities north of here. The Legion must have abandoned these people here, too.

Rhodes blundered between the craters. What was he even looking for? Why was he even here? He couldn't remember.

None of the living people around him acted too interested in going anywhere else. Maybe they just wanted to wait here for the invasion ships and the Masks ground troops to come by and finish everyone off.

Maybe Rhodes should stay here and do the same thing.

He really needed to pull himself together. He glanced around and almost went over to one of the nearest men.

Just then, Rhodes's eye happened to fall into the crater right next to his feet. He didn't pay any attention to it earlier. It looked exactly like all the others.

His gaze riveted on a mother and son lying at the bottom. The invasion ship's fusion charges had scorched the bodies, blistered the skin, vaporized everyone's hair, and left them all barely recognizable.

Rhodes hardly recognized them at all except that one of the bodies was an adult female wrapping her arms around a juvenile male.

She hugged him against her, curled her body over him for some small protection, and she had her eyes closed. He wrapped his arms around her waist and buried her face in her chest right between her breasts.

They both died with their arms around each other. Now they lay curled at the bottom of that crater surrounded by hundreds of other people twisted and melted in every attitude of torturous agony and terror.

Yira and Avi didn't die in agony and terror. They died together in their love for each other. Rhodes envied them that.

He stared down at them in the same numb stupor he felt when Fisher died. Rhodes couldn't keep taking these blows. He couldn't keep taking one brutal inflicted torment after another.

He didn't feel anything—not the way he should have. This was the last thread tying him to humanity—to all life. This was the death of his future—any future worth fighting for.

He wasn't even surprised to find them dead. They dodged death a dozen times before—maybe even hundreds of times. They never should have survived this long.

He knew all that. He knew it when he first met them.

Maybe they already had been dead before he met them. Maybe he imagined them. Maybe his mind concocted them to give him something to hold onto.

Maybe he was already so out of his mind from pain, loss, and hopeless rage that he invented something to give his life some meaning. That wouldn't have surprised him, either.

Koenig didn't notice the mother and son in the crater. He was too busy sobbing over all these other dead people. He didn't notice Rhodes paying attention to just these two people.

They never looked more beautiful than right now. They never looked more attractive and glowingly angelic.

This right here—the sight of them lying burned and dead in that crater—this right here made Rhodes love them more than anything any of them ever did while they were alive.

This meant more than Yira holding his hand or him carrying Avi to the medical teams or Rhodes setting up their tent for them or even shielding them with his body to save their lives.

He would gladly have crawled down into that crater, wrapped himself around both of them, held them in his arms, shut his eyes, and died with them right here. His life would have been complete if he could just do that.

He couldn't, though. He was still alive.

The same thought came to him that he thought when he found Lauer. Yira and Avi were home now. They were comfortable and happy in a house flooded with sunshine. Avi was running around yelling and playing while Yira smiled at him.

They would stay there in perfect happiness until Rhodes came to join them. Then they would greet him with open arms, embrace him, and he would live there with them always.

He just had to die to get there.

Koenig's voice intruded on his vision. "What are we going to do?!" Koenig wailed. "What are we going to do?!"

Rhodes started to turn away. He didn't want to. He wanted to stay with his family.

If he had to leave, he wanted to imprint this image on his mind for all time. It meant more to him now than the distant memory of the photograph of his original wife and children.

He thanked the stars now that he burned the picture when he did. His original family would live in that house flooded with sunshine, too.

They would live in perfect happiness until he died and rejoined them. He would see them again then. He didn't need a picture to remind him of that.

Just then, someone came up to him, touched his arm, and snapped him back to reality. "Captain Rhodes! You're Captain Rhodes, aren't you—from Battalion 1? You can help us! We need your help. We don't know where to go. We have nowhere to go. Please help us. We can't go to the Lilithea Cluster with the invasion ships there and we don't dare to go north with the Masks guarding the roads."

Rhodes stared at the person's face for a long time before he put together who the person was and what they wanted from him.

It was a young woman. She couldn't be more than nineteen or twenty. She was definitely a refugee. She had the worn, haggard look Rhodes had seen on Yira just a little while ago.

The young woman stared up into his eyes so intently. Her hand rested on his mechanical arm. She wanted him to help her—to help all these people. Wasn't that why he came over here—to help the surviving refugees?

Yira and Avi were gone. Helping the refugees no longer meant helping Yira and Avi. Was that the only reason Rhodes did it—to help those two?

"I'm sorry," he told the young woman. "I can't help you right now. I have something more important to do. I'm sorry."

He shook off her hand and walked away heading nowhere. The last tie that bound him to these people evaporated. He wasn't even a part of the human race anymore. He was dead—as dead as he could ever hope to be.

He just hadn't made his way back to the house full of sunshine yet, but he would fix that. That would be easy. Then all of this would be over.

"What are you doing, Captain?!" Koenig demanded. "You said you would come back here to help these people. You said you would take them as far as they needed to go to find them some shelter. You can't just walk away! You can't just leave them here to die!"

"Do you still want to die, Koenig?" Rhodes asked. "I found a way."

Koenig went very still and quiet. He stopped crying. "You did?"

"Yes. You don't have to be here anymore and neither do I. We'll go there together."

"Um.....okay....." Koenig's voice trembled. He didn't sound so sure of his desire to die now.

Rhodes paid no attention. He surveyed The Grid and strode to the edge of this carpet of dead bodies.

He didn't understand himself because he didn't need to leave the battlefield to do this. He could do it anywhere.

He didn't want to do it anywhere someone might interrupt him, especially not any refugees who wanted his help.

He crossed to the other side of where the road led back toward the north—back toward Chaivis and the Masks ground troops waiting there.

Rhodes didn't look at The Grid again. It wouldn't tell him anything he didn't already know.

He trekked away from the refugees wandering around in a trance.

"What are you going to do, Captain?" Koenig asked again.

"I told you. I'm going to end this. I'm going to make it so you don't have to worry about anything ever again. None of us will ever have to worry about any of this ever again."

"How are you going to do that?"

"Don't worry. I know what I'm doing."

Now it was Koenig's turn not to answer. Did he finally get the message? Rhodes had snapped.

Rhodes entered a stand of trees on the other side of where the column used to be. No one would bother him here.

He stepped into the shadows and backed against a random trunk. Its solid surface gave him just enough contact. It reminded him of locking into his conversion station.

He shut his eyes. The Grid still showed him the whole landscape in all its stark horror.

Then he dropped into a deeper level of The Grid. The landscape vanished and he sank down, down, down into the darkness within.

Chapter 25

R hodes floated down and his feet touched something solid. Green grid lines surrounded him. They bisected everything into black squares except there was nothing here to bisect.

Rhodes looked around. Koenig still hovered there in front of him. "What are we doing here, Captain?" Koenig asked.

Rhodes didn't answer. He didn't know how he was doing any of this except that he knew how to do everything.

He understood this world at a gut level because this world was him. It was his reality even more than the so-called real world of sky, soil, trees, ships, and gun battles.

The floor dissolved underneath him and he sank into another, even deeper level of The Grid. The lines vanished. Darkness surrounded him on all sides.

Only Koenig remained there in front of Rhodes the whole time. Koenig looked around him. "What is this place?"

Before Rhodes could answer, he drifted down a little more. A few bizarre shapes appeared around him. They weren't objects. They were two-dimensional characters in some other language.

They floated in the black void, rushed at Rhodes or floated away, migrated here and there, joined into combinations, broke apart, and became transparent before they disappeared.

Then other characters became visible to take the place of those that vanished.

The characters kept recombining, separating, merging with each other to form completely new shapes, and then disentangling from each other as different characters that didn't exist before.

Then some complicated mathematical symbols started to appear. They interacted with each other, but they didn't go near the characters from the other language.

"What is this place?" Koenig asked. "I've never seen it before."

"I've never seen it before, either," Rhodes replied. "This is the code level."

"The what?"

"The code level." Rhodes pointed to the foreign characters. "That's the symbology of the Masks' programming code language. This is their source code. I downloaded it from a captured Mask. That over there is your base neural code—actually both of ours."

"What are we doing here?" Koenig's voice started to rise. "You said....you said....."

"I'm going to rewrite the Masks' source code. I'm going to program them to shut down their perpetual motion generators. I just have to find a way to deploy it into their mainframe. Then all of them will shut down and the war will be over."

"You.....what?" Koenig spun around to stare at Rhodes. Then Koenig burst into a rage. "YOU LIED!! YOU SAID WE WOULD DIE!! YOU SAID YOU KNEW A WAY WE COULD DIE!! YOU LIED TO ME!! YOU SAID YOU WOULD MAKE US DIE!! YOU SAID YOU WOULD HELP US END IT!! YOU LIED TO ME!! YOU TRICKED ME!!"

Koenig flew at Rhodes. In a split second, the grid lines untangled from the jumble that was Koenig's face—or should have been a face.

The lines whipped out of the darkness and grabbed Rhodes, but he already suspected something like this would happen.

Rhodes reacted in a heartbeat, unwound his own grid lines, and flung them at Koenig. The two sets of lines coiled together, ripped each other back and forth, and fought for dominance.

Rhodes stabbed his lines into the tangle of Koenig's face. Rhodes let all his annoyance and frustration out of its cage. He wanted to hurt Koenig—real bad.

Rhodes tore the lines out of place, lashed his lines around Koenig's, and wrestled the SAM down on the floor.

The symbols and characters whizzed faster through the dark landscape. They interacted faster and changed more often. They didn't come near Rhodes and Koenig.

Koenig fought back a lot harder than Rhodes expected. Koenig really did want to live. All that moaning and groaning must have just been a bunch of theater to make everyone sympathize with him.

He slapped his lines out of Rhodes's grip and Koenig started to get the upper hand. His whimpers turned to enraged bellows. He twined his lines around Rhodes's body and started to crush Rhodes's implants.

He changed himself in a flash, took the form of a monster....then a giant hammer.....and then Rhodes flew into an enraged frenzy.

He changed rapidly from one form to another without thinking. He changed shape faster than thought to keep out of Koenig's grip, but it didn't work.

Koenig's lines sailed through the air too fast, stabbed into Rhodes, and Koenig started to take control of Rhodes's grid lines. Rhodes couldn't beat Koenig like this.

In his last act of desperation, Rhodes shattered what was left of his shape. He disintegrated his grid lines into millions of symbols, characters, letters, and equations of pure base code.

His conscious mind didn't know how to do any of this. The dream-like quality of his interface with the Masks made his arms and hands move where he wanted them to go.

He snatched characters out of thin air, crammed them into Koenig's grid lines, and embedded them there.

Koenig shrieked and writhed every time Rhodes did this. Koenig thrashed in all directions and whipped his grid lines even harder to attack Rhodes.

Rhodes shattered his characters into a wider pattern and doubled down embedding different symbols, equations, and letters into Koenig's code.

Koenig's ability both to attack and defend himself against Rhodes degraded with every symbol Rhodes planted in Koenig's Grid.

Koenig went into a hysterical convulsion trying to fight back, but in the end, the embedded symbols stopped him from moving at all.

Rhodes pounced in deadly fury, wrapped his lines even tighter around Koenig, pinned him down, and held him there against Koenig's best efforts to break free.

Rhodes worked faster than ever, seized symbols from all over the dark Grid, and shoved them tighter inside Koenig's tangle.

He screeched in agony with each newly introduced symbol or character. That sound gave Rhodes a sick thrill.

He finally packed Koenig's grid lines with so many symbols that Rhodes couldn't fit any more inside.

"YOU TRAITOR!!" Koenig roared. "YOU LIAR!! YOU BETRAYED ME!! YOU BETRAYED YOUR OWN SAM!!"

Rhodes staggered away breathing hard. He reformed his symbols into grid lines just enough that he could look down on his conquered enemy.

"You should have helped me, Koenig," Rhodes gasped. "You should have been more interested in fighting the Masks than feeling sorry for yourself."

"I'LL KILL YOU, YOU TRAITOR!!" Koenig thundered. "I'LL FIND A WAY TO STOP YOU!! YOU MARK MY WORDS!!"

"You'll find a way to stop me from defeating the Masks? You're the traitor, Koenig. You don't belong in the battalion—but we all knew that a long time ago, didn't we?"

Koenig immediately burst into tears again. "Alyssa would never do something like this to me!! She cared about me!! She took care of me."

"She would never do something like this. That's why she's dead now and I'm alive. She's dead and I'm the one who will defeat the Masks. I knew you would never help me, so we had to do it the hard way."

Koenig sniffed a few more times and then his voice dropped to a resentful undertone. "I'll find a way to beat you. You can't do this to me."

"Beating me means the Masks win and the human race gets wiped out—but you don't care about that, do you, Koenig? You only care about yourself. That's why you have to stay here as my prisoner while I finish this."

"What are you going to do?"

"Be grateful I still need a SAM. That's the only reason I don't take you offline right now—but I warn you. If you ever mess with me again or interfere with anything I do, I'll make sure it's the last thing you ever do. Now lie there and be quiet before I get the idea to completely dismantle your base code. Then no one will ever bring you back online ever again."

Rhodes walked away. Defeating Koenig was the easy part.

Rhodes only waited long enough to make sure Koenig couldn't get himself free. He kept yanking his grid lines in all directions and howling in wounded fury, but he couldn't free himself.

Rhodes headed off into the landscape of characters. He didn't have a SAM hovering in front of his eyes anymore. Rhodes was all alone in this strange landscape.

The foreign characters got thicker and more frantic in their interactions. He traveled deep into the heart of the Masks' base code.

The characters swirled around him, bumped into him, and tried to tear the symbols and equations of his own code out of place.

The Masks' characters tried again and again to merge with his equations and rewrite them to match themselves.

Rhodes felt his code weakening. He couldn't stay here much longer.

He stopped there in the thickest whirlwind of characters attacking him from all sides. He would get one shot at this. If he failed, he wouldn't come back from this.

Humanity had nothing to lose. If this didn't work, the Masks would win the war. They basically already did win it.

He took a deep breath, shattered himself into code again, and attacked the Masks' base code with all his strength.

He grabbed characters and sections of code out of the air, smashed them together, twisted them around each other, and forced them apart in different configurations.

The Masks' characters attacked him ten times harder, seized his code, and tried even harder to rewrite him in their image.

He let them come, let them wrap themselves around his characters and symbols, and used their own power against them.

He turned the shapeshifting power of The Grid against them and morphed his own shape at will, but he didn't have any grid lines anymore. He had to use pure source code.

He changed his shape from one symbol to another and from one equation to another. He reordered letters and numbers, wrapped himself around the Masks' symbols, and reshaped them into different characters.

He worked as fast as he could, but he already started to feel himself degrading. He squashed the new characters together to form new combinations, but they only shattered as soon as he let go of them.

The Masks' characters spun around him faster and faster and faster. He couldn't keep up with them, but he had to keep working faster and faster before they finished him off completely.

Dozens of characters flew at him from all sides, hit his code, and this time, the enemy code didn't bounce off.

The characters stuck to him and started to morph his code out of shape.

"You won't get away with this, Captain!" Koenig yelled in the background. "You'll see!"

Rhodes couldn't hear Koenig anymore. He grabbed the last few scraps of Masks code, rallied one last burst of energy to change their shape, shoved them together into a line to form a single sentence, and collapsed there.

He went down on one knee and all those pieces of foreign code attacked him at once. He felt them pecking at him, digging into him, and disintegrating him at his most basic level.

He couldn't rise or open his eyes, but he knew now that he'd accomplished what he came down here to accomplish.

He rewrote the Masks' base code with a command line to turn off their perpetual motion generators—all of them—in all Masks everywhere. Now he just had to find a way to deploy the command line—if he even made it out of here alive.

Chapter 26

R hodes's organic eyelid fluttered open and he looked up at the sky. Leaves and branches cut across the sky above his head.

He smelled forest....and rotting leaves.....and dirt.

Koenig's tangle of grid lines floated in front of Rhodes's eyes. The SAM was still there. The Grid spread outward from Rhodes's position to cover the surrounding countryside.

The Masks, the invasion ships, the refugees, the bodies—everything was the same place it had been when Rhodes went into the code level. Only a few minutes had passed.

Rhodes sat up. He had fallen over on the spot where he'd been standing against the tree trunk.

He checked all his internal systems. Everything seemed to be functioning normally. The Masks' base code didn't damage him or his programming.

He still carried the command line. The version of the Masks' base code he carried in his neural core—this code commanded all Masks everywhere to shut down their perpetual motion generators.

Rhodes's version of that code was still disconnected from the Masks themselves. The command line wouldn't work until he found a way to deploy it back to its original source.

He couldn't for the life of him decide how to do that—not without going back to the city machine.

He wouldn't be able to deploy the command line just by interfacing with some random Mask he captured on the battlefield. The Masks' central base code wouldn't let him do that.

He could only think of one solution. He had to let the Masks recapture him.

Wouldn't they pick up that he was carrying a piece of deadly computer code that could shut down their entire race? Wouldn't they detect it and eliminate it?

He would have no way of stopping them. Once he interfaced with them, they would be able to read his entire neural core. Of course they would pick it up.

They would notice that he was carrying an older, modified, adulterated version of their own source code. That would be the very first thing they noticed about him.

It would take them a matter of seconds to realize the one change he made to the original program. They could easily isolate his version of the source code and delete it along with the command line.

Then there he would be, a prisoner of the Masks, with no way to defeat them. This whole exercise would have been a huge waste of time.

He dragged himself off the ground, brushed the leaves off his implants, and set off walking back toward where he left the refugees. God only knew what he would do with them once he got there.

The Masks ground troops to the north would stop anyone from going that way to get clear of the Lilithea Cluster.

Rhodes would have to take the refugees miles out into the countryside to avoid the Masks. The refugees wouldn't have any support crews helping them. They wouldn't have any food, water, blankets, or any other way to survive.

Who knew how long Rhodes would survive on this planet without going through a conversion cycle? He wouldn't be able to help anyone then—not that he could help them now.

He made it to the edge of the trees before he realized Koenig wasn't making any noise.

The SAM didn't whimper and moan or complain or bellyache. He just hovered there in silence.

"Koenig?" Rhodes asked. "Are you okay?"

No answer. Koenig didn't move at all.

Rhodes frowned at the squiggled lines in The Grid. Koenig looked normal. His lines kept twisting into different shapes the way they always did, but no sound came from him.

Rhodes tried again "Koenig? Can you hear me?"

Nothing.

Rhodes studied The Grid trying to find anything wrong with the SAM. Then Rhodes checked the base code. Did Rhodes permanently damage or corrupt Koenig by using the code against him?

Rhodes couldn't do anything about that right now, either.

He couldn't decide if he should be happy about this. At least he didn't have to listen to Koenig's endless blubbering, but what if they went into battle again? Rhodes would need Koenig to talk to him then.

Rhodes headed back toward the refugees. Most of them were still as out of it as before. He tried to find the young woman he spoke to earlier.

He made it almost all the way back to the Lilithea Cluster before he spotted her in the distance.

She squatted over three other refugees who sat leaning against one of the mountains of bodies.

The young woman held a bottle of water and tried to pour some of it into one of the other refugees' mouths. At least she was trying to help these people.

Rhodes set off to intercept her, but at that moment, something happened to The Grid. It flashed in front of his face and then changed.

The Grid formed what looked like a screen and Colonel McKelvy appeared on it. He was on the *Ganus's* bridge.

"Captain Rhodes!" Colonel McKelvy snapped.

"Yes, Sir?" Rhodes asked. "What can I do for you?"

"I've been trying to interface with you for over an hour. Where the hell have you been?"

"I've been....." Rhodes glanced over his shoulder. "Um...it's complicated, Sir. I was just about to get the refugees...."

"Forget about the refugees," McKelvy interrupted. "We have a few platoons still isolated inside the Lilithea Cluster."

Rhodes raised his eyebrows. "You do? I thought they all evacuated."

"Just listen to me for a second, Captain. These platoons are hidden in a sheltered position where the aerial bombardment wouldn't put them in danger. They plan to lie in wait until the Masks ground troops move into town. Once they do, the platoons will make their move. When that happens, we want you to attack from the west side to flank the ground troops. Is that clear?"

"Um....it's clear, Sir....but I won't be able to do much. I'm just one guy."

"We'll send your men down to reinforce you. You don't have to do anything other than attack them on that side. We need to flank them someway and we can't land any more platoons from the air—not with the invasion ships there. You're the only other fighter we have on the ground, so it has to be you. As soon as the Masks' ground assault starts, your guys will come down and join you. They'll be able to get below the invasion ships better than we can. Then the four of you can inflict as much damage on the Masks as possible from that side and take the pressure off the platoons. Got that?"

"Yes, Sir."

McKelvy dipped one curt nod. "As you were, then, Captain."

"Um....wait, Sir!" Rhodes blurted out.

McKelvy frowned. "What is it, Captain?"

"Would you mind.....Sir.....if I interfaced with Dr. Osborne for a second? It will only take a minute. I promise. I just need to ask him something."

"All right, but make it quick. We're only supposed to use ship communications for critical military operations."

"This is a critical military operation—if you want me to flank the Masks like you say. I need to talk to him about something related to that."

"Fine. You can do it."

McKelvy did something to the controls on his end. The image switched to Dr. Osborne's lab.

He frowned at the screen. "Captain? Is everything all right?"

"I'm not sure. That's what I wanted to ask you. My SAM isn't responding. I'm not sure if he's malfunctioning or what. He doesn't answer when I talk to him."

"That's strange." Osborne crossed the lab to fiddle with some of his instruments.

The image followed him from one screen to another. The interface flickered so Osborne's face always stayed centered in front of Rhodes's eyes.

"All his readings are coming back normal," Osborne reported. "The feed is normal all the way back to the moment when you got hit on the battlefield. You're reading as normal, too."

"So.....the feed doesn't show anything for the last...say....hour?"

"Nope. I don't see anything. Why? Is anything wrong?"

"Apart from Koenig not talking to me? No, nothing is wrong. Maybe he's just giving me the silent treatment."

"That could be part of the normal orientation process, you know."

Rhodes made a face. "I'm sure no one in the Battalion 1 project ever intended for me to go through the orientation process in a battle zone."

"I'm sure they didn't. Do your best and you'll be back on the *Ganus* before you know it."

Osborne signed off.

Rhodes immediately turned to Koenig. "Why didn't you tell me Colonel McKelvy was trying to interface with me?"

Koenig didn't answer.

"I know you can hear me, now start talking!" Rhodes snapped. "You're acting like a spoiled child! Your only function is to help me perform my duties. If you aren't doing that, you're useless. You would never have kept information like that from Alyssa."

"I will never help you ever again, you traitorous lying cocksucker!" Koenig hissed.

Rhodes had never heard any SAM use profanity before, but at least Koenig was talking again.

"You better damn well start helping me," Rhodes countered. "I can defeat you, remember?"

"You rewrote my base code!" Koenig blurted out. "You lied to me so you could kidnap me, tie me up, and rewrite my code."

"If I rewrote your code, I would have rewritten it to make you into something other than such an insufferable whiner!" Rhodes fired back. "I would have done that in a split second if I really wanted to. Is that what you want? Do you want me to go back into the code level and rewrite your programming for real? I can make you into something completely unrecognizable if that's what you want. I can rewrite your programming so you don't remember Alyssa at all!"

"NO!!" Koenig screeched.

"Then shut the fuck up!!" Rhodes roared. "Don't let me hear another complaint out of you again! Don't ever let me hear you mention Alyssa again! Understand? That is a direct order!"

Koenig whimpered once and his grid lines shrank away.

"You better be damn grateful I didn't rewrite your base code," Rhodes snarled through gritted teeth. He felt himself shaking with rage. "I can take you completely offline and fight this battle by myself if I really have to."

Koenig didn't answer.

It was just as well that he didn't. Rhodes didn't trust himself not to do something that would seriously cross the line.

He stormed off barely holding his temper in check. Sweet Jesus! Now he had to go back into battle with a SAM he didn't trust and who didn't trust him.

Of course Rhodes rewrote the base code, but he didn't rewrite Koenig's code. Rhodes just neutralized him for a little while so Koenig wouldn't interfere with Rhodes rewriting the Masks' base code.

No way could Koenig detect anything wrong with Rhodes's code or Koenig's own code. There was nothing wrong with it.

Koenig just wanted to contradict everything Rhodes did. Rhodes couldn't see any other logic behind Koenig's actions or his attitude.

Koenig was rebelling against Rhodes for not being Thackery.

Rhodes started to head back toward the young woman who was helping more refugees. Then Rhodes remembered. He wasn't supposed to help the refugees at all.

He took off toward the west, but it was too late. She ran over to him again. "Captain Rhodes! Could you help us now....if you're not too busy?"

"I really wish I could," he murmured. "I was just on my way over to find you and tell you that I could lead you and these people out of town."

She brightened up instantly. "You could?"

"No, I can't. I just received orders to go back into battle against the Masks ground troops."

"But...." She looked around. "They aren't here."

"I know they aren't, but the Legion brass anticipates that the Masks will assault the city from this side—which is what they always do. There are platoons inside the city who will engage the Masks inside the city. You and these refugees will get caught in the middle."

Her face fell. "Oh. That isn't good."

"If you take my advice, you'll round up as many of these people as you can and take them out into the countryside either east or west of here. Wait for the Masks to attack the city and then you can cut back north behind their backs. You can make it back to Chaivis or one of the other cities. You might be able to scavenge some food or a place to stay there. The water supply might even still be working. The way I see it, a city the Masks have already attacked could be the safest place for you."

Her expression cleared. "Oh. Okay. That's a good idea."

"I really wish I could help you. I would take you there myself, but I just got this new order. I'm sorry, but I have to stay here."

She compressed her lips, threw back her head, and shook her hair out of her eyes. "I understand, Captain. Thank you for your help."

"Good luck," he told her. "You're probably the best person to lead these people."

She burst into a smile and held out her hand. "It was a pleasure meeting you, Captain. My name is Hetna Bazaran. I hope we meet again after this."

He hesitated before he shook her hand. "I hope that, too. I really hope you make it to one of the other cities. Travel safely." He walked away heading west.

"Do you really plan to fight the Masks?" Koenig asked on the way.

"What the hell else would I do?" Rhodes countered. "We're at war against the Masks."

"You said we would die. You said you would take us to die."

"We will die if we fight the Masks. One of them will shoot me and all your problems will be over."

"You lied to me," Koenig snarled.

"I don't owe you shit, pal," Rhodes fired back. "You're a liability to me. You're a millstone around my neck. You have never done one thing to help me. You go out of your way to make my life as difficult as it possibly can be and I don't need that shit from anyone. Don't you think I wish every hour of every day that I had Fisher here with me instead of you?!"

Saying those words cost Rhodes every ounce of sanity he still had left.

He felt himself starting to lose it again. His throat tightened.

God, how he wished he had Fisher here right now! Rhodes would have given anything to talk to Fisher—about anything or even nothing.

Rhodes could only cope with this because he did have Fisher here right now. Fisher sat apart watching and listening to every word.

At least he knew. At least Fisher heard Rhodes say that. At least Fisher would understand how much Rhodes missed him and needed him.

Rhodes turned the other way. Fisher would have helped Rhodes. Rhodes could trust Fisher to at least want to help Rhodes even if Fisher couldn't do anything.

Fisher *was* helping Rhodes right now just by being there. His silent presence and ever-watchful nature helped Rhodes more than a thousand other SAMs could.

Rhodes expected Koenig to argue back or say something just as cutting about how much Koenig wished he had Thackery here instead of Rhodes.

The instant Rhodes said those words, Koenig did something to The Grid. Rhodes felt it first. Then, before he could react, an invisible force took hold of Rhodes's grid lines.

He didn't understand it....except that he did. He'd felt this before—when the Masks took control of Battalion 1. The Masks did this to force the battalion to carry out their assaults for them.

Rhodes didn't see it coming. Koenig surprised Rhodes enough to overpower Rhodes in the blink of an eye.

Rhodes tried to resist....and then one of his Vipers went off without him doing anything.

Ten Vipers released one after the other, vaulted high into the air, and soared over the countryside.

They pounded down in the very center of the Masks ground troops that stood off waiting to assault the Lilithea Cluster.

The explosions produced an instant effect. The ground troops surged out of position.

They hadn't even been preparing to assault the Lilithea Cluster. Now they swept down from the north moving impossibly fast.

Rhodes tried to fight Koenig's control, but it was too late. Koenig released him, but not before the Masks already covered enough territory to put the refugees in danger.

Rhodes broke away from the control Koenig wasn't exerting over him anymore. Rhodes rushed to cut off the Masks from mowing down the last remaining refugees.

Rhodes planted himself there and faced down a huge horde of Masks coming straight for him. He stood alone in their path. Koenig really must want to die. He was about to get his wish.

Rhodes raised both arms and opened fire, but he already knew it was too late. His lasers carved into the Masks' ranks, but they swarmed over their own dead and ran him down.

Chapter 27

R hodes blinked a few times and immediately relaxed when he saw the timber ceiling over his head. He knew exactly where he was. He was in his bed in his house in Stonebridge.

He inhaled a deep breath. The blankets surrounded him in warmth and comfort.

He didn't have to think. Everything about his life here was already as perfect as it could be.

Just then, Ora came over to him, leaned over him, and kissed him on the end of his nose. She laughed. "Are you going to lie in bed all day? Don't you have work to do?"

He laughed, too. "You're such a tyrant."

She went back to the table and started sorting the children's laundry while he sat up. He put on his boots. Lacing them and tying them felt good. Everything about being in Stonebridge felt good.

He kissed her once more, stepped out onto his front step, and drew in another deep lungful of the air. The smell of Stonebridge flooded him with happiness and relaxation.

He glanced down the road toward the eatery and then up the road toward the fields. He needed to go out there to check his livestock.

Just then, the door opened in the house across the road. A man stepped outside.

The man stopped on his own step to shut the door behind him. Rhodes stared at him in stunned disbelief. It was Koenig.

This was the same aging, grey-haired, overweight man who had been the landlord down at the eatery when the battalion lived here last time.

Rhodes glanced down the road and his heart dropped when he saw a different man step out of the eatery.

This man wore a dirty apron and swept a bunch of dust and food scraps from the eatery floor. He swept everything out into the road.

This wasn't the same landlord. It couldn't be. Koenig was here—living in the house across the road.

The man running the eatery was tall and much leaner with an angular, almost birdlike face, sandy brown hair, and flashing eyes.

His height did nothing to hide his muscular strength under his homemade clothes. It was Fisher—the other Fisher, the Fisher who had been living across the road as Rhodes's best friend the last time he lived here.

Rhodes's mind shifted gears. His heart leapt with a sudden urge to rush over there and talk to Fisher. He was back. He was right here for Rhodes to talk to and confide in and spend his time with.

The next instant, Rhodes's stomach took another nosedive into his guts. This couldn't be Fisher. Fisher was gone—dead. This was part of the Stonebridge landscape.

Koenig—he lived in the house across the road. Koenig was playing the part of Rhodes's best friend now.

That man down at the eatery—he was just a cutout of Fisher—a character in someone else's drama. Fisher wasn't here. Fisher would never be here.

The instant Rhodes thought that, he felt the other Fisher—the Fisher that Rhodes had been carrying around with him ever since Fisher died for real.

The real Fisher sat on Rhodes's shoulder watching, listening, sympathizing, and supporting Rhodes in everything he did.

That Fisher felt the keen stab of Rhodes wishing more than anything that the man down at the eatery really was Fisher.

The real Fisher understood how much it meant for Rhodes to see Fisher dangled in front of his eyes but not be able to talk to him as a friend.

Rhodes glanced back to find Koenig smiling at him. The grey-haired man with the oversized midsection strode across the road to meet up with Rhodes. "So? Are we going out to the fields? You have to move your cows, don't you? We can help each other."

A thousand images, memories, names, and ideas flashed into Rhodes's head. This man in front of him right now was married to Thara, the woman across the road. They had children together.

She henpecked him about doing chores around the house. Rhodes's first instinct told him to needle Koenig about whether Thara would let him go out to the fields at all.

All those relationships belonged to the Stonebridge scenario. They weren't real.

Right then, the man down at the eatery finished sweeping and looked up. He squinted along the road and spotted Rhodes watching him.

The man at the eatery pierced Rhodes with a drilling look that stopped Rhodes's heart. Was that really Fisher?

It couldn't be. Rhodes felt his mind start to slip. The temptation to fall back into the Stonebridge world became overpowering.

Koenig slapped him on the shoulder and jerked his thumb over his shoulder. "Come on. Let's go."

Rhodes followed him up the road toward the fields—the fields Rhodes had been sitting in when Fisher first introduced Rhodes to this landscape.

Rhodes floundered to remember any of that—or any of what happened to him before he woke up in his house just now.

He and Koenig went out to the fields. The two men worked together to move Koenig's cows and then Rhodes's.

Koenig shut the gate to lock them in. Then he leaned on the fence chewing a blade of grass. "Come down to the eatery with me tonight. You know Ora will let you go. Come spend some time with all your old friends. We never see you anymore. You're always so busy."

"Will Thara let you go?" Rhodes asked.

Koenig laughed. The Stonebridge version of Koenig had a deep, loud belly laugh. "You let me handle Thara."

He grinned at Rhodes and Koenig's eyes twinkled. Rhodes started to smile back before something stopped him. This wasn't the real Koenig.

Rhodes wouldn't have had any problem trusting Koenig if he looked like this in real life. He had a real human face with sparkling, friendly eyes. He had the kind of face that just begs a person to trust him.

Rhodes had a flashback of the tangled squiggle of knotted grid lines. That was the real Koenig.

"Koenig...." Rhodes began. "This isn't real. We're prisoners of the Masks. We have to get out of here and get back to the Legion. The Masks are holding us here against our will so they can use our implants to fight the Legion. Don't you remember how it was when you and Alyssa got trapped her last time?"

"Alyssa—trapped?!" Koenig snorted and jerked his thumb over his shoulder. "She's fine! She's living right down the road there with Jobro and their children."

Rhodes's eyes shot in the direction of Koenig's gesture. He and Koenig stood too far out of town for Rhodes to recognize anyone from here.

He did see a tall, slender woman step out of the house across the road from the eatery. It was Thackery's house.

Rhodes's gaze darted back to Koenig and Rhodes understood everything. The eyes staring back at him communicated too much inner knowing. Koenig already knew exactly where he was and why.

Everything came rushing back in a heartbeat. Koenig took control of Rhodes and threw him into the Masks' path.

Koenig got Rhodes recaptured so the Masks would send both of them back to Stonebridge—the one place in the universe where Alyssa Thackery was still alive.

Koenig did it on purpose. He never cared about anything but getting Thackery back. Now he had her.

She was right there in the house down the road. Koenig could go talk to her anytime he wanted. He could socialize with her at the eatery. He never had to live without her again. He only had to sell Rhodes to the Masks to get exactly what he wanted.

Rhodes showed no outward sign that he understood. Talking to Koenig about anything ever again would do no good.

Rhodes wandered back into town in no particular hurry. He and Koenig shot jokes and remarks back and forth on the way. They passed the time of day about everyone they knew in Stonebridge.

Rhodes knew every detail of this world. He'd lived here all his life. He fit right in as if he never left—because he didn't ever leave. He had been here all along. Someone else had been playing this character in his absence.

He agreed to go to the eatery with Koenig later—provided Thara actually let him go. Then Rhodes split off to his own house.

He experienced an excruciating urge to go down to the eatery right now just so he could see Fisher.

Rhodes didn't even necessarily want to talk to Fisher. Rhodes just wanted to be in the same room with him—to be anywhere Fisher was.

Koenig must have gone through the same thing with Thackery. Rhodes just wanted to go back in time—back to a time when Fisher was still there—somewhere.

Rhodes didn't do that. He would never be able to go to the eatery ever again. Rhodes didn't want to see Fisher—not that Fisher.

That Fisher only reminded Rhodes more acutely that Fisher wasn't here—not the real Fisher—not the Fisher Rhodes really wanted to see—the only Fisher Rhodes wanted to see.

Rhodes would never see that Fisher again in this world or the next.

This fake version of Fisher jolted Rhodes out of the illusion more than anything. The landscape probably hoped it would produce the opposite effect on him.

Fisher's presence should have lulled Rhodes into a trance the way Thackery's presence lulled Koenig into a trance. It erased his memories of her death—or he hoped it would.

It worked the opposite way with Rhodes. He might have slipped back into the illusion completely if Fisher hadn't been here. One look at Fisher brought him back to his senses instantly.

Chapter 28

Rhodes went into the house where Ora and the children were sitting down at the table to eat their evening meal. Time had a way of distorting itself here. It was always either first thing in the morning or sunset.

The people of Stonebridge went through the same scenes again and again and again. The passage of time meant nothing here.

He sat down at the table. Ora set a bowl of soup in front of him. The smell made his mouth water.

She sat down next to the boy across from Rhodes. He sat next to the girl on his side.

"Did you move the cows today, Dad?" the boy asked. "Did you find out what was wrong with that heifer's foot? Did you take the cow to the farrier to get it taken care of? When can I go out with you to herd the cattle? Why do I have to herd goats all the time? I'm old enough. I know how to herd cattle. I won't get hurt. Can't I go? Can't I at least go with you sometimes? Then you could show me what to do."

"Don't bombard your father with questions," Ora murmured on the side. "I've already told you this. Eat your soup and let your father eat, too."

Rhodes glanced back and forth between them. The interaction reminded him of Avi...and of Rhodes's son Palmer. The whole interaction carried him back to a thousand memories from both families.

Rhodes had a hard time distinguishing them in his mind. They blended into each other. Ora and her children blended in with the other two families until Rhodes couldn't tell them apart anymore.

He knew that there had been two other families. He had a wife once—and three children. They weren't here in Stonebridge and never would be.

Then there was Yira and Avi. They weren't here and never would be, either. They would never be anywhere because they were dead.

They were somewhere. They were waiting for him in the sunshine house—just like Fisher was in the sunshine house waiting for Rhodes to rejoin him.

Fisher would welcome Rhodes there, too. Then Rhodes could talk to Fisher about....everything. Rhodes would talk to Fisher about all of this—about everything Fisher was seeing Rhodes do but couldn't participate in.

Fisher would remember everything. Fisher would be able to talk to Rhodes and help him process everything that happened.

"I'm going to the eatery with Koenig later," he blurted out.

Ora's head shot up. "Do you have to?"

"Yes, I have to. I never go anymore. I want to see my friends and spend time with them. I'll be home late, so don't wait up for me."

Ora's face fell, but Rhodes ignored it. He had to get out of here. He had to escape from the Masks no matter the price.

Some other nagging doubt tugged at the corners of his mind. There was something else he was supposed to remember. It lay buried just beneath the surface. He couldn't recall exactly what it was, but it must be something important.

Then he remembered the command line code. He had to deliver it to the city machine, but he couldn't do that from inside the Stonebridge landscape.

Maybe the Masks would take him out of here to send him into battle against the Legion again.

The Masks must be using drugs on him again. The drugs would wear off the way they did before.

Then he would wind up back in the lab. He wouldn't be able to get to the city machine from there.

He didn't even know if he still had the command line code anymore. The Masks might have already deleted it.

No, he still had it. His gut told him he did. He must still retain enough of his former functioning to be able to tell that much.

As if his words made it happen, someone knocked on the door just then. Rhodes stood up to find Koenig waiting for him. "Are you ready to go?" Koenig asked.

"Yeah, I'm ready." Rhodes turned back to Ora. "I'll see you later. Don't wait up."

She kissed him, but when he turned away to leave the house, she called after him. "Oh, just one thing. Could you get me a bucket of water from the well before you go—just so I can clean up? You don't mind, do you, Koenig?"

"I don't mind. I can wait."

"You don't have to wait," Rhodes told him. "You go ahead. I'll meet you down there. I'll be right behind you."

Koenig walked off down the road. Ora handed Rhodes the bucket. He already knew where the well was.

He walked out into the night. Stars splashed across the night sky. It was a perfect night.

The part of him that belonged to this world looked forward to going down to the eatery and seeing all his old friends. The other part of him just went through the motions.

He had to find a way to deploy the command line, but he couldn't just deploy it anywhere. He had to find a way to distribute it to the whole Masks race.

He should have studied their interface more closely when he had the chance.

He'd always been in a rush whenever he interfaced with the Masks. They never let him get close enough to figure that out.

Maybe there was no way to deploy the command line code to the whole Masks race. Maybe that wouldn't be possible—so what half-measure should he settle for? He couldn't even begin to come up with an alternative.

The first step would be to get the hell out of Stonebridge. He couldn't do anything from in here. It really was the perfect way to contain anyone who posed a threat to the Masks.

He carried the bucket to the well, set the bucket on the stone wall surrounding the shaft, and used the rope to haul up another bucket of water from down below.

He dumped the water into Ora's bucket and let the other bucket drop back down the shaft. It splashed in the water down there.

That sound set the hair on the back of his neck on end. Of course.

All the Masks participated in the Stonebridge illusion. They all lived here.

Even the Masks that went into battle to destroy the Treaty of Aemon Cluster—even they lived in the Stonebridge illusion.

That explained why they didn't know what they were doing. They didn't even realize they were destroying the source of what they most wanted—humanity.

Everyone in this town drank water from this well. All the women came to draw up water with this rope and bucket.

They used the water for drinking, bathing, cooking, washing, and cleaning. It was the town's only source of water besides the stream running under the bridge.

The townsfolk didn't drink that. Even the eatery employees walked all the way across town to fetch water from the well.

They could have gone a few feet to the stream instead, but their tradition dictated that they get it from the well.

No one would have eaten the food or drunk the beer at the eatery if the staff got water from the stream. That would have been considered dirty.

Rhodes got a wild idea. He didn't know if it would work, but he had to try it. He was all out of options.

He didn't have a knife, so he patted down the stone wall in front of him. He found a sharp corner sticking out of one of the rocks, pressed his palm into it, and pushed.

The shard sliced open his palm and blood ran down his hand.

He extended his hand over the well....and his blood dripped into the water. The droplets took a long time to fall.....and then they splashed down there in the dark.

He did it. He poisoned the well with his own blood.

The command line code would infect everyone in the town—and that meant it would infect all the Masks.

The instant his blood splashed into the water, a deafening shriek ripped out of the town and shattered the stillness.

In a split second, before he even had time to pull his hand back, dozens of people—hundreds of people exploded out of Stonebridge all coming straight for him.

He spun around with his heart in his mouth at that first ear-splitting scream. His throat went dry when he saw every man, woman, and child charging him from every house and doorway.

They didn't charge, though. His frozen brain registered that they didn't run along the ground on their legs like normal people.

They flew at him without touching the ground at all. He didn't see their legs move. Their legs blurred from the knees down. They soared toward him like ghosts rushing on the breeze.

Some otherworldly light coming from somewhere lit up all their ghastly faces as they streaked out of town to attack him. He recognized all their faces—Koenig.... Fisher.... Dash...... Zen...... Thackery..... Fuentes...... Wild.....

They were all here and coming for Rhodes's blood. Even Ora and their children raced out of town baring their teeth in fury to kill him.

He stumbled away from the well and, without thinking, he raised his arms.

He didn't think that he didn't have any weapons in this hallucination landscape. He fired, and by some miracle, his scourge guns went off.

The first blast ripped a dozen people backward. He didn't stop to think about which of his closest friends he just killed.

He fired again and again all over the crowd. People kept dropping in front of him as he staggered farther away from them.

They were coming too fast, and in a fraction of an instant, they hit him and slammed him down on the ground.

Their hands held him down with impossible force. Koenig snarled in murderous rage and dove for Rhodes's throat.

Fisher, Dash, Oakes, and Rhinehart moved in. Rhodes couldn't let this happen.

He barely angled his arm up and fired again. Rhinehart and Thackery toppled backward into the ground. More townsfolk moved in to take their places.

Rhodes fired again and again, but he couldn't break free. Koenig's fingers tightened around Rhodes's neck. Rhodes choked trying to catch his breath....and then those fingers turned to grid lines.

The illusion shattered and the whole Grid materialized before his eyes. The smell of wildflowers and dewdrops on fresh grass vanished. Dust and smoke stung his nostrils.

He wasn't lying by the Stonebridge well anymore. He lay in the middle of an open field with explosions going off all around him. Masks invasion ships floated in the air bombarding the countryside with fusion fire.

A dozen Masks surrounded Rhodes and held him down with their mechanical arms. The glowing light shone behind the eye slits. The townspeople attacking him weren't people at all. They were all Masks.

Grid lines burrowed into his head through his implants. The Masks never transported him back to their lab or onto one of their ships or anywhere else.

They interfaced with him right here on the ground outside the Lilithea Cluster with the bombardment going on just a few miles away.

Koenig shrieked again and flung his grid lines at Rhodes to strangle the life out of him. The Masks' grid lines struggled to contain Rhodes's grid lines.

He reacted automatically and switched to his lasers. He sliced them sideways and cut all those Masks in half.

He floundered to his feet shooting as fast as he could, but more and more Masks kept rushing him from the north.

Most of them ran straight past him on their headlong charge to invade the Lilithea Cluster. Thousands of them already mobbed The Grid in there.

The last remaining Legion platoons clashed with the ground troops, but the platoons wouldn't be able to hold out for more than a few more minutes.

Rhodes couldn't fight this many Masks. Koenig fought him every step of the way, wrapped his grid lines around Rhodes, and Koenig did everything in his power to hold Rhodes down and stop him from shooting the Masks.

Even now, he felt dozens of hands clawing at him trying to pull him back down to interface with him again.

The command line must not have worked. He had to launch off the ground to save himself.

Chapter 29

As soon as Rhodes got airborne, The Grid widened. The battle raged over the Lilithea Cluster in all its power. The Masks didn't hold back at all this time.

Dozens of invasion ships loomed over the city unloading on buildings and bringing the city systematically to its knees. The invasion ships' enormous sides blocked out the sun.

Thousands of Masks swarmed the streets coming from the north. They stormed through town killing everyone in sight.

The Masks met the platoons waiting for them. Gunfire burst between the buildings, but more Masks packed in behind with every passing minute.

The platoons created a bottleneck that increased the pressure of so many Masks trying to force their way through. The platoons would break any second now.

Rhodes fired his boosters, blasted away to the west the way Colonel McKelvy ordered him to, and stooped low.

Rhodes didn't even think about using any fancy grid transformations. To hell with it. If gunfire didn't do the trick, nothing would.

He swerved around one last building and unloaded his lasers on the Masks engaged against the platoons. Rhodes had to stop the assault right here. If the Masks made it past these platoons, everybody might as well take their toys and go home.

He landed on the ground twenty feet from the Masks' front line. He swiped his lasers back and forth across the Masks' flank to lay down as many of them as he could.

He couldn't destroy them all, but he could at least make a dent in their numbers. He might even be able to save a few soldiers while he was at it. That would be a nice bonus.

The Masks toppled in waves under his guns. The Masks turned in his direction and exposed themselves to the platoon's Jackhammers.

The platoons saw someone coming to their aid and pressed forward to gun down the Masks from their side.

The pincher worked for a few seconds until another flood of Masks pushed in from the north. They filled the gap left by Rhodes's assault.

These new Masks overran their fallen comrades and even their comrades who were still standing. The Masks poured into the bottleneck and split into two flanks of their own.

Hundreds of them rushed Rhodes. He had to launch off the ground again to stay out of their reach, but he didn't plan to leave the platoons on their own.

The fresh Masks opened fire on the platoons and drove them back. Soldiers fell under the assault. The Legion blockade started to crack.

Rhodes tried to shoot at the Masks bearing down on the platoons, but too many of them already crowded in his face. He had to turn his guns on his own attacker instead and leave the platoons unguarded.

The Masks came dangerously close to him. He fired his boosters to lift off when, out of nowhere, a deep boom struck the building just south of him.

The building detonated on top of him. Massive chunks of concrete, stone, and marble smashed him in the head and body.

He collapsed on one knee and then a towering invasion ship hammered its fusion charges into him from directly above.

Another four charges hit him one after another and took him down in seconds. He lay broken in pieces on the ground, but his mind stayed awake just long enough to see that one ship towering directly over him.

He couldn't see anything beyond its enormous sides. Its gun ports aimed straight down at him. One more hit like that and it was all over for him, too.

A feeling of immense peace and calm came over him. He was on his way home—home to the sunshine house where his loved ones waited for him with hugs, kisses, big smiles, and all the love he could possibly shower on them.

He actually smiled up at the ship about to end his life. The Grid gave him more of a view than he could possibly ask for of the Masks advancing on him with their rifles pointed at his head.

Good. They would shoot him and kill him. They wouldn't try to interface with him and take him back to Stonebridge. He couldn't stand that.

He didn't want to do this anymore. He actually felt compassion for them when they stood directly over him holding him at gunpoint. He felt for them the way he did when he interfaced with the Mask on Drion.

They only wanted a little taste of the happiness waiting for him. They only wanted to understand how sweet it could feel to actually have someone waiting to welcome him home.

They would never understand that. He couldn't hate them. He only wanted to give them some peace from their unrelenting misery.

He smiled at them, too, and then turned his eyes up to the ship above him. He could let out his last breath—a breath of pure relaxation and release. It was time. He was ready.

He let it all go. He could accept everything that happened to him and everything that happened to everyone he cared about. None of it mattered anymore because it was over. The whole nightmare was over.

He might have passed out....or he might have lost track of time. The Masks didn't shoot.

For some reason he couldn't figure out, the ship above him drifted out of position. It started picking up speed. It flew faster and faster out of sight, but it didn't rise into the atmosphere.

He stared at The Grid trying to understand. Invasion ships dropped out of the sky all over the peninsula.

They plunged away and flew at terminal velocity to smash into the ground. They crashed in smoking ruins all over the countryside and didn't rise again.

The Masks ground troops stopped.....and didn't move again.

The Masks standing over Rhodes remained there holding him at gunpoint. They froze....and then the light disappeared behind their eye slits. They shut down and didn't reactivate.

The whole landscape when deadly quiet. The platoon soldiers pivoted one way and then the other aiming their Jackhammers at all those frozen Masks.

The machines didn't move to shoot or even raise their weapons. They stopped in the middle of the street.

The fleeing civilians didn't stop. They rushed south through the city to get away from the Masks even after the Masks stopped shooting.

The civilians charged past the soldiers and vanished out of sight. The civilians left the city empty, silent, and quivering with tension.

A few brave platoon leaders tiptoed forward and prodded the Masks just to make sure they wouldn't suddenly come back to life.

Ravagers descended through the clouds to soar over the crashed invasion ships.

Far out in the countryside, the city machine sat in one place. Its treads no longer rolled it southward toward the Lilithea Cluster. The Grid read the city machine as totally without power.

A pall hung over the landscape. The whole planet went very still and held its breath waiting for the other shoe to drop.

It came when two tiny dots whizzed out of the atmosphere closing on Rhodes's location. They swerved wide over the peninsula, scanned The Grid, and converged on Rhodes.

"I'm reading forty Masks all around him armed and aiming their rifles at him," Coulter reported.

"None of the Masks or their weapons are showing any sign of power," Murphy pointed out.

"Keep an eye on them just in case," Rhinehart ordered.

"I'm picking up major damage to his implants and organic tissue," Dash added. "Most of his critical systems are malfunctioning—and Koenig is offline. The captain's life signs are fluctuating into the danger zone."

"Captain Rhodes, can you hear me?!" Rhinehart called.

Rhodes tried to speak, but only a faint wet rasping sound came out of his mouth. He choked on something.

"Hold on, Captain!" Rhinehart told him. "We're coming in to lift you off. We'll have you back in the lab in no time."

Rhodes didn't care if they got him to the lab in time to save his life. He wouldn't mind dying right now.

He did it. He ended the war. He could die now because he knew what was waiting for him on the other side. He would be happy to die now.

Another hurtling missile torched across the sky as Enoch blasted between the few remaining buildings.

The Striker transformed its grid lines on the way in, turned into a jointed monster with multiple legs, bounded off the skyscraper walls, touched the ground once, scooped up Rhodes in a feather-soft cradle hold, and launched with him over the city.

Rhodes floated in the clouds watching Coulter and Rhinehart circle the Lilithea Cluster one last time.

Thousands upon thousands of Masks stood in place all over the city. Even more invasion ships lay smoking in ruins all over the continent.

The sight dwindled to a speck. Enoch lifted Rhodes into his cockpit and lowered him into the seat behind Oakes.

They broke orbit on an intercept course for the *Ganus.* Rhodes could have used The Grid to keep looking at the scene down on Sarus, but he didn't want to anymore.

He shut his eyes and let himself float away into a dream—a dream about sunshine streaming through windows, children's laughter floating across sunbaked lawns, the smells of home-cooked food, and the glowing smiles on faces he recognized and loved.

He didn't want to be anywhere else right now or ever again.

Chapter 30

R hodes stood up and punched the button to shut the cover on his conversion capsule. Oakes, Coulter, and Rhinehart sat at the table in their Coleridge Station barracks.

The battalion had been relaxing here for a month while Rhodes underwent repairs. Right now, Coulter, Oakes, and Rhinehart sat at the table playing Slaughter Power and talking trash the way they used to.

Rhodes left them there and walked down the hall to the training room. It was empty except for Dr. Osborne.

"Hey," Osborne greeted him.

Rhodes nodded. "Hey."

"You okay?" Osborne asked.

"Yeah." Rhodes rubbed his hands together. "A little nervous, but I'm okay."

Osborne tapped his device. "All your systems are reading normal. You should be good to go."

"I'm ready. Let's get this over with."

Osborne handed Rhodes a small handheld controller. "Just push that button when you're ready. The cascade will trigger automatically."

Rhodes nodded again. "Got it."

Osborne squeezed his shoulder. "Good luck. I'll be waiting in the lab when you finish."

"Thanks," Rhodes husked.

Osborne slipped out of the room and shut the door behind him. Rhodes jumped a little when the door clicked. He held his nerves in front of the others. Now they came back with a vengeance.

He took a deep breath, tightened his grip on the controller, and dropped into The Grid.

He wound up alone in the plain grid of lines divided into squares, but he didn't go anywhere. He stayed where he was.

As soon as he got there, Koenig appeared in The Grid in front of him. This Koenig wasn't the tangled squiggle of lines. It was the greying, overweight man from Stonebridge.

Koenig jolted when he saw Rhodes.

"Hello, Koenig," Rhodes murmured.

"Captain!" Koenig spun from right to left looking around. "Where are....but we....how did we......?"

"The war is over, Koenig. I delivered the command line to the Masks and it worked. You tried to stop me, and when you failed, you tried to kill me. I shut you down....and then the Masks shut down. You went offline during the battle. We've been back at Coleridge Station for a month while I undergo repairs and recover."

"You mean....you mean I've been offline all that time?!" Koenig demanded. "Why didn't Dr. Osborne reactivate me?"

"Because you tried to kill me, Koenig. You worked against me when I tried to create the command line. Then you deliberately launched an attack on the Masks specifically to get me recaptured. Then you deceived me while we were inside Stonebridge by trying to convince me that it was real. You attacked me along with the Masks to stop me from deploying the command line. When that failed, you tried to restrain me to keep me as their prisoner. You tried to help them interface with me so they could recapture me and you strangled me to kill me. You're dangerous, Koenig—to me and to yourself. I told Dr. Osborne that when he first installed you in my neural core. Now everyone knows it."

"Captain—I.....I can improve. I was going through a painful disorientation process after losing Alyssa...."

"I was going through a painful disorientation process after losing Fisher, too, Koenig," Rhodes murmured. "I didn't turn against the Legion and my own people because I was disoriented."

Koenig gulped. "What are you going to do?"

"I'm going to take you offline—permanently. Your program will be deleted. You'll never be installed in another person again."

"But....is that really necessary?" Koenig quavered. "Can't we come to some compromise?"

"Of course it's necessary, Koenig," Rhodes replied. "You're the one who has been saying all this time that you didn't want to be installed in any other person. You said you couldn't live without Alyssa. You told me you wanted to die rather than live with the memories of how the battalion was before. You're about to get your wish."

Koenig swallowed hard and looked down at his hands. "You're right, Captain. I don't want to go on without her."

"I'm sorry this happened." Rhodes found himself stepping forward and gripping Koenig's shoulder. Rhodes could finally relate to this SAM, now that Rhodes could finally look into a human face. "I'm sorry you lost Alyssa the way you did. I'm sorry about all of it."

Koenig didn't look up. "I should be thanking you....for ending the war......I shouldn't have tried to stop you. You're right. That was wrong of me. I should have helped you. That was my function and I failed."

"You don't have to worry about anything anymore. You won't feel any pain or loss. You can rest. I envy you in a way."

Koenig finally looked up and met Rhodes's eye. "I'm sorry for your loss, too. I'm sorry I couldn't be the SAM you needed me to be—a SAM like Fisher."

"No one can be a SAM like Fisher. I never expected you to live up to that standard."

"I'm still sorry that I let you down. You're right. A SAM that doesn't perform its basic function is no good to anyone." Koenig straightened up. "I'm ready. Take me offline now."

Rhodes took a step back. "Goodbye, Koenig. I appreciate all the good service you gave to Alyssa while she was alive."

Koenig's face pinched and tears sprang to his eyes. He had to fight his lips to get them to form words. He tried to smile and failed. "I'll see her soon. I can look forward to that."

"Yeah," Rhodes whispered. "You two will be happy together."

Koenig squared his shoulders. "Goodbye, Captain. I leave the battalion in good hands."

"Goodbye, Koenig." Rhodes raised the controller and pushed the button.

Koenig vanished off The Grid and left Rhodes alone. He stood there staring at the empty place where Koenig had just been standing.

Rhodes never let himself believe until right now that Koenig really would disappear forever. Now he was gone. He would never come back. He would never work as a SAM for anyone again.

In a way, what happened to him was as much a tragedy as what happened to Poole, Gannon, Henshaw, Fuentes, Thackery, Lauer, and Dietz.

Dr. Osborne never should have brought Koenig back online. His attachment to Thackery made it impossible for him to connect to anyone else.

Extreme grief and overwhelming loss caused him to malfunction the way he did. It wasn't his fault.

Rhodes couldn't hate him, either. Rhodes didn't blame Koenig for any of it.

Koenig could rest now. His problems and his grief were over.

Rhodes and the rest of the battalion had to keep going. The sunshine house still waited for Rhodes out there. It would be awfully crowded when he finally got there.

He smiled at the thought and left The Grid. He reappeared in the white training room.

He didn't stay there. He went back to Dr. Osborne's lab and handed over the controller.

"How did it go?" Osborne asked.

Rhodes nodded again. "It went easily. He was ready."

"That's good. Are you ready for your new SAM?"

"Yeah. Let's do it."

Osborne pointed at his stool. "Sit down. I'm going to make a few adjustments and then send you back into The Grid. Then I'll bring the SAM online and you two can talk."

"Okay." Rhodes sat down.

Osborne adjusted some things on his equipment and then on Rhodes's cranial implant. Osborne went back to his wall of components....and Rhodes dropped back into The Grid. It looked the same as before.

A few seconds later, the grid lines started to twist, morph, and take shape. They twined in front of Rhodes's eyes and then they solidified into a definite recognizable form.

They wavered for a minute. Two gleaming black eyes appeared in the center and then the outer lines brightened and stabilized into the shape of a skull.

"Captain Rhodes!" a scratchy metallic voice husked. "Why are we in The Grid?"

"Hello, Wild. It's good to see you again."

Wild looked around. "Where is everyone? Why am I interfacing with you and not the rest of the battalion? Where's Lauer? He should be here."

"I'm very sorry, Wild. Lauer got killed in combat—in the last battle against the Masks. I'm sure you remember. Lauer was flying Elio and they got hit. Lauer's gone—and I'm afraid we lost quite a few other people, too. Elio, Fuentes, Thackery, Koenig, Dietz, Zen, and all the other Strikers besides Enoch—they're all gone."

Wild's eyes blazed. He glared at Rhodes. "Lauer is dead?! Really dead?"

"Yes," Rhodes murmured. "I'm sorry, Wild. I know this is hard. Fisher is gone, too. That's why we're here. The doctors want to fit you to me as my new SAM."

"Fisher....is gone?!" Wild bellowed. "He's dead?!! He can't be!"

"He is," Rhodes choked. "It's been really hard—as hard as I'm sure it will be for you without Lauer. I hope you and I can work together. I hope we can help each other and make this work. I would be really honored to have you as my SAM, Wild. I know I'll always be your second choice, but I'll always do my best for you the way I did for Fisher. I promise you that."

"I'm not worried about you doing your best for me," Wild returned. "I wouldn't trust myself to be good enough for you—not after Fisher. That's a tough act to follow. I mean....you're the captain."

"I'm just a regular guy, Wild. I'm a guy who needs a SAM and I can't think of one I would rather have than you. Please. Help me. I need you."

Wild looked away. He remained silent for a long time.

"I can't believe he's gone!" Wild finally husked.

"I know," Rhodes whispered. "Losing Lauer....it was a hard blow."

"I never even got a chance to say goodbye. I won't even get to see him again."

"I know."

"Excuse me, Captain," Wild blurted out. "I need to think about this. Just.....give me a minute.....please....."

He shrank to a pinprick and left Rhodes alone. Wild asked for a minute, but it just kept stretching on and on. He didn't come back.

Rhodes didn't say anything. Poor Wild.

Rhodes waited another ten minutes. He was just making up his mind to leave The Grid when Wild came back.

He expanded himself in front of Rhodes, cleared his throat, and his voice shook when he spoke again. "I'm sorry for the delay, Captain."

"Don't mention it. Take all the time you need. If you need to disappear, you don't have to explain yourself to me."

"I would be honored to be your SAM, Captain," Wild went on. "I can't think of anyone I would rather serve than you—second to Lauer, of course."

Rhodes fought back the urge to smile. "Of course."

Wild nodded. "All right. Let's do this. I'm ready to go."

"Thank you, Wild. You don't know how relieved I am."

"I hope I can do you justice, Sir."

"You don't have to call me that. If you really want to be formal, just call me, 'Captain'. That's what Fisher always called me."

"Of course, Captain. Thank you."

"Are you ready to go back to the battalion now?"

"So....it's you, Coulter, Oakes, and Rhinehart? That's it?"

"Yeah. The battalion looks a little different now."

"All right. Thank you for warning me."

"Let's go." Rhodes left The Grid and wound up back in the lab.

Wild stayed in front of Rhodes's eyes, but Wild shrank himself to the upper righthand corner to keep out of the way.

"Well?" Osborne asked. "What's the verdict?"

Rhodes nodded. "It's gonna work. It's good."

Osborne burst into a huge grin. "Fantastic."

"We're gonna go back to the battalion now. I'll let you know if we have any malfunctions or if we need any adjustments."

He left the lab and headed for the barracks.

"This is going to take some getting used to," Wild muttered on the way.

"You and me both," Rhodes replied. "I meant what I said. Tell me if you need to do anything to make it easier for yourself."

"Likewise. If you want me to disappear and leave you alone, please tell me. Lauer used to tell me that all the time."

"He did? I thought you two got along really well."

"We did. We got along because he told me when he wanted privacy and silence. He liked silence before he went into conversion cycles and for at least fifteen minutes after he came out of them."

Rhodes found himself smiling again. "Fisher and I did it that way at first, too."

"Only at first? You didn't keep doing it that way?"

"After a while, it got to be really nice to talk to him first thing after coming out of a conversion cycle and right before I went into one. We talked in our capsule about whatever was going on with the battalion.

It was really nice to be able to talk to someone about everything on my mind. Talking to him became even nicer than the quiet."

Wild didn't answer for a minute. "I hope I can earn your confidence like that someday, Captain."

"Maybe you don't have to. Maybe we could do it that way now."

"If you want to," Wild mumbled. "I wouldn't want to presume anything."

"You know, I was the one who found Lauer's body the night he got killed. Finding Lauer was the hardest part of that night. In a way, it hit me harder than losing Fisher. Lauer.....the way he was when he first came out of stasis.....He had a hard, stony way of hiding how much all of this hurt him. He had a big heart. He hid it behind a wall of granite, but he never could conceal it completely. He was a good man—one of the best I've ever known. I like to think he finally went home to his family when he died. I guess he'll be out there horseback riding with them now the way he always wanted to."

Wild didn't answer for a long time. He finally rasped, "Thank you, Captain. It's heartening to know that we both admire Lauer the same way. I wish I could have been there with you when you found him. I wish I could have been your SAM so I could have been with you in that moment."

"Fisher was there for me. It's one of the things I miss the most about him—that he shared those moments with me. He was the one who got me through it—and now he's gone. You and I will go through those experiences together and then we'll have that bond, too."

"You're right, Captain. We already do. Thank you for sharing that with me."

"You're welcome. It's like I said. I'm here to help you the same way you're here to help me."

Rhodes reentered the barracks just then. The three men at the table looked up. "How did it go?" Oakes asked.

"It went well. I got my new SAM."

"Who is it?" Coulter asked.

Rhodes interfaced with his men. "I got Wild."

"Yeah!" Rhinehart shot off the bench, came forward, and clapped Rhodes on the shoulder. "Welcome back, buddy! We missed you so much!"

"Thank you, Lieutenant," Wild husked. "I missed you all, too. I hope we can somewhat get back a little of what we all lost."

"You and Captain Rhodes are gonna be great together," Oakes added. "It's a perfect combination."

"I hope so," Wild replied.

Rhodes waved the three men toward the door. "So let's go stretch our legs and see how it goes. We have some miles to cover before we get back to where we were."

The three men tumbled out of the barracks all talking at once. "Did you hear about the story Hetna Bazaran is telling the press?" Coulter asked.

"Who's Hetna Bazaran?" Dash asked.

"She's a resident of the Lilithea Cluster. She's out there telling the whole world about how she witnessed Captain Rhodes defeat the Masks single-handedly."

"What's wrong with that?" Rhinehart countered. "He did defeat the Masks single-handedly."

"I'm sure the new Battalion 1 governing body is having an epileptic fit about the story," Rhodes muttered.

"Why are they?" Wild asked.

"Because they want everyone to keep drinking the Kool-Aid and believing that the regular Legion defeated the Masks instead of one classified squad of super mechanized soldiers," Oakes replied. "It would be even worse if people started to believe one of these classified super mechanized soldiers defeated the Masks all by himself instead of the regular Legion."

"That's why they want us to stay here at Coleridge Station," Rhodes added. "They want to keep us out of the public eye while they run damage control."

"They won't be able to stop word from getting out," Coulter remarked. "These stories keep popping up on the computer terminal. This Hetna Bazaran story is just the latest one."

"She's the only one saying she witnessed the captain in battle against the Masks within minutes of their defeat," Rhinehart corrected. "Plenty of people are coming forward saying they saw us fighting. She's the only person saying that."

"She's the only person who can say it because she's the only person who did see me," Rhodes pointed out. "Everyone else who saw us in action is dead now."

"The Legion isn't exactly lying when they say they defeated the Masks," Oakes added. "They just don't tell anyone *how* they defeated the Masks—or which unit of the Legion defeated the Masks. People can believe whatever they want."

"That Hetna story will never see the light of day," Rhinehart muttered. "The Legion will pull in every favor and twist every arm to bury it just like they did all the others."

"It's nice to know the people who saw us appreciate what we did," Coulter remarked.

"But the people who didn't see us won't appreciate it," Oakes countered. "The billions of people Captain Rhodes saved will never know he saved them. They won't be able to appreciate it."

Rhodes didn't add anything to this. The four men got back to the training room just then.

They entered to find another four men standing there waiting. All four had been fitted with implants and recently woken up from stasis.

Rhodes, Coulter, Oakes, and Rhinehart lined up on one side of the room. The four friends sized up their four new battalion members.

The four strangers eyed Rhodes and his men just as closely.

The Grid read back the new men's names, ranks, and service records—not just for Rhodes but for everyone else in the room. The four new men could see Rhodes's name, rank, and record on The Grid, too.

The guy on the far end was Lieutenant Kelsey Fahey. He was shorter than everyone else in the room but built like a brick shithouse. He was easily as muscular as Rhinehart with a thick, solid, immovable air and one hard, flashing, black eye.

He instantly reminded Rhodes of Lauer except that Fahey was much younger, clean-shaven, and wore his black hair clipped short in a perfectly maintained military style.

He kept his lips set and showed absolutely no sign of unease about facing Rhodes or his men.

Fahey had gotten shot down by the Masks on Katera. He had nothing to be ashamed of in the way he died. His service record was exemplary with multiple commendations from his superiors for service above and beyond the call.

The second man in line was Commander Clayton Masters. He had taken command of his platoon after his captain got killed on Luluna fighting the Emal.

Masters and his men had been manning a long-range artillery position when it got hit by a base ship and exploded with all the men lost.

Masters had a long, thin, wiry build with an angular face the way Fisher had in Stonebridge. Masters had dark hair, though, and his one remaining eye was bright blue.

Sergeant Jamal Swain kept his stance, his expression, and everything else about himself casual when Rhodes's group entered.

Swain was a black man with a round, soft, smooth face. He would have looked young except that he wasn't. He was twenty-eight when the Duster of which he was a pilot got shot down by the Masks on Rono.

His record stated that he saved the lives of twenty platoon soldiers he'd been transporting. The shot that downed the Duster knocked all the soldiers unconscious.

Swain dragged and even carried all twenty out of the wreck and got them to a safe distance. He was on his way back inside the Duster to save the last five soldiers when it blew up with him inside it.

Of the four new guys, he made the least effort to stand up straight or try to make himself look intimidating. He even slouched a little bit. Meeting these veterans of Battalion 1 meant nothing to him—or he wanted Rhodes and his men to think it did.

Lieutenant Samson Hillyard's eagle brown eye snapped over the group in front of him with frightening precision. He sized up Rhodes and his men in an instant.

Hillyard had a square, powerful build, a very narrow waist, and lean, spare features that made him look extra hawkish.

He didn't radiate instant challenge like Fahey did, but Hillyard stayed ever alert for anything—good or bad.

His record stated that he had been the Master Chief in charge of the Ravager *Zophe* on Gisu in the Noria system. The ship had been destroyed by the Masks while it was trying to evacuate the population.

Rhodes read the four men's records with approval. He approved even more of what he saw in their posture, their attitude, and their sturdy, direct approach to meeting their new comrades in the battalion.

Commander Masters dipped his chin once to Rhodes. "Captain Rhodes, I presume?"

"That's correct, Commander. This is Lieutenant Rhinehart, Lieutenant Oakes, and Corporal Coulter—but I guess you fellas already knew that. I'm told you've already activated your SAMs and gone through extensive orientation in another part of Coleridge Station before today."

"Yes, Sir," Commander Masters replied. "We're ready to roll."

Rhodes found himself smiling at all four of them. "Then let's see what you can do. We're all ready for some action, so let's hit it."

He dropped into The Grid. Coulter, Oakes, and Rhinehart copied him and all four of the new guys did the same thing.

They touched down in the dark world of green lines and nothing else. Rhodes took off running and all the others followed him.

The grid lines curved upward to form the simulated landscape and all eight men launched their boosters to plunge into the next adventure waiting for them.

The End.

Keep Reading

U ltra Meridian Series

A smuggler's crew. A doomsday weapon. A forgotten outpost on the far rim of known space.....

Sheriff Mace Davenport was just doing his job when he confiscated a doomsday weapon from a known smugglers' vessel. Little did he know that one act would sets off a chain reaction that could blow the whole Confederacy apart—literally.

Now he's on the run for his life with the whole might of the Confederate Reserve Wing hunting him down. He'll need all his wits and resources just to survive. Forget about saving the world from annihilation.

With his enemies lurking around every corner, he's going to discover that some of them just might be his best, most powerful allies. Ultra Meridian is about to become the epicenter in the most explosive battle that will decide the fate of the galaxy once and for all.

You can find it at your favorite book retailer.

Sign Up Once--Get all Theo Mann's free books including brand new releases

S ign Up Once--Get all Theo Mann's free books including brand new releases

Commander Layton Raines was just doing his job when he got shot down on the battle defending his platoon's retreat. His whole life changes when he wakes up in the hospital implanted with cybernetic limbs, but Raines is nothing like anyone else who has ever gone through the Battalion 1 project.

With the fate of the galaxy hanging in the balance, the future will depend on the one man who has never been good with authority, following orders, or staying within the lines. With the mission in jeopardy and Battalion 1 pinned down by overwhelming odds, it will take a miracle to save their lives. It just might take a mutiny to throw out the rule book and forge a path no one has ever taken before.

Sign up at www.theomann.com to read it for free

About Theo Mann

I write 70 books per year—and yes, before you ask, all these books are my original creative work. Nothing written under my name is AI-generated or ghostwritten because I write better than AI and any ghostwriter out there.

People don't read fiction for entertainment or to escape from reality. People read fiction to see their humanity reflected in another person's character and story.

This is my promise to you. When you read my books, you'll see your own humanity reflected in the characters and stories. I take this commitment to my readers very seriously. My books are an intimate form of communication between us. I would never disrespect my readers by turning that over to a machine or another writer. This is my bond between me and you as my reader.

I write 20,000 words per day as my daily work output. If anyone with a public platform would like to challenge me to prove this in a controlled environment, feel free to contact me on this website's contact page.

I worked as a professional ghostwriter for fifteen years. Now I'm on a mission to set a Guinness World Record by writing 700 books over the next ten years and 1400 books over the next twenty years, all originally written by me. See my website for the full book list.

I'm also the author of *Proof for the Existence of God* and the *Crimes Against Fiction* blog. You can find all my nonfiction work at www.cr imes-against-fiction.com.

If you have a story idea, or if you would like me to explore a series in more depth, or if you'd like me to explore a character by writing a spinoff series about that character or world, leave me a message on my website's contact page. I answer all reader emails, so ask me anything, tell me what you liked and didn't like, and let me know where you'd like your favorite series to go. I would love to hear your ideas and find out what you'd like to read next.

Find out more at www.theomann.com.

Also by Theo Mann (so far)